Cover Designed By
Covers by Juan

Jessica Rousseau
Elemental Editing and Proofreading
Missy Stewart
Ms. Correct All's Editing and Proofreading

SHADOW TOUCHED

THE VEIL KEEPER BOOK ONE

HARPER WYLDE

ACKNOWLEDGMENTS

I have to start by saying thank you to all of the wonderful readers who have my book in their hands, reading this acknowledgment. Your love, support, encouragement, and enthusiasm have made my publishing journey incredible. Thank you for reading and for being a part of my book world family.

To my editor, Jessica Rousseau. I can't give you a big enough thank you for allowing me to bounce ideas off of you, for the wonderful edits that polished my manuscript into what it is today, and for the long hours and dedication you've given me during the editing process. You are amazing and I'm sending you all the virtual hugs!

To my second editor, Missy Stewart. Thank you for always supporting me, allowing me to run ideas by you, and helping me edit my novel. Your friendship is a blessing and I can't wait to see all the wonderful places editing and publishing takes you!

HARPER'S DEDICATION

This book is for my family. I love you so much. Thank you for understanding the long hours, late nights, and piles of dishes. Your love, support, and encouragement mean the world to me. And to my little sidekick who was growing inside of me during the writing of this book, I can't wait to meet you soon!

WARNING

Shadow Touched is a reverse harem novel which means our heroine doesn't have to choose between her love interests. Really, though, that's just more fun for everyone!

ONE

LORN

I had never been normal. It was a fact I'd known about myself my entire life, and one I'd learned to live with. So I guess it stood to reason that like my life, my death would be anything but mundane.

I stood riveted to my spot as dark red eyes stared down at me, boring into my flesh like burning lasers. The breath of the beast was rancid as it bared its blood-red fangs, the unearthly slits in its eyes widening as a puff of hot breath washed over my face, chest, and arms. Magick tinged through my veins as I narrowed my gaze and assessed the enemy, looking for the best way to end it before it ended me.

Everything about the creature was unformed, its edges undefined. Instead, its body was a pitch-black mass of thick, swirling, cloudlike whisps, but that did nothing to detract from its deadly appearance. It did, however, make it hard to figure out where the beast was most vulnerable. Lethal claws tipped each of the creature's long fingers, and horns jutted out from the top of its wide, triangular shaped head. When it blinked, the beast's eyelids lifted from both the bottom and the top, meeting in the middle in an unsettling, otherworldly display that had panic squeezing my heart in a vice-like grip. A piercing, all-encompassing roar unleashed from the beast spurring me into action, and I raised my hands, letting go of the carefully guarded magick that I always kept locked away. Adrenaline coursed through my body and my heart started racing just before I jolted awake on a scream.

Panting from my subsiding nightmare, I groaned as aware-ness seeped back into my body. It took a few moments for my thoughts to find their way to the present, and I pushed myself up, my palms meeting the rough texture of what could only be the forest floor. The sticks, stones, and leaves of my impromptu bed stuck to me as my shaking arms lifted my upper body off the ground. Every muscle ached, giving homage to a wicked workout session that I knew I hadn't done. I was completely exhausted down to a soul level, but I forced myself to crack my eyes open. Bright, blinding daylight greeted me, filtering down through the trees, their green, swaying leaves dancing in a cheery display that did no match my pre-coffee mood.

"Shit. No. Not again!" The adrenaline that was dying off after my nightmare surged back to life within my chest as reality crashed over me. My cheek stung from the sharp stone I must have used as a pillow and dirt clung to dark hair that tumbled freely around my shoulders. My very *naked* shoulders.

Wincing, I glanced down before shutting my eyes again with a disheartened sigh. Totally. Naked.

This is not happening. Not today! I scrambled to my feet while embarrassment ate at me and my worry became nearly tangible. The possibility of being discovered like this made my stomach drop and my pulse race much like it had during my overly realistic dream. Getting my bare ass into motion, I hurried through the thick forest, hoping the trees would offer up enough camouflage that I'd make it home unnoticed. The soles of my feet were sore after only a few steps, but I pressed on anyway, heading to the extra stash of clothing I kept outside for exactly this occasion.

This wasn't the first time I'd found myself outdoors, naked, with no idea how I'd gotten there. And it probably wouldn't be the last. These 'episodes,' as I called them, were happening more frequently. The fact I'd had one last night, just two days after my previous one, was more than a little concerning, but I needed to handle getting home before I let myself freak out. They'd never happened in such quick succession before, and deep down I recognized this change for the bad omen it was.

After a year full of dealing with them, I was still no closer to figuring out what the 'episodes' were about, or what happened when I was 'under.' As far as I could tell, there were no patterns or commonalities. The one thing I did know was that I couldn't blame them on alcohol and bad decisions. At nearly twenty, I was still under drinking age and a strict rule follower. You had to be when your adopted father was a warlock on the High Coven. Eyes were always turned in our direction, and as the blemish that already stained the Kentwell name, I did everything in my power to stay as unnoticeable as possible.

The sun was well over the horizon line, and I knew there was a possibility it would be too late to sneak back into the house and pretend nothing unusual had happened. Especially if my absence had been noted. So far, I'd been able to hide these weird occurrences from my family, but today might require some creative storytelling.

A whoosh sounded, and a hawk flew overhead, deftly moving through the branches before extending its wings and gliding to perch in a nearby tree. My heart nearly leapt from my body as I momentarily freaked out, throwing my hands over my nude body while a scared, embarrassed shriek left my lips. I skidded to a halt just as the ground beneath my feet trembled with unrestrained magick that slipped out unwarranted, taking advantage of my heightened emotions. It was a dangerous oddity of mine, this magick I wasn't supposed to possess. I looked around frantically while I calmed myself and processed that the noises had simply come from a bird and not a person. Working to retract the free rein energy, I mentally contained it all back in the box I kept it hidden in. With sharp movements, the creature watched me through it all.

"You get off on scaring people?" I scolded the hawk with an icy glower. It simply tilted its head—like it was actually listening to me. I knew hawks were known for being incredibly smart, but it seemed impossible that it actually understood the accusation I'd thrown at it.

Thoroughly shaken by the entire morning, my rising anxiety had my feet moving again as I sped toward home. The very last thing I needed was to be discovered by an actual person in the state I was in. I had no way to explain any of this, and if word got out, it would probably mean the ruination of the sliver of reputation I had left.

Taking in my surroundings, I knew I was getting closer to my house. Almost there. At least this time it seemed as though I'd stayed on my parents' property. A few nights ago, I had ventured far enough away that I'd ended up in the state game lands. Easily a five-mile hike from home. If there was one shining bright spot in having returned home from the Witching Academy—a two-year, college-like program all witches and warlocks had to attend—it was that these odd occurrences were easier to hide here than they had been when I lived in a dorm room full of other students.

I drew a lungful of clean—albeit humid—air, while the

unsettling dream I'd had buzzed in the back of my mind. It wasn't the first time I'd awoken to the nightmare, either. The eerie creatures stalked my sleep, and while it wasn't the same monster every night, each was just as deadly and creepy as the last. Despite the summer heat, a shiver raced down my spine, but I suppressed the memory of those eerie red eyes and buried the haunting remnants away as deeply as possible.

"Well hello there." A deep, masculine voice washed over me, freezing me in my tracks. I whipped around, which I realized too late was a terrible, terrible idea. The dark, handsome stranger let out a low whistle, openly appreciating the curves I was flashing him. Quickly crossing my arms over my chest, I darted behind a tree and used the trunk for cover.

Peeking around the bark, I let myself study the guy. He was tall, tanned, and sexy, and my cheeks, which were already heated with embarrassment, blazed as I realized just how good looking he was.

Holy bad luck batman! Humiliation burned through me and I decided the earth could officially open up and swallow me whole. I'd never seen such a handsome man before and, of course, out of everyone in the entire world fate dictated that he was the one to stumble across me while I was in such a state. Such a bare-naked state. Karma was definitely a bitch, I just had no idea what I'd done to deserve her wrath for all these years. It seemed to be cruel and unusual punishment.

The mysterious stranger took me in equally while I regarded him. His posture was casual—in complete contrast to mine—and nothing about him immediately screamed "danger Will Robinson," but I wasn't about to let my guard down. If there was one thing I'd learned as a witch, it was that looks could be deceiving.

The man smiled at me and the crooked slant of his lips and

the sparkle in his eyes were enough to have me squirming in place, but I willed myself to hold still and stand up straight. My mother's words ricocheted through my head 'appearance is everything.' The non-loving lecture had come after a particularly bad day of teasing when I was in middle school, and the lesson stuck with me through all these years. It was probably the only one that had ever actually been helpful rather than degrading or mean mannered.

Narrowing my gaze slightly, I tried to appear in charge. He didn't need to know that inside I was a quaking mess. "Who are you and what are you doing on our property?"

The stranger glanced away, rubbing a thumb under his lower lip before his gaze found mine again. The motion almost seemed like a nervous tick, but then he responded.

"I'm working here today." It was all he offered, but I closed my eyes and pressed my forehead to the rough texture of the tree. Of course, he was. It was a valid excuse. The grounds of the Kentwell estate would be crawling with extra help today in preparation for the Summer Solstice event this evening.

I sighed.

Now what? This guy was well within his right to be here and my leverage was exactly zero. *How was I going to get out of this situation relatively unscathed?* I'd long given up giving people the benefit of the doubt and I prepared for the worst as I opened my eyes. I wasn't sure what I expected to see, but his mischievous smirk and the intense glimmer of interest reflecting in his gaze caught me off guard.

The man couldn't have been much older than me, but he was quite a bit taller. Dark hair hung across his forehead, making him flick his head to swish the locks back. His eyes gleamed in the sunlight, and while there were a few feet of distance between us, I could see the varying shades of brown that made up their depths. They reminded me of roasted coffee beans, the color dark yet warm. His tanned arms were perfectly muscled, just enough not to be overwhelming but plenty to make a woman swoon. He looked strong. The black tee-shirt he wore stretched across a broad chest and covered a set of rippling abs that I could barely make out under the fabric. Dark jeans hung off of his hips and I knew if he turned around, he'd have a perfect ass to accompany his toned physique.

Holy shit. He is beautiful. Something about him had me swaying closer. His warm gaze was glued to mine, and I could have sworn I saw a flash of heat flare to life within making the breath catch in my lungs. The strength of his magick was like a magnet, the pull of it drawing me in, the tingling power mingling with my own in the space between us.

I'd never reacted to a guy so strongly before and I mentally filed the interaction away for later inspection as a slight breeze tickled across my skin, reminding me of the precarious situation I was still in. I redirected my attention elsewhere before I started drooling, stammering, or blushing. I wasn't known for my prowess around the male species, and I was sure I'd make an idiot out of myself if I continued to ogle him. Besides, I was pretty sure I looked like some crazy swamp thing right now. I quickly reached up and plucked a leaf from my hair. Definitely not the best first impression.

"The question is," he continued in a low, sexy drawl, "what are *you* doing outside sans clothing... not that I'm complaining."

"That is..." I floundered for what to say. "... none of your business," I stammered, realizing that I probably sounded rude. It had been ingrained in my upbringing to be respectful, but everything about this day was turning out utterly wrong. Trying to save myself, I pushed through the awkwardness and pretended like I wasn't naked... outside... hiding behind a tree. This wasn't my life. Or maybe this was *exactly* my life. My luck had always been non-existent. If I could have dropped my face into my palm, I would have. Instead, I responded to the magick I could feel thrumming through the air. "Which coven are you from?"

He chuckled. "So, you can dish out the questions, but you can't take them, huh?"

I arched an eyebrow at him with a small smile curving my lips. "It's a simple question."

He crossed his arms casually over his chest, appearing relaxed as we bantered. Humor sparked in his brown eyes and he lifted his chin up just slightly in a nod. "So was mine." His head tilted to the side, studying me like I was a puzzle he couldn't figure out. If only I was actually that interesting.

Shaking my head with a small laugh, I took a deep breath. I glanced over my shoulder and eyed the distance I needed to travel to get back home. I wasn't far, but I wasn't fully out of sight from the house either. The grey Victorian house I called home peeked through the trees. I was too close for comfort to be caught au natural, yet not close enough to seek refuge within its walls so I could put this entire morning behind me and focus on what today was *really* supposed to be about.

You know, today... the day I would be assigned a witching specialty and a *fiancé* during the Summer Solstice event. The day every good emerging witch looked forward to her entire life. It was only held once a year and it was finally my turn to be presented, which was enough to give me anxiety all on its own. As much as I'd have liked to spend some time getting to know this mysterious guy and figure out why I was so drawn to him, I didn't need any extra complications or distractions right now.

Pull yourself together, Lorn, I chastised myself. *Focus.* In a handful of hours, I'd be as good as engaged to some random guy I probably didn't know. It was a sobering thought.

My eyes trained back on the mystery man's face, and I took a brief moment to soak up the attraction I felt. If the guy was truly a powerful as the magick I sensed in him indicated, then there was little doubt that we would ever be matched together—if he was even available. I'd be lucky if I received a decent placement tonight. Sending a plea to the stars that I'd be as drawn to my future match as I was to this stranger, I forced words to come out of my mouth, ending what had to have been the weirdest conversation of my life thus far.

"Well, I should get going. The longer I stand here... the worse this gets... so..." I fumbled as it dawned on me that my dignity was about to become non-existent.

Squeezing my arm over my breasts more tightly, I tried to cover the rest of myself as best I could with my free hand. I realized no matter how I maneuvered, I would be flashing the stranger more of my body the moment I moved away from the tree. A stranger who apparently had not one polite or chivalrous bone in his body. I mean, couldn't the guy at least turn around?

With a look somewhere between smoldering and mischievous, Mr. Tall-Dark-And-Handsome swiftly reached behind him and pulled his shirt over his head, flashing the defined ridges of his abs at me.

"What? Are you trying to level the playing field?" I arched an eyebrow, but I was sure the effect was lost due to the fact that my attention was glued to the hard planes of his body.

Holding the black fabric in his hand, the man's fingers found the button of his jeans and my face flamed again.

"I... I was kidding," I stammered, but despite my blush and the rapid beat of my heart, I almost wished he would continue.

He chuckled as though he could read my mind. "Nice to see

the interest on your face, but no… I wasn't planning to strip for you. Although, I'm a willing negotiator." My gaze flitted to his face and the sinful smirk I found curving his lips. Everything about his demeanor radiated confidence from the way his arms flexed to the way he unabashedly looked at me.

"You're evil." I refused to let my attention slide back down his body. He may be hot, but he seemed to have an ego the size of Mars.

"So I've been told." Holding out a hand, he offered the shirt to me, making me eat my words.

"You're giving me your shirt?" I questioned hesitantly. It was rare that anyone ever went out of their way to help me.

I must have appeared shocked because his features softened.

"I am, but I require a favor in return." His voice was gentle, and he dipped his head, catching my full attention.

"This shirt comes with strings, then?" I was sure my face looked as confused as I felt.

"Only one." The quality of his smile was irresistible, and his muscles rippled as he leaned closer as if he was going to confide a secret. His eyes were bright, and he drew a deep inhale into his lungs before sating my curiosity with his answer. "I want to know your name."

A sigh of relief left my lips. The request was easy enough to fulfil. "Oh, uh… I'm Lorn." I went to reach out a hand only to quickly put it back in its place, keeping the essentials blocked from view. I ended up doing a weird shrug that I was sure made me look spastic, adding to the awkward allure I was expertly spinning. *Not.*

The smile on his face was genuine as he laughed at my distress and I couldn't help but smirk at him and the whole weird situation.

"I like that." He took a tentative step closer, extending his arm as far as he could to hand me the shirt while still keeping a respectable distance. It was a move I appreciated.

With a rueful smile, I stepped from my hiding spot and took the offering. Just as my hand closed around the soft fabric, his smile faltered, and his eyes widened just enough that I noticed. He inhaled deeply and then released the shirt. Brows furrowed in confusion, I ducked quickly back behind the blessedly wide tree trunk. His reaction to me had me lifting an arm to smell myself. Seriously? I didn't smell shower fresh after waking up in a freaking forest, but I certainly didn't smell terrible enough to warrant that kind of response. Frowning, I pulled the fabric over my head fully encasing myself in the shirt. The spicy outdoor scent of the still nameless man assaulted me in the best way. The fabric smelled good. Incredibly good. The mixture of spice, woods, and something sweet washed over me, and an involuntary shudder raced down my body.

Stars, get ahold of yourself! I smoothed my hands down the shirt, making sure it covered everything while I tried to shake off my reaction. The black tee-shirt hit mid-thigh, and for the first time since I awoke that morning, I finally relaxed.

I stepped from around the tree. "Thank you—" I held the note, waiting for him to fill in the blank.

"Axel."

Nodding, I tucked my hair behind my ear. "Nice name." *Smooth, Lorn. Real smooth.* I internally rolled my eyes at myself and hurriedly covered my artlessness with another question. "You sure you can survive without your shirt?"

More like was he sure he could avoid being jumped now that all his gorgeous, golden skin was out on display, but I didn't think that would be appropriate to voice out loud. Besides, he looked more than capable of handling himself if he needed too.

"I'll survive, and I think you needed it more than I did." He winked at me, but I didn't miss how his eyes scanned down my body, taking in the bare skin of my legs before his focus returned to my face. "Besides," he held up his hands and wiggled his fingers, "I'll survive. I can just magick another one."

"Right. Thanks then." I gave him a tiny wave as I started walking backward, nearly tripping in my hasty escape. The last thing I needed was him questioning why I didn't magick *myself* any clothing. The truth was, magick and I had a love-hate relationship. I loved to try and use it, and it hated to work correctly. I was safer walking around in the buff than I was trying to summon and use my wand. Every spell I tried to cast ended in disastrous chaos. I gave him one last cursory glance and then turned and high tailed it toward my destination.

"Just as beautiful going as you were *coming*!" he teased, the scintillating notes of his lowered voice clearly relaying the dirty innuendo of his words. I pursed my lips trying not to smile. The pervert. Anyone could be listening, and I knew that had been the point. From knight in shining armor right back down to hellion.

"You just had to make that sound dirty, didn't you?" I called over my shoulder, just loud enough to reach him as I retreated.

Axel's hands were tucked into the pockets of his low hanging jeans as he watched me go, every defined ridge on display. "It wouldn't be fun if I didn't, sweet cheeks." The grin on his face was also present in his tone.

I shook my head, but my lips were permanently tipped upward. Axel was by far the most interesting guy I had ever spoken to, and I didn't even know him.

"Will I see you again?" he asked when I didn't dignify his vexatious flirting with a response.

I stopped and turned around. Such a large part of me wanted to stay outside and spend time getting to know him. I longed to hide away from the world and forget that today existed, and the allure he presented was hard to pass up. But I needed to get back inside. Every minute I wasted outdoors was just an increased risk in being found out, and I had no idea what the repercussions of bailing on the Solstice would be. Nothing good.

With a sigh, I resigned myself to my fate. "I'll be at the Solstice tonight." Biting my lip, I didn't wait for his reply. I turned and hightailed it through the forest.

Moving from tree to tree, I tried to stay out of view of the house as I made my way to the gnarly old oak with a hollowed-out trunk I'd used since I was a child. It was my perfect hiding place, but lately all it held was an extra pair of clothing.

A sense of nostalgia flared in my chest as I reached into the familiar knot of the tree and retrieved my clothes. I'd spent my childhood in this yard, playing in this forest, and I ached for just one more day of carefree living before my life changed permanently. A lazy afternoon spent outdoors with a favorite book sounded like heaven, and I let myself dream for a second more before I shut down my delusional musings to get back to the task at hand. Adulting sucked.

Slipping into a pair of cotton shorts, I stripped out of the good smelling shirt and donned a sports bra and my own loose, oversized tee-shirt. If I walked back indoors wearing clothing that clearly smelled like the handsome man I'd left behind, my parents would be sure to notice and draw their own conclusions. It wouldn't matter that those conclusions would be inaccurate, the evidence would be implicating. I threw on my old pair of tennis shoes, combed my hair with my fingers, and called it as good as it was going to get.

Quickly coming up with a plan, I tucked the guy's shirt under my arm, started jogging, and left the tree line. The property was crawling with maids and ground staff, and they glanced up from their work as I made my way toward the house. Ducking my head, my footsteps thudded against the wooden decking as I made my way up and inside.

Cool air greeted me as I slid the back door shut, enjoying how refreshing it felt against my overheated skin. The back entrance led into the kitchen area, and I glanced longingly at the fridge, desperate for a cold drink—maybe some much needed iced coffee—but the sound of my mother's voice from deep within the house had my feet moving past the appliance as I scrambled for the stairs. It was best to try and avoid her at all costs.

My perfectly coiffed adopted mother walked into the entryway, dictating to the floating notebook next to her. The pen scribbled furiously to keep up with her notes, undoubtedly about the Summer Solstice event. Since my father was on the High Coven—a council of powerful witches and warlocks formed from the various covens around the United States—it was my parents' turn to host the event for our region of magick users. As much as I was dreading having to attend, I was happy that it had brought my father home. His position so often kept him out of the house, leaving me alone with my mother.

Avalon Castalia came from powerful witching bloodlines. Her family was considered royalty among the covens, and it was no surprise that she had married a man just as powerful—merging her family line with the Kentwells. She ran her household with an iron fist, and I'd never felt like I measured up to her high expectations. My adopted father, on the other hand, I adored. Cardoc Kentwell was a religious rule follower and believed in the old ways of the witches and warlocks, but when it came to me, he was just a big softy.

Our vastly different appearances were a constant reminder that I wasn't blood related—a fact that Avalon liked to make sure I never forgot. Both of my parents had golden blonde hair —my father's a bit darker than my mother's—and their skin was creamy white. I, on the other hand, was their complete opposite with a head full of dark brown hair, and golden skin. The only thing I had in common with either of them was the cornflower blue color of my eyes.

"Lorn, there you are!" My mother's call floated toward me, making me pause right as my foot hit the first stair. *So close and yet so fucking far.*

Turning slowly, I hid the black shirt I was holding behind my back.

When her blue eyes locked with mine, I offered her a tentative smile. Confusion crossed her face as she evaluated my appearance. With a wave of her wand, the notebook snapped closed, and it and the pen promptly vanished into thin air.

"What on earth happened to you?" she queried, her eyes racking me from head to toe. I knew my mother was a clean freak and wouldn't appreciate me dirtying her foyer—or her stylish, crisp, white outfit.

I tried not to let the disappointment I saw on her face get to me. I hated lying, but I also knew there was no way I could explain the odd sleepwalking that had been happening to me lately. They'd never done well with the oddities that surrounded me, and I'd spent the last number of years trying to appear as normal as possible.

Downplaying the morning's events, I took a deep breath and dove in. "I went for a run but I tripped and the ground broke my fall." I hoped my absence this morning hadn't been noted. It was completely possible for us to miss each other in this big house, as long as none of us went looking for the other.

She tsked and shook her head. "Lorn, today of all days you decide to go running?" She looked exasperated. In her defense, running never had been my thing. Who the hell liked to run? "While I appreciate your effort toward physical fitness, you've got just over an hour to clean and prep, but then we have nail, hair, and makeup appointments this afternoon to get ready for tonight." Her phone jingled, saving me from the scolding and gloating portion of the conversation about how I could work harder, how wonderful her own Solstice was, and all the minute details that would make tonight's event a smashing success—as long as I didn't ruin all her hard work with a crappy placement. I escaped to my room as she answered her cell and quickly became preoccupied.

The covers on my bed were still a mess, and I scrutinized every inch of my room, searching for clues as to what happened last night. Other than having left the sheets in a tangle—a federal crime according to Avalon—nothing looked out of place other than the neglected suitcases in the corner that I hadn't put away after returning home from the academy following graduation.

Huffing out a frustrated sound, I plunked myself down on the bed and fell backward across the mattress, letting my hair hang over the other side while I rested my hands on my stomach. The softness of my mattress was a welcome comfort compared to my inner turmoil. Nothing about my life made sense any longer, or maybe it never had. Maybe all the small, weird occurrences that had happened to me fit together like jagged pieces to a larger puzzle.

I reached into my nightstand and pulled out my journal flipping to the next available blank page. Writing as fast as I could,

I detailed everything I could remember about the night before, noting down all my observations about the episode. Writing everything down had become my salvation when I had no one else to confide in, and it also allowed me to look back over each occurrence to check for similarities and differences, hoping that someday I'd be able to connect the dots and figure out what the hell was going on.

Glancing at the clock, I knew I was out of time to stew as I tried to figure everything out. The Summer Solstice was hours away, and Avalon's strict schedule was not to be trifled with. Apprehension settled in the pit of my stomach.

There was no way that my being assigned a witching specialty was going to go well, and if it didn't then I held no hope of snaring myself a good match.

I lifted my hand, cupping it as I brought my fingers together and whispered, "Suvasa."

Magick gathered at my fingertips, and with a quick downward sweep of my hand, my wand appeared. Tentatively, I reached for it, wrapping my palm around the beautiful wooden handle. The moment my skin made contact sparks flew, branding the palm of my hand with a wicked shock.

I dropped the wand and rubbed at the black soot marks left behind.

This was hopeless. Growing up, I'd always tried my very best in the witching schools my parents had sent me to. I'd never had the knack for magick, and neither of them could understand my struggles. I was an anomaly among my own kind —the witch who couldn't even use her wand without wreaking havoc on the world around me.

Sighing, I picked up the black tee-shirt I'd dropped onto the bed, hugged it to my chest, and buried my nose in it. Axel's scent was somehow calming, an earthy mix all his own.

With a groan, I pulled myself up and headed for the bathroom, flipping on the shower. It was time to get ready and face the music. Whatever the outcome of the Solstice, I'd deal with it. I'd been juggling difficult situations my entire life, and this was no different. No matter what specialty I ended up with, I'd make the most of it, and if I was matched with someone I didn't like, I simply wouldn't marry them. It wasn't a common option, but I was sure it had to have happened in the past. And if not, I'd just have to be the first. I wasn't going to let one night change my entire life.

TWO

AXEL

I ran my hand through my hair and swept it off of my forehead. Everything about this morning had been surprising, from spotting Lorn fleeing through the forest naked to reacting so strongly to her scent when she reached out to take my shirt. Her rich fragrance still teased my memory even as she retreated into the trees and disappeared from sight. I swore her scent—an intoxicating combination of lush forest, blackberries, and violets—stayed with me as I turned and strode through the forest, heading for the tree line so I could observe the house that was seated at the center of the property.

Property I was currently trespassing on. I'd been careful to open the portal on the edge of the warlock's forest, wary of setting off any warded alarms that may still be activated as I entered into dangerous territory. Then I'd gone and announced myself to a witch like an idiot. A very beautiful witch.

Witches and warlocks were our greatest enemy, and I was infiltrating their domain. It wasn't just any magick user's land I stood on, either. No, that would have been too easy. Instead, I stood entrenched in a fucking High Coven member's private property. If any of my pack-mates knew what I was up to, they'd probably kill me themselves for taking such a dangerous risk.

The way I saw it, we put our lives on the line every day by existing, not to mention the work we did, and if I was successful today, the reward would far outweigh the risk. I could only hope my friends—practically my brothers—would understand.

The sound of murmured voices up ahead had me pausing as I reached the clearing, keeping to the tree line and crouching in the brush for cover. Calling forth my magick, I summoned a black tee-shirt to replace the one I'd given to Lorn, quickly pulling the black fabric over my upper body. Then I held my forearm up and, with my other hand, directed magick through my finger to start tracing symbols on my exposed flesh.

Slashing lines of pulsing magick glowed as I finished the symbol I needed, and after a moment it seared itself into my skin, the glow sinking below the surface of my flesh and disappearing while giving me the invisibility I'd called upon. My hands faded from sight and the rest of my body followed suit until I was nothing more than a glimmer in the sunlight. Tracing my forearm one more time I drew another rune, this one for increased hearing, and let the magick get to work as it crashed over me, the volume of the world rising.

I could hear every scampering squirrel and the rustle of every leaf in the trees overhead. Dimming the noise of my surroundings, I focused on the talk of the workers who buzzed around the large gray Victorian mansion like little bees, obeying the king or queen who dished out orders from indoors. I tried to listen for any gossip that would be useful and aid my plans, but I soon found my thoughts straying back to the enigma of the girl.

My muscles tensed as I closed my eyes and pictured the

curves Lorn sported; her breasts looked big enough to fill my hands, and her waist flared into curving hips and a beautiful ass that men should worship. I loved the way her bow-shaped lips tilted when she smiled and the sparkle in her blue eyes when her words sparred with my own.

The thought of other men seeing her the way I had this morning sent a wave of irrational jealousy rocketing through me, and I tipped my face skyward while I tried to calm myself and the magick that surged strongly through my veins. I was insanely glad that I'd been the one to find her, but now all I wanted to do was see her again. Maybe tonight at the Solstice I could...

I gritted my teeth. Being here that long was not in the plans. This was supposed to be an in and out kind of mission, and to hang around would be the worst kind of foolish. I took a few measured deep breaths, hoping the familiar pine-scented air would help clear my head. The last thing I needed was complications, and I knew Lorn fell into that category.

What the hell had she been doing outside without any clothing on in the first place? A ton of questions plagued me as my mind refused to stray far from the mysterious girl. While nudity wasn't uncommon in many types of supernatural groups, it wasn't commonplace for witches, and there'd been an uneasiness about her as she ran through the forest. The closer I'd flown toward her in my alternate form, the more I felt the tingle of the girl's magick and a niggling need to help her. A feeling that wouldn't let up until I'd landed, shifted from a hawk back to my human form, and struck up a conversation.

I didn't know how or why I was drawn to her when we were from different species. I was a skinwalker. A powerful breed of magick users of Native American descent with the ability to shift into animal forms.

Rumored to be touched by dark magick and far more powerful than the typical witch or warlock, they had deemed us their mortal enemies and began killing us off one by one.

I'd felt more alive just being around Lorn for those few short minutes, but fraternizing with supernaturals was always risky, and the fact that she was a witch made it downright deadly.

Shaking off my thoughts of her, I glanced around for another vantage point, so I could get closer to the mansion.

I was about to change up my spying tactics when a figure broke from the tree line, heading toward the house, and I watched transfixed as Lorn jogged up the stairs of the back porch and slipped inside.

Oh, fuck. I drove a hand into my hair, pushing it away from my face. Not only was she a witch but she was the daughter of the fucking High Coven member? I knew the guy had a daughter. I'd done a minuscule amount of research before portal jumping, but it hadn't occurred to me when I met Lorn. What was it about her that had made me so fucking blind?

I groaned quietly and rubbed at my eyes with my palms. More damn obstacles.

Turning up my hearing to a near painful volume, I closed my eyes in focus, tilted my head, and listened to see if she would out my presence to her parents. I was pretty sure she'd bought my story of working on the property, but it wasn't a risk I was willing to take. My mission was too important for chances like that.

While eavesdropping on Lorn's private conversation made me feel slightly uneasy, I was happy to know she hadn't mentioned me or our encounter in the woods at all. The best news I had was that they would be heading out in preparation for their event this evening, which meant I only had to wait for them to leave before making my move.

Sliding back into the woods to wait, I found a hidden spot with a clear view of the driveway and made myself comfortable against a large, towering oak.

Digging into my back pocket, I produced a crinkled note I'd looked at a dozen times—the entire reason I was taking such a massive risk in the first place. Its creased lines were becoming soft from overuse, and I stared at the scrawl written in dark ink. There were only a few words written down.

Possible unidentified walker followed by coordinates—which I'd used to magick a portal—and the name of an artifact that I was supposed to extract for the Fae Prince, Rook Oberan. Without the artifact, he'd never share the information he had on the supposed skinwalker. Information like where I could find them.

The Fae, like all supernaturals, were self-serving. There was no way he'd share what he knew without a trade, and the importance of the artifact matched the importance I levied on the knowledge he held for ransom.

My younger brother's happy voice echoed in my head, and I squeezed my eyes shut against the onslaught of memories. Pain and guilt assuaged me. The air felt thinner and I found it harder to breathe. Tilting my head back against the trunk of the tree I swallowed hard, trying to regain control of my spiraling regret. It'd been over a year since I'd last been attacked by grief of this level, but I shouldn't have been surprised. The idea of another young skinwalker staring down death unknowingly—alone—was bound to uncover the emotions I'd worked so hard to bury. I should have been there for my brother. It should have been me who died in his place. I wasn't going to let another kid die on my watch. Not when I knew about their existence and could do something to save their life. I was sure it was why Rook targeted me with his letter. He knew I'd bite and bring him back what he wanted, and I fucking would.

What seemed like a simple transaction was anything but because the artifact I needed to retrieve currently resided inside that house. My gaze flicked back to the mansion as I re-pocketed the missive and pushed away the gloom my thoughts had conjured.

Exactly an hour later, I watched Lorn trail her mother out of the house. I drank in the sight of her. Wet hair was piled high on her head in a messy bun and she wore jean shorts that showcased her long legs with a tee-shirt sporting the name of a band with their logo on it. My eyes were riveted to her form until she climbed into a black Lincoln Town Car and drove out of view.

The house was as empty as it was going to get. Checking that my runes were still activated, I stood and stretched before I prowled on silent feet across the green grass of the lawn. My back met modern vinyl siding as I pressed myself against the mansion, looking around to make sure no one had noticed me. The invisibility rune worked to an extent, but anyone who looked hard enough would be able to make out my shimmering outline as it caught the sunlight.

Drawing another rune on my skin, I let the locator magick sink into my body before I closed my eyes and pictured the artifact I was after. The Tavia Glass. From my research, it was a small glass bottle containing a strong potion that would give anyone who drank from it the ability to slip between the realms without leaving any kind of calling mark behind. Essentially, whoever consumed the liquid would be unnoticeable and untraceable. A powerful and potentially dangerous combination.

Since I'd seen a picture of what the glass looked like, the locator magick I'd used was able to latch onto it faintly. The more familiar I was with an object or a person the easier they were to locate. Out of all my packmates I was the most skilled with using this rune, another reason I was sure Rook picked me to lure into this task for him. If I'd only had a little information on the skinwalker, I might have been able to track them on my own, without this vigilante mission. Closing my eyes, I let the magick work as it showed me glowing, neon blueprints that outlined the house. A thrumming orb gleamed on the blueprints, confirming the treasure I sought was indeed indoors.

Circling the property, I searched for the best way inside. For a place that let their wards down they were much more secure with their actual dwelling. All the windows on the first floor were locked but the back door was propped open for the staff carrying items in and out as they set up for tonight's event. Rounding the back of the house, I ducked into the tree line and let my primal side surge forward, the runes disengaging in my shift. I chose an animal form from my arsenal, picturing a sleek black house cat as magick grew heavy in my limbs. The give of muscle and bone shifted with the image in my mind's eye.

The world spun and dropped as my perspective changed. Every blade of grass appeared larger from my feline form, and I circled the tree I was next to unable to resist rubbing my fur covered body on the bark to scratch before sauntering off toward the house at a lope. Around my neck was a red collar I'd envisioned with my shift, ensuring I seemed like a pet rather than a feral feline. Cats weren't my favorite form, but it was the one most likely to get me inside.

Traipsing toward the house, I let the natural reflexes of my cat take over as I jumped up onto the railing of the porch, balancing before hopping down in a seamless, graceful motion. Padding my way toward the door, I slipped easily through the opening as the hired help scurried this way and that, deeply focused on their preparations.

I headed through the kitchen, following the directions I'd memorized from the blueprints. The smell of fresh seafood pulled at my senses, and I had to fight my feline instincts not to go after the scent. As much as my animal and I acted as one, we were technically separate beings co-existing in the same body through magick. Whatever animal I took on had a will of its own, but it bequeathed control to me while I wore its skin.

The map led me to a doorway, and I batted at the partially closed door, opening it enough to slip inside. The staircase beyond was dark, and I prowled on padded feet down the stairs, taking a sharp right at the bottom and heading into a vast basement complete with three couches and a massive entertainment system, all shrouded by darkness. The guys would fucking love the setup the Kentwells had going here, and I mentally logged the layout for future discussion. Enemy or not, they had good taste in electronics.

Using the night vision that came equipped with this animal form, I hurried to the back room I'd seen on the map. Which happened to be hidden behind a closed door.

Fucking great. I grumbled to myself as I paced, looking up at the door handle. There was no way I was going to switch back to a human to open the door. Not when the risk was so monumental. I could hear the thudding of footsteps overhead. There was nothing to do now except...

I groaned as I slunk between the sofas, finding a private spot. Closing my eyes, I tilted my head and let the magick flow over my body, changing from a cat into a mouse.

Changing into something so small was painful but the discomfort would be worth it. Scurrying from my hiding place I squeezed myself under the door. The room was littered with cluttered tables, bookshelves full of jars and bottles, and herbs growing in pots along the far wall. Two small windows on the outside walls of the room near the ceiling let in shafts of sunlight that filtered into the darkened space. The overhead lights were off and I had no way to turn them on, so I was grateful for the ambient light that allowed me to make out where to start investigating first.

Thank fuck mice were damn good climbers, because I quickly scaled a wooden work table, and wove my way through various plants, herbs, and jars filled with gross looking concoctions. I studied each one I passed, keeping an eye out for the Tavia Glass that I had to be nearly on top of. The map had been clear. The Glass was in this room.

By the time I spotted it I was thoroughly revolted by some of the contents spread across the work table. I'd seen a lot of shit in my lifetime thus far, but witches used disgusting things in their spells. Tongues, eyeballs, and disgusting slimy shit filled the jars, and I had to force myself to look away. I was damn glad we didn't need to stoop to such levels for our own magick. If we ever needed more than the magick thrumming through our veins, we generally worked with plants and herbs.

Climbing my way up a tall bookshelf, I scampered down the wooden plank until I was staring at my reflection in the curved surface of the Tavia Glass. I looked around and tried to figure out the best course of action to get the artifact and get the hell out of dodge.

I was so close now… If I could just figure out how to pick up the vial and…

The sound of a low male voice had me freezing in my perusal of the room as I worked up a solid exit strategy. A key slid into the lock at the door and my eyes widened as I watched the door handle turn. Darting for cover, I dove behind some horizontally stacked books on the shelf, making sure every part of my small, furry body was out of view. I hated being such a small creature, but at that very moment I was grateful for my ability to slip out of sight so easily. A cat would have been much harder to hide from the warlock currently entering the room.

The blond man strode inside with a phone held to his ear, pocketing the set of keys he'd used to unlock the door to the workshop.

His workshop, because the man was none other than Cardoc Kentwell himself. Owner of the property I was trespassing on, coven leader for the Winston-Salem regional coven, a High Coven member, and Lorn's father.

"Don't take this the wrong way, but why are you calling? It's been years since I've heard from you, not that I'm not happy you're finally reaching out." He spoke into the phone, but no matter how hard I stretched my hearing in this form, I couldn't make out more than the muffled sound of another male voice on the other end of the line. The conversation I could make out was solely one sided.

"She'll be happy to hear you cared enough to call and wish her well on the eve of her Solstice. After all, she barely knows you outside of the birthday cards you send her every summer." Sarcasm tinged Cardoc's words as he braced a hand against his work table and hung his head as he listened to the retort on the other end of the phone.

"I'm her father. I think I know what's best for her." His tone was decidedly less friendly with each passing comment, the conversation clearly deteriorating as he and the other man spoke.

"You don't need to worry about Lorn—"

"She's been improving. I've been taking care of her for her

entire life, you really think I'd let anything—" His words clipped at the end as he was continually interrupted.

"I appreciate your concern, but it's unfounded." Turning around, Cardoc leaned his hips against the worktable, the contents in the jars sloshing around as the table rocked from the addition of his weight against it. Reaching up, he pinched the bridge of his nose and closed his eyes, clearly upset or stressed about the discussion he was having.

"I have to run. We have a lot to accomplish before tonight's event. I... I hope you'll call again sometime. When things are less... hectic." He stuttered over his words, growing quieter with each passing one.

He pulled the phone away from his ear and stared down at it while the garbled voice continued pleading their case. Clicking it off, he squeezed it tightly in his hand before placing it in his pocket. The sigh he released sounded as haggard as he looked, and he ran his hand through his hair before straightening his posture, picking up a bowl full of crushed plants, and leaving the workshop. The door clicked shut behind him, and I waited for the jingle of keys before I dared to move.

Playing it safe, I waited an extra few minutes before exhaling the breath I seemed to be holding and allowing myself to relax. That was way too damn close.

My magick played over my small body and I let bone and muscle expand until I was back in my favorite form: a red-tailed hawk. Grasping the Glass carefully in a talon, I spread my wings, ruffling my feathers, and took flight. Soaring to the small glass widow, I bit at the lock until it moved and then put my weight into the glass pane. The window fell open, the glass pane hinging into the grass. Not bothering to worry about the evidence of the open window, I spread my wings and left the ground, soaring into the safety of the forest.

Once I was far enough away, I landed and shifted back to my human form—summoning the clothing I was wearing before my shift to appear before me. It was a handy trick that meant less naked time outdoors. I stepped into my clothing as my mind immediately fell back to a naked Lorn. What the hell had the guy on the other end of the line been so concerned with? Whatever it was, the guy had seemed adamant in his worry over her.

Something stirred deeply inside while I eyed the distance to the edge of the property and weighed my options. I'd done what I came here to do. I palmed the Tavia Glass and held it up for inspection, before spelling it to my person and allowing it to disappear from sight. With the object safely tucked away where no one would find it, I glanced over my shoulder in the direction of the preparations for the Solstice Lorn would be attending.

"Fuck," I whispered into the trees. There was no doubt in my mind. Every cell of my being was being called to stay and see her again. And with what I'd overheard, I wasn't sure I could leave until I was certain she was all right.

My packmates were going to kill me for this, but I was going to hell anyway...

I shifted, took to the sky, and found a place to wait.

THREE

LORN

The heels decorating my feet were killing me as I strode through the foyer. If I had to listen to another litany of well-wishes and excited proclamations over my ceremony tonight, I was going to keel over dead. Or, at least, I would wish for it to happen. Spending an entire afternoon with Avalon dropping veiled, passive-aggressive comments about how her disappointment in me would be sealed if I didn't place well tonight had been exhausting and frustrating and had only served to make me more nervous—which I hadn't even realized was possible. I'd been dreading this night for as long as I could remember, and a minuscule amount of relief shot through me as my hand landed on the cool metal handle that led into my father's office. It was the one room where none of the guests would dare go, and that made it my personal haven for as long as I could hide.

The familiar scent of books surrounded me like a warm blanket as I slipped inside and carefully shut the door. I inhaled deeply and focused on relaxing one muscle at a time. The happy chatter of the party was blessedly muted by the heavy white wooden door, becoming a soft soundtrack that I could easily tune out. My magick was a constant agitated buzz inside of me reacting to my frazzled feelings, but it finally quieted at the solace of the study and my nerves soothed. My biggest fear was losing control of it and outing myself and my unique abilities to the congregation of magick users amassed on our property.

My phone dinged as I made my way to the plush sofa that sat in the middle of the room facing a set of tall windows that overlooked the front yard. Unwilling to care about the fancy dress I was wearing, I plopped down on the couch, wishing for my yoga pants and favorite tee-shirt as I nearly lost myself in a sea of tulle and lace. Once the layers were tamed I dug my phone out of my small purse and smiled when I saw my best friend's name on the screen.

Emmaline: Are you wearing the shoes? You better be wearing the heels, LoLo.

Her text message made me grin, and I quickly snapped a picture of the beautiful shoes she'd made me swear to wear tonight and sent the picture to her.

Emmaline: Eek! Those look fab! I'm getting ready to leave. I am so freakin' excited! See you soon, boo!

Her enthusiasm over tonight's festivities was the one bright shining spot in having to attend the Solstice tonight.

The door clicked open, increasing the party's volume again and setting me on high alert.

"Hiding out, are you?" My father smiled at me from the

doorway and I relaxed from the tension of the intrusion. There was no reason to feel guilty for skipping out on the party when he himself seemed to be doing the same thing.

My father's tuxedo was tailored perfectly, squaring his shoulders and framing his medium build with a double-breasted lapel. Golden cufflinks winked in the overhead lights from their place at the ends of his sleeves, nearly matching the color of his hair. The black of the suit was stark against his pale skin. He looked dignified, refined, traditional, and rich. I had no doubt that it was the precise look he was after.

I wasn't ashamed to answer him when I knew he was just as guilty as I was. "Absolutely. And so are you!" A smile broke across my lips when he chuckled and walked further into the room, thankfully closing the door behind him to keep other partygoers at bay. I wasn't quite ready to surrender the solitude.

Swirling some amber liquid in his crystal glass, he strode over and took a seat in a wingback chair. The dark grey upholstery made the chair stand out like a dark throne. Fitting for one of the highest coven members in the country. It was his favorite. I had so many memories of him sitting in that chair reading to me as I grew up. My love of literature may have progressed without my father in my life, but I knew he played a big part in my bookish personality. He never minded my introverted demeanor. In fact, I'd concluded that he had some of that in himself, as well. Large parties like this were much more Avalon's cup of tea.

His blue gaze found mine. "So, what has you hiding out? I was sure you'd be with your friends tonight. Emmaline, at least." His smile was gentle, but I knew he was curious as to what I was doing in his office. The Solstice was a larger event than prom, and just about everyone my age would be gathering in the clearing to hang out together before the event began and our lives changed monumentally. It was a time to mingle and be seen.

The truth was, my father had no idea about my trepidations. I'd never told him how much I was dreading my placement. Suddenly the secrets I was keeping from him felt like a chasm between us, and I traced the oriental pattern of the sofa fabric with one elegantly painted finger, giving him an unladylike shrug while I avoided eye contact.

If there was one person who could see straight through me —straight through my lies and half-truths—it was my father.

The overwhelming urge to open up and tell him what was bothering me nearly knocked me over with its force, but tonight wasn't the right time. There was too much going on. Too many people around. Not to mention he also held high hopes for my witching ceremony tonight. I'd done my best over the last few years to hide my oddities from my parents' knowledge, trying to appear as normal as possible. It'd become necessary, especially after I saw how my differences affected my parents: my father's constant worry and my mother's constant disdain.

The pressure was real, and my stomach was alight with nerves.

"Lorn," my father said softly, leaning back into his chair to get comfortable as he crossed one ankle over his knee. "I know you're nervous about tonight. I remember feeling the same way when it was my Solstice. Just know that whatever specialty you receive, we will be happy with. All we've ever asked for is that you try your best. I know that sometimes magick doesn't come as naturally to you as it does for others, but you've always worked hard, and that goes farther than natural talent. It doesn't matter which specialty you're placed within, as long as you apply yourself."

I took a seat on the couch and nodded, trying not to take his pep talk too personally. I wasn't a good witch. We all knew that. My hard work may mean something to him—and I appreciated that—but it wouldn't placate my mother, nor would it help me land a good match. I'd already lost the attention of the only guy I'd cared about, and apparently his affection had always been tainted with an ulterior motive. While I'd been left with a mountain of hurt, he'd already moved on to Kadence Witherstone, a witch who would undoubtedly end up with a good placement.

I sighed but gave my father a weak smile. Downing his drink and leaving the crystal glass on the end table, he stood and ran a hand through his golden hair. He straightened his tuxedo jacket and moved behind the couch on his way to the door.

"I won't let anything bad happen tonight, I promise. You're going to make a good match. You're part of *my* family. The best day of my life was finding you on my doorstep."

I nodded, swallowing back the rising emotion that threatened to spill out. Being adopted by Cardoc was the best thing that had ever happened to me. It was as if he'd read my mind, and the conviction in the tone of his voice helped lend me some of his confidence. I took a bolstered breath, feeling more myself again as he patted my head, gently ruffling the careful half up, half down style the salon had perfected.

"Careful, or Avalon will hex you for that!" I laughed.

"Lorn…" The warning in his tone was clear, and I immediately straightened my posture.

"Sorry… I meant Mother, not Avalon," I mumbled. It was something he'd criticized me on before, and I winced as I realized my screw up. I tried to call her mother when I was around him, but her non-maternal attitude toward me had made me lean toward calling her by her actual name rather than the endearment—it'd been that way since I became a teenager. Still, I knew better and I felt sheepish for the slip-up.

The soles of his shiny black shoes were a soft thud on the hardwood as he moved to the door, choosing to let my faux pas slide. "I'll see you out there soon?" He checked his watch. "Festivities start in ten minutes."

"I'm just going to take one more minute to myself and then I'll be out to join the masses." I stood, brushing my hands down the black tulle and lace skirt of my dress to straighten it.

"You look lovely." His smile was warm, and it helped ease some of my fears for a moment. No matter what happened tonight, my father would be there looking out for me. With his power and position, I shouldn't stress. At least, that's what I tried telling myself, however my latest episode just this morning made me more worried than I'd been in a while.

Squaring his posture and looking every bit the rigid 'politician,' he headed back out into the crowd.

My arms found their way around my body and I ran my hands up and down the bare skin of my arms. Pacing the length of the room, I tried to keep my balance on the three-inch heels Emmaline had insisted on. I loved her and hated her all at the same time for that fashion decision. On one hand, my legs looked great and the shoes were sexy. On the other? My feet were already aching, and I had to get through an entire night of standing.

I missed my favorite pair of flip flops.

Dropping my arms, I shook out my hands while I crossed the room on wobbly ankles. A bad omen felt like it followed me from one end of the study to the other and back again. The invisible dark cloud just grew as my stomach churned. As much as I wished for it to be otherwise, I just knew that tonight wasn't going to go well. I squeezed my eyes shut, trying to ward off the negative feelings and will my rising panic to subside.

Magick doesn't come as naturally to you, my father's words rebounded through my head, and I let out a self-deprecating laugh looking down at my hands. If he only understood how wrong that statement was. Even now I could feel the magick thrumming through my veins—a constant electric current that I suppressed. No. Magick came *too* naturally to me. What didn't come intrinsically was using a wand to cast magick the way other witches could. Witches and warlocks weren't able to access the magick that lived inside themselves without wielding their wands. My wand, however, might as well have just been any old wooden stick for the way my magick rebelled against it. I didn't need the wand to use my magick, and the way it manifested was just one more oddity that set me apart—made me 'other.' Made me less.

It made me feel like a failure.

A bell tolled in the distance calling everyone to gather in the clearing for the start of the event, and magick rocketed out of me as my anxiety spiked. I contained the mishap quickly and sent a plea skyward that no one outside of this room had noticed. When everything remained quiet, I let out the breath I was holding on a long sigh. In my magickal outburst, the walls had shaken, knocking the pictures they held askew, and I set off to straighten them—more for something to do with my hands than for aesthetic reasons.

Memories of a happy childhood filled the walls, and each one brought a grin to my face as I set them all back to rights. My father and I at the carnival, birthdays, beach trips. My entire life was up on this wall right down to my graduation from the Witching Academy just a few weeks earlier. There were also images of Avalon and Cardoc's wedding and my late grandparents. The last image on the wall was one of my father with his brother. The image was photographed in black and white, but the resemblance between my father and the uncle I hadn't seen in more years than I could remember was uncanny. They had their arms thrown around each other with smiles on their handsome faces. Since the picture was devoid of color, I couldn't tell if all of their features were similar, but they shared the same eye shape, nose, and smile. I wasn't sure what had happened between them, but the picture screamed of happier times. With so much that could go wrong tonight, I just hoped that whatever happened this evening didn't leave me looking back on a similar picture years from now, remembering the times before the Solstice with a wistful longing for the better days of my youth.

My phone had been chiming from across the room, and I hurriedly finished my task, looking over the wall before I walked back to where I'd left the cell on the sofa.

Emmaline: Where are you?

Emmaline: Everything is starting, and I can't find you!

Emmaline: You know you can't bail on this, right?

Emmaline: Unless you're dead, you better get your cute butt out here!

I grinned at the last one. I could picture her now, impatiently tapping the toe of her very expensive shoes as she waited for me. She'd probably be livid by now. Unlike me, she was giddy for the Solstice. Her enthusiasm was the one shining bright spot in my having to attend the Solstice tonight. As a star student and a talented witch, Emmaline was bound to get an amazing placement, and I wanted to be there to support her.

The bell tolled three times in a row, signaling the start of the festivities, and I scooped up my things and ran—as fast as an inexperienced heel wearer could run—to the door. Wrenching it open, I left the study and the house behind as I hurried into the backyard.

FOUR

LORN

"I can't believe you!" Emmaline screeched quietly from her place near the back of the gathered crowd. I rushed through the forest to her side, one hand holding my dress up, so I didn't ruin it in my haste, and the other clutching my purse and the black fabric of Axel's t-shirt that I'd brought along with me, hoping it'd give me an opening to talk to him again if he was at the event tonight. Anxiously, I peered around to make sure my absence hadn't been noticed. Avalon was standing on the elevated dais that sat at the front of the gathering, and when my eyes collided with hers, I knew I was in deep shit. The angry, disappointed look she sent my direction sliced through me like a knife through butter, and I turned away from her, trying to ignore the invisible impact.

"Sorry! I got distracted." I reached Em's side and let her loop her arm through mine, almost like she was afraid I'd disappear if she let me go.

"What could possibly distract you from the *Solstice*?!" she scolded with a hiss, already working her way through the party. Emmaline dragged me bodily through the crowd to the front of the gathering. Even though she was small, she was strong and determined, and I murmured apologies to the other witches and warlocks as she—unapologetically—secured us a prime spot at the front of the bonfire with a perfect view of the raised platform beyond.

Grumbling, Em pried her heels from the soft earth below our feet, and I laughed quietly at her distress. "The heels were your idea. I said we should have worn flats." I smiled angelically as she looked crestfallen at the dirt covered spikes of her strappy green heels. The designer shoes matched her dress perfectly, the straps crisscrossing over her feet like her dress crisscrossed over her back. The red locks of her hair were elegantly gathered on top of her head, cascading down the center of her back in carefully set curls. A strand of feathers and beads added decoration that hung down one side of her face, framing her green eyes and adding whimsy to the simple, yet classy, green dress she wore. It hung flawlessly off of her lithe figure, the silk a perfect contrast to her milky pale skin. She looked elegant, regal, and magickal... so unlike myself.

My black dress hugged my curves, a tulle skirt flaring at my waist and draping to the ground in sweeping A-line fashion. Sheer black fabric covered me from the edge of my shoulders to my neck, featuring a small collar that made the bodice look like a fitted blouse rather than a dress. I'd fallen in love with the style the moment I'd tried it on. The neckline of the dress was open, a deep 'V' that plunged more than I'd preferred, but now that I saw the gowns adorning the other witches at the ceremony, I was grateful that Em had pushed me to buy the dress. Black lace decorated the whimsical fabric. Still, while the dress was gorgeous, I was sure I didn't wear it as confidently as the other girls wore theirs. I wasn't one to dress up often, more comfortable in my jeans and flip flops or boots than I was in formal attire.

"I would have worn flats if I had even two more inches of height. I'm too short," Em whined good-naturedly as she called forth her wand. I arched an eyebrow at her, wondering what she was up to. With a grin, she wiggled her eyebrows at me. "Magick, my dear friend. It will get you everywhere." With a flick of her wrist and a murmured spell, she cleaned her heels and magicked them, so they would no longer sink into the ground. A handy trick.

Honestly, the idea was brilliant, and I debated doing the same thing for about two seconds before every magickal debacle I'd ever had resurfaced in my mind. *Yeah, no.* A little mud on my heels was totally fine. Didn't bother me in the least.

Em chuckled next to me, clearly reading some semblance of my thoughts on my face.

"Don't worry, girl. I got you. Just promise me that you're going to keep your wand stashed away for the evening." She leveled me with a serious look and I nodded wholeheartedly. I didn't have any desire to dabble with magick tonight. Nothing short of life and death could get me to call for my wand with so many witnesses around.

With a wave of her hand my heels were magicked as well, the black satin cleaned and no longer digging into the soft padding of the forest floor.

"Having a talented friend sure has its benefits." I sent her a grin and scanned the gathered witches and warlocks.

Covens upon covens that I rarely saw or had never met filled the clearing set back in the woods behind our home. Candles lined the perimeter of the open space and glowing lanterns hung from tree branches, giving off a soft yellow glow that added a romantic feeling to the forest. Earthen smells of moss, dirt, and pine mixed with the scent of wood smoke from the bonfire, creating my favorite aroma. It helped me relax and I tried to shake off the anxiety and gloom I felt pressing in.

The crowd was hushed as they listened to Cardoc speak, calling the Solstice to order. After a lengthy introduction that I tried to pay attention to, he officially opened the ceremony by dropping a powdered substance—a specific recipe of plants and herbs that Cardoc had crushed himself with his mortar and pestle—into the fire, which not only fueled the flames but prepared the fire for the sorting.

A leader from each coven stepped forth, taking a seat on the large dais to wait for their turn to present their coven members to the masses.

Atticus Morgan, Master of the Blackthorn coven outfitted in his usual all black, stepped up to the small podium at the front of the dais. His tuxedo was tailored to perfection, outfitted with long tails that reached his knees. The look was so dramatic that it actually took me by surprise when he began to speak in an utterly drab tone of voice.

"Coven Blackthorn." His dark eyes scanned over our heads, locating his coven toward the back of the clearing and summoning them forward. The witches and warlocks chatted excitedly as they headed toward the dais. One by one they lined up, ready to receive their placement.

"Agatha Searce," Atticus droned. Raising her chin, a beautiful blonde girl at the front of the line climbed the stairs with a confident smirk. When she reached her coven master, she presented her palm to him. Cupping her hand in his, he procured a dagger that had been concealed on his person. Each dagger had the crest of the coven engraved on it—in this case, a black rose intertwined in thorns. I watched, riveted, as he sliced her palm with quick, deft movements.

Emmaline drew air in through her teeth and squeezed my arm tighter as she watched the scene, just as fascinated as I was. I knew she hated the sight of blood, which was ironic given that it was the main component in much of our potion and spell work. I squeezed her back, lending my support, impressed when she didn't look away. Red blood pooled in Agatha's palm, and the coven master yanked the girl's hand over the railing of the dais and guided her until her palm faced the fire, the flames nearly close enough to singe her skin.

Red liquid dripped from her hand, and the fire consumed it. For one anxious moment, nothing happened. Then, without warning, the flames changed color, turning shades of blue before our eyes as the fire crackled and popped.

"Elemental!" The coven leader's smile shocked me. It was the most expression I'd seen from the stoic man, and the look seemed almost out of place curving his features. "Well done, Agatha!" He praised her as if she'd had any control over the results. I rolled my eyes at his accolade while the girl beamed at a cheering crowd. The placement was among the highest one could earn, and I was yanked into Emmaline's side as she joined in the clapping.

Mothers with bubbling potion punch began whispering amongst themselves, already working on speculating matches, all which would be made after every witch and warlock had a declared specialty. A warlock was called forward as Agatha descended the stairs on the far side of the stage, greeted by a group of other elemental witches. Each specialty was eager to gain a new crop of young witches and warlocks.

The evening continued in much the same vein, and I shifted uncomfortably on my heels. Every muscle in my body grew more tense as I watched witches and warlocks receive their placements.

"If you get any more tense, you're going to crack like a board." Em's low admonishment had me trying to relax, but it was a futile task. There was no way I would be able to breathe normally again until I had my specialty and it wasn't something horrible.

I twisted my fingers together and chewed on the inside of my cheek to the point that I tasted blood. As one coven finished and another started, I grew cold for no other reason than my body's reaction to the stress. I searched for any scrap of enthusiasm I could muster to make this evening more tolerable. Sadly, my internal search yielded nothing.

"What's that?" Em asked me, finally turning her attention away from the stage. Peering down, I realized she was motioning to Axel's shirt which I had placed next to my clutch at my feet. Stooping, I quickly snatched it up and held it close.

"It's just a shirt." I tried to deflect, but my best friend was like a hound dog once she caught a scent.

"Whose shirt?" She narrowed her green eyes and propped her hands on her hips. The look she shot me appeared menacing under the red flash from the bonfire that announced a Fire witch.

"Just someone I met." I shrugged, trying to downplay the encounter I'd had this morning. How was I supposed to explain the shirt if I didn't tell her about the episode I'd had? I really should have thought things through better before bringing the shirt with me, but the lure of talking to the handsomely irritating stranger again had won out over having to cart the fabric around all evening. Axel was an enigma. An intriguing mystery. I wanted to know more about him, but it wasn't in my repertoire to simply march up to a hot guy and start making conversation. Hence, the shirt. I hoped it would give me the 'in' I needed.

I searched the crowd, scanning the faces as I tried to find

him. I had no idea if he would even be here, but I looked for him anyway.

One of the benefits of having a parent on the High Coven was the fact that I knew just about all the members of the neighboring covens, if not by name then by face. The fact that I'd never met Axel before—because let's face it, if I had, I'd have remembered him—only solidified the fact that he wasn't from around here.

"Someone? Or a male someone?" The inflection in Em's words made me grin sheepishly to myself. I should have known I wouldn't be able to keep anything from her. I wasn't a good liar, and she knew me better than anyone else in the world. Schooling my features, I made eye contact and arched an eyebrow in her direction, daring her to continue with her interrogation.

She wasn't fazed. "I knew it. It's a guy. Spill everything now!" She stepped closer, dropping her intimidating stature and pulling on my arm excitedly. The fire gleamed green and a warlock was announced as a Garden warlock. As sexist as it sounded, it wasn't a highly appraised placement for a male, and he walked off the other side of the stage looking slightly dejected. My heart went out to him as he was greeted by a fluttering flock of witches all rushing the stage. Apparently, they were much happier than he was to have gained a warlock among their ranks.

Slightly distracted, I waved Em off. "I ran into him on the grounds this morning." I chose to stick to the same story I'd told Avalon earlier. "I went running, tripped, and fell. In the process I'd ruined my top. On my way home, I ran into this guy and he offered me his shirt." My lips curved as I replayed the actual events in my head instead of the fib I'd had to tell by necessity.

Her eyes narrowed skeptically as she digested my story. "You don't run."

"I decided to try it." I shrugged.

"You hate running." She knew my answer was bullshit, and her stare almost had me breaking down—ready to tell her everything—but the extra second I held out seemed to do the trick because her entire face changed as she decided to latch onto the topic she deemed more important. A sly smile worked its way onto her lips.

"Finally, you're moving on!" She was practically beaming. "It's about time you let go of Mr. Hufflepuff over there."

"That is not his name." Why I instantly jumped to William's defense was beyond me, and I realized the error of my ways before Emmaline had even had time to roll her eyes at me. Standing tall in the crowd beyond was William Thunderbach— my tall, blond, handsome, magickally inclined ex-boyfriend. While I was bitter over our break-up, it was only because I realized that his attentions had been fake from the start.

A month before graduation I'd heard a few girls talking in the bathroom about how he'd only gotten close to me to get into my father's good graces. Unbeknownst to them, I was in the next stall over, humiliated, heartbroken, and angry. What made the entire escapade worse was that when I tried to ask him about it, he didn't deny it as a fallacy. Instead, he looked guilty as fuck and I'd ended things... by punching him in the stomach. It was a little too late though because he'd already been cheating on me with Kadence. I shook off the memory. It didn't matter. I chose not to give that man any more power over my life and emotions. Good riddance. I was sure he would end up with some sort of elemental power, which meant he would probably be a perfect match for the beautiful girl he currently had his arm thrown around.

I, on the other hand, had no idea which specialty I was inclined toward. I brushed the thought away. If I started down that never-ending rabbit hole again, I'd be more of a mess than I already was.

If anyone knew about my reservations regarding this evening, it was Em. In fact, while she didn't know all the details, she was probably the only one who knew just how much I wanted this night to be over already. Em was my best friend and she'd always stuck up for me. As my closest neighbor, it made sense that we would have bonded as children, but our friendship had only grown and strengthened over the years. Having grown up in the same coven, we'd stayed close through our time in high school followed by the Witching Academy. And here we were, on the Solstice, like we'd always talked about.

"He was a grade A asshole, and you know it," Em scolded, but I didn't blame her. She spoke the truth.

I reached over and squeezed her arm gently. "I know he was, and I promise you, I'm not hung up on him or what happened anymore."

Choosing to be gracious, she let the conversation veer back to the previous topic. "And now we have a new hottie to talk about! Which one is he?" She stretched her small frame as tall as she could make herself and started glancing around. "Please tell me he's one of those badass looking men from the Haven Fall's coven!" She nearly squealed her excitement as she took in the sight of the bad boys in the back.

"Will you stop that people are starting to notice." I chuckled as I pulled her back down on her heels. "Honestly," I leaned in and spoke quietly, "I don't know which coven he's from."

Em scrunched her face up. "You didn't think to ask?"

"Of course, I did, but we had a bit of a banter going and I never actually got an answer."

"Ooo! A mystery man! Well that just adds to his allure." She wiggled her eyebrows at me and I rolled my eyes playfully.

Our attention was brought back to the present by sneering voices to our left.

"What do you think she's going to be chosen as?" Tabitha Krick, a previous classmate of mine, taunted, the twisted look on her face in direct contrast to the beautiful purple dress she wore. Her stark black hair hung perfectly straight around her shoulders, her bangs a sharp line across her forehead.

"Probably a Chaos witch! She hasn't even bonded with her wand!" Tabitha's crony, Janice Vale, joined in the teasing, laughing at the absurdity of her statement. The beautiful blonde was decked out in a deep red, nearly inappropriate dress. Unfortunately, her words were true—even though they were said with evil intent—and I worked to suppress my reaction from showing on my face. The poison tipped insults used to hurt, but after years of their torture I'd learned not to let it show. The more I let them affect me, the worse their taunts and jeers became. I'd hardened myself over time, and simply sent them an overly sweet, sarcastic smile.

"Just ignore them." I gripped my best friend's arm, holding her back. I saw the angry, scathing glare she sent in their direction. Choosing not to waste any more time on us, they slid easily through the crowd to a set of handsome men and began flirting. I rolled my eyes. God help the men who ended up with either of them.

The magick in my fingertips was pulsing from the confrontation and I curled my fingers into my palm, begging the magick to behave and listen to my plea. *Not here. Not tonight. Please!*

The last thing I needed was another magickal misfire. With so many people around, it would be ruinous to both me and my parents. I refused to be any more of an embarrassment.

Against my will Janice's ugly words replayed through my mind. *Chaos witch.* While it was an actual specialty, it was rare and considered a curse. The bottom of the witching totem pole. I knew of only one other witch who'd received the placement. Remilda Gelden was a spinster. Never matched, she'd lived her life alone on the edge of the Silver Moon coven. If the rumors were to be believed, she practiced crazy, untamed, dangerous magick that bordered the line of black magick. An unwarranted shiver raced down my spine, and I swallowed as my heart pounded heavily in my chest. I did *not* want to become Remilda.

The noise surrounding me became muffled and I sucked short gulps of air, my breathing turning rapid.

"Stop panicking!" Emmaline delivered a sharp, painful pinch to my arm that pulled me out of my spiraling gloom. "You just need to embrace who you are, Lorn. You don't give yourself enough credit. Your differences make you who you are, and until you yourself learn to accept them, you'll never feel like you fit in anywhere—even when you do."

She reached for my hand and gave it a squeeze as I thought over what she'd said. The problem was that I had no idea who I was. There was a hole inside of myself that I couldn't fill, and she didn't even know the half of it. It was my fault for not confiding in her—or anyone—sooner. I felt like I was floundering, one small fish in a large ocean full of unknowns with no idea which direction I should swim.

It was a feeling I couldn't shake, even as our coven name boomed over the crowd.

"Triple Moon Coven."

My feet stayed rooted to the spot, but my friend was a force to be reckoned with, and she used her considerable strength to haul me along behind her as she headed to the dais to get in line.

"Come on. It's now or never," she grunted as she pulled.

"Can I choose never?" I mumbled, but finally relented and stepped up beside her. I could almost feel Avalon's disapproval burning into my profile as I lined up behind Em.

I watched as my fellow coven members received their placements and clapped wildly when Emmaline was ruled a Hedge witch, a perfectly respectable placement. She was beaming as she descended the far side of the stage, turning to give me two thumbs up and a cheesy cheer that made me smile and helped ease my tension and fear.

Maybe this wouldn't end in disaster.

Either way, I was out of time to mull it over as my name was called by my father himself.

"Lorn Kentwell." His voice rang with pride.

I stepped up to meet my fate. Maybe after this, I'd know which direction to swim.

FIVE

LORN

The fire crackled through the clearing, and the bright glow of the orange flames made the shadows dance around me. Soft-spoken conversations rushed through the air as I climbed the wooden stairs of the dais to my smiling father. He seemed relaxed. I didn't know how he did it. Being watched by so many people had me fidgeting in my uncomfortable heels, wishing that I was anywhere else but on that stage.

The coven's dagger was clutched in his hand, the silver metal decorated with ruby gems that glinted in the firelight. Engraved on the handle was the emblem of our coven: a full moon in the center bracketed by a crescent moon facing outward on each side; the triple goddess symbol. I'd always thought it was beautiful, but now I looked down at it with trepidation.

My father held his hand out, waiting for me to offer up my palm. I clutched my purse and the shirt in my other hand, squeezing them until my knuckles turned white. From the corner of my eye, I saw my mother shake her head in exasperation due to my hesitance. I wanted to roll my eyes at her critical attitude, but I blocked her out instead, gritting my teeth and preparing myself for what was about to happen. The culmination of my entire life had led up to this moment.

No pressure. I had the insane, inappropriate urge to laugh at the stress weighing down my shoulders, but I held it in as I carefully set my things on the ground beside me.

The humidity in the air settled along my skin, the heat—even in the dark of night—made everything feel heavier. With a steadying breath I lifted my arm, placing my hand in my father's, my palm facing the glowing moon that had risen high in the sky. His calm manner was reassuring, and I watched in rapt fascination as he brought the dagger to my flesh. I barely felt the sting of the pain, too fixated on the pooling blood that traveled along my lifelines. Maneuvering my hand, he held it over the fire, the warmth of the flames flickering in his blue eyes.

"Ready?" My father's familiar tenor washed over me. One of the things I loved most about him was that he never forced his timing or opinion on you. He had a way of encouraging people and bringing them around to his point of view. It was why he was excellent at the politics of our world.

The woodsy scent of smoke filled my lungs as I took a deep breath, blowing it out slowly as I held my father's gaze. My nerves quieted as our eyes remained locked, and before long, I nodded, moving with him as he guided my hand, flipping it over and feeding my blood into the hungry flames.

A hush fell over the assembly as everyone watched on eagerly. I was hyper-aware of every crackle and pop that sounded as I awaited my results.

Without warning, the fire roared thunderously, and flames shot into the air. As if that wasn't enough to stun everyone in the clearing, the natural orange color of the bonfire turned black, and smoke poured from it in thick, choking ribbons.

Shit! Shit! Shit! The curses flew through my mind as cries of outrage from the crowd had my heart pounding loudly in my chest. Stumbling away from the fire, I looked around with wide eyes as the smoke wound around me, depriving my lungs and making me cough.

I was unsure which specialty was assigned the color black, and my panic addled brain spun as I tried to furiously ferret out the answers I needed.

My magick burned in my veins, threatening to escape, as the crowd grew louder in their restlessness. The scene below the dais turned into a twisted mosh pit—some people pressing closer while others fled toward the outer edges of the gathering like I was Voldemort and this was some scene in a Harry Potter movie.

I could actually feel the repulsion aimed in my direction. My ears rang, and I could hear every breath I took.

My dismayed gaze swung to my father. If anyone knew what was going on right now, it would be him. I watched in what felt like slow motion as he stepped away from me, his own eyes wide as he stared at me in shock. I felt like an observer in my own life, the whole world going on around me while I watched on from somewhere else.

Somewhere in the distance a hawk screeched loudly, but it barely registered as movement behind my father caught my attention. The coven leaders on the dais were on their feet, their wands being called forth and aimed in my direction. A quick glance thrown over my shoulder showed me flocks of witches and warlocks on the ground were also armed. Sparking magick threatened me from all sides. I was completely surrounded.

Confusion addled everything and before I knew what I was doing, my hands flew up in the air in the universal sign of surrender. The powerful magick inside of me swirled like a wild tempest, rebelling against the motion. My fingers twitched as I gritted my teeth and held it back with all my strength. I'd never felt it want to burst forth so badly, but I'd also never been in such a life or death situation. And I had no doubt that's what this was.

My movement must have startled my father out of his stunned state because the next thing I knew, he was standing in front of me, placing himself between me and one set of deadly wands.

Tears pricked behind my eyes at the gesture. Besides Emmaline, he was the only other person who had been on my side my entire life, and the gravity of his actions sunk in. I wasn't his blood relative, but I was his daughter, and he would die for me. I had to swallow a few times to get the knot in my throat to lessen. Showing weakness right now would be my undoing.

Weakness would be like blood in the water to a school of hungry sharks.

"Skinwalker!" The deep, condescending voice drew my attention back to the coven leaders and other members of the High Coven who were standing on the stage, their wooden chairs long forgotten. The man who'd spoken was old, his hair a distinguished silver grey that was slicked back from his forehead. Remiken Kingston was the oldest and most feared member on the High Coven, and the intense fury on his face sliced fear through my heart.

The word 'skinwalker' reverberated around my head and my heart dropped to my feet. My hands were ice cold as I mentally repeated the word over and over again.

Skinwalker. Wasn't that... I couldn't even complete the

thought, but I didn't have to because the next words out of Kingston's mouth confirmed my suspicions.

"Dark magick!" The man's bony, accusatory finger was pointing and shaking in my direction like a parent reprimanding a child.

"Well this just got interesting." A distinguished looking man in his thirties stepped forward and I recognized him as my father's good friend and fellow High Coven member, Buford Darbonne. His thick, Creole accent was hard to miss. He ran one of the larger covens in the country, covering all of New Orleans, Louisiana and was the youngest member on the High Coven at a mere thirty years old. Firelight warmed the appearance of his umber skin, and while he normally appeared put out and bored by such functions as the Solstice, his light green eyes were now alight with interest. One of his dark eyebrows arched upward, and his hands casually rested in the pockets of his perfectly tailored black slacks.

His posture was much too relaxed for the tense situation, and he strutted forward, placing himself between the two sides. Behind him, mirroring his movements, was a man I didn't know by name but recognized as Darbonne's protege. His dark hair, beard, and eyes accentuated the dark malice he shot in my direction and marked him as someone who was clearly not on my side. I wondered what he was doing, following his master if he clearly had made up his mind about me.

"Cardoc." Darbonne spoke again, using my father's given name instead of his last name, as was formally done. "What is the meaning of this?"

"I assure you, I had no idea. Lorn is our adopted child. She's no danger to anyone." My father stepped forward again, trying to bear the brunt of the angry reactions of those around us. My arms shook as I held them aloft, but I didn't dare drop them.

Instead, I found my grit and steel and stood up straighter, drawing deep breaths in through my nose and out through my mouth while I prepared to plead my case and stand my ground. "Step aside, Kentwell." Kingston pressed forward, the position marking him as the clear leader in the rally against me—and my father by association. Others soon took up his flank, positioning themselves as his backup. Whispered words hissed through the air as wands were jabbed forward in antsy anticipation. My magick flared, and I begged it back.

One thing was clear. We were wildly out numbered.

However, we were long past flight or fight, and I'd chosen my side. I was going to fight. Glancing around, I searched for anyone who would stand on our side. My gaze landed briefly on my mother, but her eyes were wide and locked on Cardoc, begging him to abandon me and go to her instead. My heart squeezed in my chest at the idea of facing the firing squad alone, but I didn't want my father in the middle of my mess either. Even if it was unknowingly and accidentally created, this entire situation revolved around me.

Behind us, coven members continued to band together on the ground, offering their support to Kingston, their wands leveled on my back. A strange, tingling energy zipped through the tense atmosphere, making the hair on my arms stand on end. Dark red, sparkling magick sizzled at the ends of each wand, marking me for death. A strangled sound wanted to escape my throat, but I choked it back.

I called on every last reserve of strength I had inside of me and garnered it like armor.

"Father," I whispered, "we're surrounded on all sides." My hushed notes were spoken only loud enough for him to hear. Adrenaline surged through my veins in time with the thrumming, rhythmic pulse of magick that burned in my icy fingertips. I gritted my teeth and kept careful control over the energy. I knew if I let even the smallest bit slip without my wand present, it would seal my fate. Witches and warlocks couldn't use magick without their wands. So why the hell could I?

"I said, step aside," Kingston barked, each word enunciated to the extreme. The magick at the end of his wand flared with his command.

"This is my daughter we are talking about." The word daughter shook with emotion, but otherwise, my father's words were cold and serious, the authoritative bite of them lending credence to why he was a well-respected member of the High Coven.

The lack of response from Kingston told me all I needed to know.

This was no longer a party but an execution. I'd like to say that I stood by bravely like a captain who goes down with her ship, but inside I was freaking out from the threat to my life. Breathing rapidly, I scanned the cold faces around me, some who used to be like extended family to me.

I spotted Em on the sidelines. Her eyes were wild, and she was caught in a lunge, the other hedge witches holding her back from rushing forward to join in my fight. Her devotion as my best friend melted the ice that had temporarily frozen my brain, and I was finally able to think once more as my self-preservation kicked in.

Turning back to Kingston, I blurted, "I'm not dangerous. I'm a terrible witch, but I'm not a threat to anyone. I don't practice black magick." I shook my head, finally lowering my arms slowly. I ignored the tingling in my arms as blood rushed back to my hands, and I took two steps forward, bringing myself even with my father, making myself a contender. I avoided the sharp look he shot in my direction, instead narrowing my eyes just slightly on the older gentlemen set on killing me. I wanted him to look me in the eye and acknowledge me. If he was going to kill me, I'd make sure he truly saw me first. The standoff with the High Coven leader felt oddly reminiscent of my reoccurring dreams, and that idea was somehow calming. I'd done this nearly every night for as long as I could remember. This was just a different kind of monster. The fact that I'd always woken up before I'd won the fight was a small fact I was willing to overlook for the moment.

I just needed to find Kingston's weakness.

"I've grown up in the coven, following their rules religiously. You don't grow up in the Kentwell household without learning to become a rule follower." I spoke proudly, owning the name my father had given me all those years ago. "It's true that I'm adopted. It's true that I don't know anything about my origins, but I am a witch. I've been raised by the best." I motioned a hand toward my father. "I'm not evil. I'm a good witch who just happens to be bad at magick. I'm a danger to no one." I took a deep breath and made sure I had Kingston's attention, hoping the crowd was listening because my next words were the only ones I could think of that might get me out of this situation alive. "I'll hand over my wand."

Gasps rose, and a low chatter broke out. I wanted to smile in victory for having roused a reaction from the assembly, but I didn't allow my serious features to break nor my attention to sway from the ringleader. His eyes were sparking fire in my direction, much like his outstretched wand was still doing. I held his gaze, refusing to be the one who relented first while I waited to see if plan A worked.

Hell, who was I kidding? Plan A was all I had.

Kingston raised a hand in the air, effectively silencing the onlookers. The heated sizzling of the fire behind us became the only sound in the clearing until Darbonne started to slowly clap his hands together. Whether mockingly or in actual praise, I wasn't sure. He'd never been an easy man to read.

"Well done. I think she makes a convincing case, don't you Kingston?" Darbonne turned his attention to the old man, waiting for him to volley back a response. "Surely, given the situation, we can change protocol this one time. Let the girl turn in her wand."

"Her wand won't make a difference! Our laws have always been clear. Laws that you both uphold and believe in!" He eyed both Darbonne and my father. "We cannot endanger our wives, children, and covens by allowing the girl to live! The rule has always been death." He spit his venom and I wanted to roll my eyes at the perceived threat he thought I was, but my heart squeezed in my chest instead as I realized my speech had failed. Cheers of assent lifted in response to Kingston's statement, and my rollercoaster of emotions quickly morphed into anger.

"The circumstances here are different and you know it. Lorn was raised within the covens. She's been brought up as one of us. She's the daughter of a High Coven master who also happens to be our friend. Surely we can start by taking her into custody and making an educated decision once we've had the chance to investigate the matter more fully." Darbonne, not to be outdone—and having way too much fun with the serious situation we were in—stepped closer yet to Kingston, challenging him with a gleam in his light eyes as he pleaded his, or our, case.

I narrowed my eyes at Darbonne, wondering what his investment was in all of this, but I wasn't one to quibble over where the help came from right now. Even if he was essentially trying to send me to jail. Anything other than death was a good option right about now. As long as I was alive, I could figure the rest out later.

The truth was, at the heart of the matter, this was the same old argument the High Coven had been in flux about for the last few years. Many of the younger members wanted to see change brought to the ancient, dusty rules the older members governed by, while the elders wanted to keep our old-world traditions intact.

"You are young and naive, boy! You don't know what the skinwalkers are capable of." Kingston's face turned redder the more he argued, and I saw the moment he was done.

Magick burned in my clenched fingers and I tightened my hands into fists. I ground my jaw together and worked to keep careful control over the power inside of myself. This time, however, I didn't hold it back. I felt it grow heavy as it tingled up my arms, fueled by my temper and my frustration, but I didn't let even one spark free. I wouldn't be the one to lodge the first attack. That was a sure-fire way to sign my death certificate.

I didn't have to wait long.

Kingston reared back, whipping his wand over his head as he lobbed a bolt of magick directly at me and my father. My eyes tracked the blast and my magick begged to be released, but just before I let it loose, my father blocked the attack with his own magick, waving his acquired wand and throwing up a protective shield that surrounded us.

"Come now, Kingston. Let's negotiate! This is an overreaction!" My father yelled over the low roar of building power. The air was charged with static energy, all of it aimed at me.

My gaze flew around the stage, taking in all the threats at once. The roar of an engine kicked up and steadily grew louder as it kicked into gear. It was the last thing that registered before another attack of magick flew at the protective shield that my father had placed over us.

Everything happened so fast after that. Determination was set like stone on my father's face as he turned me and ordered me to run, and that split second of inattention was all it took for Kingston to lob another blast that took down our shield. Kingston—followed by his followers—let a stream of white magick lash out at my father, entrapping him in a rope made of pure energy that wrapped around his body, immobilizing him and taking him to the ground.

"No!" I lunged forward, dropping to my knees and pulling at his binds. The magick burned my hands as I tried to free him. Avalon's hysterical cries echoed from the other side of the stage through all the chaos.

"Run, Lorn. Now!" my father pleaded. "Go!"

The magick wrapped around my father jerked wildly, and before I knew what was happening, he was yanked away from me, bound at Kingston's feet.

Magick raged within me, and for the first time in my life, I didn't hold it back. I let it fill me. I had no idea how my power worked. I'd been afraid of it my entire life, but this time, I begged it for help. Holding up my hands, I closed my eyes and threw back my head, letting the magick burst forth on a scream. The release was more painful than I'd expected, the excess of magick ripping out of me in uncontrollable waves. When I finally opened my eyes, I saw a wall of purple fire burning between the coven leaders and myself. It didn't burn the wood, but it acted as a clear dividing line between us. I had no doubt that it would harm anyone who touched it. A quick look over my shoulder showed the same had happened on the ground, providing me with protection and a chance to get away.

I was momentarily relieved I hadn't hurt anyone, but when I

noticed my father on the other side of the line, my stomach twisted. The magickal binds that were wrapped around him had fallen away and he was being held captive by other members of the High Coven.

Every single person, including my father, had their attention leveled on me, and their dismay was palpable. The absence of the sparking magickal attack finally registered and that's when I noticed that every single witch and warlock in the clearing was disarmed, their wands floating ten feet above us, suspended in air.

Slowly, I stood.

My gaze fell on my father once more, and I was sure my own expression mirrored what I saw on his face. Shock, a little bit of awe, fear, and a whole shit load of confusion. Regret was a heavy feeling as I stared at him for a moment longer. I had no idea what I was capable of, but my power was no longer a secret and I was no longer safe here.

I wished I had told him everything. This was my fault, and he was on the other side being held in the custody of men who were suddenly my enemy. And I realized that there was nothing I could do to fix it.

For the first time that night, I felt truly alone.

A loud roar pierced the air, and I whipped my body toward the sound, already letting my magick build to fend off another attack. If I thought the night couldn't get any worse, I'd been terribly, ridiculously mistaken.

There, forming from the smoke that rose from my magickal fire was my living nightmare reincarnate. The twisting, cloudlike wisps of a hideous monster seemingly formed from nothing, it's glowing red eyes unmistakably recognizable.

Screams rent the air as people began to flee.

"You see! Dark magick. She's summoning demons!" Kingston bellowed, his eyes wild from the danger in our midst.

I looked down at my hands with wide, scared eyes, utterly horrified. Was I truly a dark witch? Had I summoned that... monster? My stomach churned like a raging sea in the middle of a tempest, and I scrambled backward as the creature threw back its head and let out a thunderous howl.

Hair prickled along my arms, and terror ripped me apart as it finally sunk in that the thing I'd been dreaming of just that morning was *legitimately* standing in front of me. Somehow, I'd brought the creature of my nightmares into my reality.

My head vibrated with the sound, but all I could think about was stopping that... thing. I continued to stumble backward and held my hands up again. Pulse frantic, I breathed erratically as I threw a blast of magick at the beast. I'd never gotten this far in my dreams. I didn't know how to destroy it. I just knew I had to stop it. Preferably before it started hurting people. Or... you know... killed *me*.

Lights flashed to my right drawing my attention to a motorcycle propelling itself up the stairs of the dais and onto the stage. The stranger on the bike shot out a hand, aiming a destructive hit of magick directly at the monster. I knew damage had been done when the beast growled menacingly.

"Come on! We've got to draw that thing away from the crowd!" the stranger yelled as he slowed the bike. Reaching my side, he held out the same hand he'd blasted the creature with. "Get on!"

Jumping on the back of some stranger's bike wasn't a thing I did. However, I had two choices. Stay and die or take my chances with the biker and try to save the people I cared about. It wasn't hard to logic out my best course of action, and with a look at the helmeted man, I grasped his hand and let him help me swing onto the back of the bike. The entire exchange happened in seconds, and we were off.

The last thing I saw was the relief that covered my father's face as the bike jerked to life underneath me and the world became a hazy blur of movement. My heart ached as I left him behind.

The motorcycle lurched forward as the driver picked up speed, and I squealed, quickly wrapping my arms around my savior's stomach. Hard abdominals met my hands and I clung to him as he aimed the bike for the stairs on the opposite side of the stage.

As the bike bumped down the steps, I was pressed fully against the man's back, and I hung on for dear life. The motorcycle sped past the remaining bystanders.

"Lorn!" Emmaline cried from the sidelines as other witches in her specialty dragged her out of the path of the demon. Tears leaked from my eyes, flying off my cheeks as the stranger drove the bike into the forest.

The ground shook around us and I dared a look backward. The beast was hot on our trail, following us at a fast clip as trees I'd grown up looking at my entire life flew past.

"It's following us!" I knew there was a panicked edge to my growing hysteria, but I didn't care to try and play it cool. Cool went out the window a hell of a long time ago.

"Good," was the only response I got.

"Do you happen to have a plan? Because I think we could really use a plan!" I rambled past the emotion clogging my throat and the danger that chased us into the night.

"Don't worry, sweet cheeks, I've got this." I could feel the rumble of the stranger's words in his chest as I hung on for the ride. And then my brain finally processed what he'd said.

"Axel?"

"The one and only." Even now, fleeing for our lives, he sounded cocky and sure of himself. And I hoped to hell he was because I was completely out of my element. He thrust a hand out in front of us as the bike hurtled through the rough terrain.

"Oh yeah, this seems like a great freakin' time let go of the handles!" The words were ripped from my mouth and lost to the forest as we flew, my sarcasm a band-aid for the hurt searing my chest.

"Lenavas!" I could barely make out his chant over the wind flying past my ears, but the spell left his lips and soared ahead of us, the magick gathering in a dense circle that began to grow. A portal, as clear as glass and glowing orange around the edges, expanded until it was large enough for us to fit through, and my grip grew even stronger as he angled us directly for the forest clearing I could see shimmering on the other side.

"Hang on, sweets. It's about to get real!"

"Real? Have you not witnessed how 'real' my night has been already? I think I can handle a portal." I felt his body shake slightly as he chuckled at me, but I simply pressed my cheek to the back of his black tee-shirt as the pulsating magick of the portal engulfed us, stinging over my skin as it swallowed us whole.

The bike landed with a jarring hit, listing precariously sideways. My grip on Axel was tight, but the harsh clash of our landing threw me from the bike, and I hit the ground hard before I rolled into the impact. My head ached, and spots swam in front of my vision, but I pushed myself up onto one arm and quickly found Axel, who was still seated on his motorcycle. His hands were out in front of him again and he was chanting wildly at the portal. I could hear the outcry of the beast and see it charging for us, but right before it landed in front of us, it screamed as the portal changed from orange to a deep red. And then it slammed closed.

"Is it still there? At the Solstice?" I asked breathily, instantly worried about my father and Emmaline.

Axel's chest heaved, but he shook his head. "No. I sent it somewhere else."

It was all I needed to hear. I dropped down onto the grass and squeezed my eyes closed, letting pain consume me on a groan. The fall had hurt like a bitch, and my leg stung fiercely where something sharp had cut into it.

It was all I had time to process before our small victory of escape was cut short, tarnished by another deep, dark voice.

"What the hell have you done?"

SIX

AXEL

My shoulders sagged after the portal sealed shut, and I could finally breathe again. I drew a deep lungful of air, and every muscle in my body froze.

Blood. The sweet coppery scent of it lit up my senses while I inhaled deeply. Like a wave crashing over a rocky shoreline, the primal energy within me surged forward in response. Nothing had ever smelled as intoxicating as the claiming scent of Lorn's blood calling me home.

A shiver raced down my spine, spreading outward until all the nerves in my body were alight. My heart pounded strongly beneath my breastbone as the entire world shifted and refocused, centering around Lorn, who was undeniably my mate.

The effect was ruining. Devastating in the best way. Wreaking havoc on the shambles that used to be my life and restoring every solitary piece until everything in my world was made whole. I hadn't even realized how empty my existence had been until I felt my connection to Lorn solidify in place.

Every animal spirit I possessed swirled through me, each calling out and lending their voice in synchronized harmony to the primal spirit that I felt alive and energetic inside myself. My head tilted back, eyes shut tight, while the magick that bound Lorn and me together finished knitting our connection.

Mate. The word simmered in my thoughts, both lighting a fire in my blood yet soothing me at the same time. I never thought I'd ever have a chance to truly call someone by that word. The claiming was so much more than I thought it would be. Since there were so few female skinwalkers and true mating occurred so rarely, all I'd had to go by was lore and legend, and nothing in any of those tales could have prepared me for the intensity of the moment I'd just experienced.

In fact, the claiming was so overwhelming, so fucking consuming, that I hadn't even heard the obvious snapping of branches littering the forest floor or register what the scent truly meant until a grating voice roared from behind me.

"What the hell have you done?" Dason stormed into the small clearing I had landed in, thusly snapping me out of my bliss with a sharp tug that grounded me solidly back in reality.

Fuck.

Blood.

The potency of the Lorn's scent suddenly weighed heavily on my shoulders as I swung my leg over the motorcycle in quick, deft movements, threw the kickstand, and rushed to the girl's side. Dark hair fanned haphazardly around her beautiful face. Her piercing ice blue eyes were wide as she looked up and over my shoulder at a towering Dason. He had that kind of effect on people. And not so much the jaw-dropping, panty melting kind, but more of the 'instill fear into the heart of your enemies' kind. But Lorn was far from an enemy. And any second, my lug of an alpha asshole was going to realize exactly who she was to us. Because if she meant something to me, there was no way she didn't belong to him as well.

Mine. I couldn't stop the possessive declaration from forming in my mind. The primal spirit within pressed against the barrier I kept my arsenal of alternate forms locked behind. I wanted nothing more than to shift into my wolf or my bear skin and roar my claim into the dark surrounding night for all to hear, but I choked off any sounds that threatened to escape my lips and suppressed my shift before I frightened the girl to death. She'd already survived a shitty evening—fucked up demon included.

My earlier reaction to her suddenly made so much sense. The way I was drawn to her, how amazing she smelled, even to my human side, and how protective I felt over her.

She was mine.

Watching her on that stage tonight had been one of the hardest things I'd ever had to endure. I had no idea what the black smoke meant, but the moment that old asshole had called her a skinwalker, my entire world had narrowed in on Lorn, standing in front of hundreds of our enemies. She was the one I was looking for, and she'd been under my nose the whole time. I cursed myself for not realizing it when I'd met her. The allure of her scent had called to me, but I hadn't known she was mine without having scented her blood. It was that way for all skin-walkers.

Come on. Deep breath there, buddy, I prompted Dason. Now that he was standing closer, there was no way he'd miss the claiming aroma. I pushed my thoughts toward him hoping he'd do a partial shift, open our connection, and comply. But who the fuck was I kidding? Dason listened to no one.

My shoulders tensed as I heard him inhale and I couldn't contain the way my mouth quirked up on one side when he let out a low, menacing, possessive rumble, his jaw clenching as he rode out the claim.

My mirth quickly disappeared, however, when Lorn scrambled backwards, trying to get herself into a sitting position even as she winced in pain. Her blood stained the ground, and the strong smell of it had me pressing forward wildly, determined and desperate to help her. My eyes flashed with the power of my primal side and I reached for the girl, my hand landing gently on her knee. The soft tulle of her gown was askew, ridden up from her fall and corresponding shuffle. Her palms were pressed into the leaves and grime of the forest clearing, fingers digging into the dirt as she propped herself up with ramrod straight arms.

And then she narrowed her eyes on us, staring down Dason and me.

"What are you?" It wasn't a question so much as it was a demand. I flicked my hair to the side with a quick jerk of my head to remove it from my eyes and let my gaze wander over her form. Just like she'd been this morning, she was covered in dirt and completely out of her element, and yet she was strong. Fucking determined. I liked that about her already. This mate of mine.

Before Dason could open his big mouth, I chimed in, hesitant to share too much information after what she'd just been through. I wanted to get her home and healed first before we dove into all the overwhelming details.

Trying to appear non-threatening, I spoke gently, but firmly. "We're on your side, is what we are. You're hurt and bleeding. The way I see it, you have two options: You can either choose to stay out here in the forest, or you can come with us and get patched and cleaned up." I pressed my palms against my knees and pushed myself off the ground. "Let us help you." Extending a hand to her, I waited for her decision, reminding myself to breathe as her gaze flicked between the two of us standing before her and then to the spot where the portal had disappeared, as if weighing the greater of the two dangers.

Dason's chest heaved, but he stayed blessedly silent, waiting on her answer as much as I.

I could see the thoughts playing out on her face as she considered her options. My teeth clamped down on my tongue to keep myself from smiling at her expressive features. Knowing the little I did about her, I figured she'd probably take my smile as a challenge and defy me just for the hell of it.

The moment the soft skin of her hand closed around mine, the tension seeped from my shoulders in relief that we'd be able to get the hell out of the forest and back to the safety of our place.

"Where are we going?" she asked as I flexed and hauled her easily back to her feet. Her dress fluttered around shapely hips, falling in a tattered mess around her legs. Realizing her disheveled state, she quickly retracted her hand from mine and smoothed her palms over her ruined, ripped gown, being careful around the injury on her thigh. She'd looked gorgeous earlier in the evening and honestly, the grime and leaves sticking to her didn't diminish her beauty. In fact, I was enjoying the slightly wild look about her. Hell, she could wear a garbage bag and neither Dason nor I would care.

Pulling myself from my thoughts, I ran a hand through my hair to push it back off my forehead.

"We don't live far from here." I reached for my shirt while I spoke and ripped a thick strip free from the bottom. "You're bleeding, though, and I'd like to get that looked at before we start walking. Will you allow me to help?" I asked, holding my hands out slowly like I had when I'd offered her my shirt this morning. A small smile curved one side of her lips as though she realized the gesture was similar as well, and she nodded, biting at her lower lip as she lifted the hem of her dress, baring her outer upper thigh to me. Squatting down, I took a look at the nasty gash slashed across her leg.

"I'm going to bind this around the wound to help staunch the bleeding. It looks like it's already slowing down." Her fast healing was already helping to clot the injury, but the depth of the cut was serious enough to require aid in its healing process. We needed Kota.

I slid the fabric around her thigh, being careful not to touch her more than necessary. We'd only just met and I didn't want to take familiar liberties that weren't yet mine to possess. Tying the knot tightly enough to bind against the wound, I stood back up, satisfied that the bandage would hold until we could get home and fix her up properly.

"Thank you," she mumbled quietly as she fixed her dress back into place. "That's the second shirt you've sacrificed for me." When her blue eyes met mine, they sparkled in the moonlight, the sincerity of her gratitude shining in their expressive depths. I nodded, an odd sort of pride filling my chest at having helped my mate.

Turning to my bike, I waved a hand, disintegrating the magick that made up the motorcycle and letting it melt from sight. Lorn gaped as she watched the show, but I didn't explain, and she didn't ask. There would be time for that, and Lorn already had enough to process right now.

I motioned for her to join me and after only a few seconds of hesitation, she stepped up to my side as we headed through the dense cover of trees along paths I would know in my sleep. I'd grown up around here. This forest, the mountain, it was home.

It didn't escape my notice that Dason took up position on Lorn's other side, leaving her enough personal space to feel comfortable but unwilling to leave her exposed. That one small move spoke volumes.

It'd been much too long since our pack had truly cared about anything other than each other, although Dason would argue the case. Females of our kind were rare, and the call of a mate was nearly unheard of given our diminished numbers. With only a handful of us left, the members of our pack had resigned themselves to a life of meaningless flings and one-night stands with human women who had no idea who or what we were. All of us except for Dason. He'd refused to settle, and he'd dragged us all along with him under the guise of what was best for our pack—and for our species. He'd found us a female to mate with, even though none of us felt called to her, and I was now insanely grateful we hadn't finalized claiming Mara as our own.

Still unsettled by the strong smell of Lorn's blood, I picked up my pace, hurrying us along a little faster as I pushed the complicated thoughts to the background and focused on what was important. The sooner we got home, the sooner I could get Lorn healed. Knowing she was hurt had me on edge. I fucking hated that she was injured, and I took that blame solely on my own shoulders.

Her small strides hurried along with our longer ones and I forced myself to slow again when I noticed a small limp in her walk.

"We need to call for Kota." The demand in my tone caused Dason to bristle, but he didn't argue with me. While we all had healing abilities, my brother Kota had an extra knack for medicine that the rest of us didn't possess, and his magick only strengthened his skills. He was the one to call when our medical needs outweighed the rate of our accelerated healing. The tick in Dason's jaw was indicative that he was controlling the alpha spirit inside of himself. Hell, if his primal side was riding him the way mine was me, I couldn't even imagine how much harder it was for him to keep his cool while Lorn hobbled along beside us.

"I can pick you up," he nearly growled, and Lorn's steps faltered as she walked.

"Thanks, but no thanks. I can make it." Small hands clenched into fists around the delicate fabric of her dress as she hiked it up even higher, exposing the sexy black heels adorning her feet before she stomped off ahead of us like she knew where the hell we were going.

A chuckle escaped my smirking lips, and I slapped Dason on the back. Jogging a few steps to catch up with Lorn, I threw a retort over my shoulder. "I think things just got a lot more interesting around here."

"Don't expect this level of interesting," Lorn murmured while trying to pick her way through the foliage on those spiked heels of hers. "I swear I'm normally a very boring person. This is probably the most interesting day of my entire life, thus far." Her voice wobbled with emotion just as her heels caught on a stone and she flailed before catching her balance. Dason and I both had hands out to catch her, when she righted herself and continued on like she wasn't driving us both insane with her near misses and current catalogue of injuries.

Tucking my hands into the pockets of my dark wash jeans to keep myself from snagging her off her own two feet, I sauntered after her.

"Oh, I don't know, everything about you has proven incredibly interesting since we met." I tried to lighten the mood. I knew there was very little I could do to make her feel better, but I hoped that answering her questions once we got settled at the cabin would be a good step in the right direction.

"And how long have you known her, Axel?" The accusation, flung from Dason, didn't faze me. As our alpha, he'd more than earned his spot as our leader, but we were a group of strong males, and deep down, he wouldn't have wanted it any other way. Only the strong survived in a life like ours, and when we banded together, we'd only become a stronger force. The most sought-after group of walkers in the country.

It was why Lorn's appearance in our lives was significant. As one of the only female walkers in existence, she was important in her own right, but as our mate, she was everything. Mating with her would only intensify the strength of our bonded team.

"Only since this morning." Lorn came to my rescue, but her voice was strained, and she slowed her pace, looking around as if finally realizing she had no idea where she was or which direction she should be heading. In that moment, it was like the world came bearing down on her at once. Her features openly fell as she went back through the events of her day. "He was working on my father's property, getting ready for the Solstice event. I... was in need of some assistance."

The way she said the last line made me smile to myself, my lips curving up at the endearing embarrassment I could hear a hint of in her words.

"You were with the witches?" The rage in Dason vibrated outward at her admission, and I pinched the bridge of my nose. I may have had the good sense to be cowed but nothing would make me regret a decision that led us to Lorn.

"I'd say the risk was well worth the outcome." I leveled a hard look at my leader, daring him to contradict the truth of the matter that was literally staring him in the face. I knew once we got home, I'd have some explaining to do. I just hoped he'd let me do it in private. Call me selfish but the last thing I wanted to do was start my relationship off with Lorn with her knowing I was on her property to steal from her father. They were obviously close. Good intentions or not, I wasn't sure how she'd respond to that tidbit of information.

Lorn had turned, her wide blue eyes taking in the scene we were making as we all stood just outside the barrier of our land. The itch to get her onto protected territory was unbearable, and I rolled my shoulders, trying to lessen the tension I was feeling and hold my primal side at bay. Lorn didn't need to see either one of us lose control like temperamental teenagers and shift. I had a sneaking suspicion that she truly had no idea who or what she was. Her shock at the Solstice couldn't have been faked, and this situation called for more tact than either one of us could or should handle. We needed the others. Chayton in particular, for this matter. The male had a gentler way about him. Where I could be a smart ass at times and Dason was our occasionally overbearing leader, both of us were too hard headed and blunt to ease her into her new reality. And let's face it, she had nowhere else to go. Not that we'd let her simply waltz back out of our lives.

Things had changed the moment I'd scented her as my mate. And it would be the same for my packmates.

If one thing was painfully obvious, it was that she would need time to adjust to everything that had been thrown at her already, let alone everything she still had left to learn. Right now, she needed us as much as we needed her. I just hoped with time, she'd get to know us and want to stay for more reasons than just the mating call. Sadly, there weren't enough documented matings among walkers to know what to expect from all of this, and I just hoped that none of us fucked it up as we entered unknown terrain.

Especially Dason.

Before we could worry about anything in the future though, we needed to get her through the fucking barrier and onto protected land, and this standoff with my alpha was impeding the most important goal.

Keeping Lorn safe.

"Can we do this later? I'd like to get Lorn safely inside our territory." Every muscle in my body was tense, but I wasn't above begging if that's what it took. I may challenge Dason, but he was my alpha and I'd never blatantly defy him.

It's also why he had no idea about my little self-imposed mission to retrieve the Tavia Glass. What he didn't know about, he couldn't forbid.

It's why he was so damn pissed at me.

And I understood it. We were a pack. A family. As close as brothers. I couldn't even imagine losing one of them, and unsanctioned, vigilante missions were a sure-fire way to get yourself killed. Especially when they involved witches. The devastation such a loss would deliver to a pack... a hundred gunshot wounds would be less painful.

Still, even given the risk and the potentially fatal outcome, I wouldn't have changed a thing now that I knew how the day had turned out. Finding Lorn was like breathing fresh air after a decade of holding your breath. It was like living in a black and white world only to finally discover color. Like eating bland, dry food when you could have been enjoying fruit. You couldn't even fathom what you were missing until you got a taste of something better... sweeter.

His hand ran through his short hair as Dason paced in front of me, too pent up with aggressive, dominant energy to hold still. "Did you even check to see if she was being tracked?"

"Trust me, with the way the night went, I don't think anyone had time to hit her with a tracking spell."

"Did it ever occur to you that this whole thing could be a trap, so they can figure out where the fuck we are?"

"Not even a little bit. They had no idea that she was one of us. I highly doubt they would have wasted a spell to place a tracer on her. Not when they didn't plan for her to get out of there *alive*." I stressed the last word, hoping the threat to her life would finally sink in.

His eyes snapped to mine, and I saw every sharp intake of air he dragged into his lungs. The warring conflict of emotions he always tried to hide behind that badass facade of his now played plainly across his face. The news that she was in danger bothered him. And it should.

Mate. The resounding call of my primal spirit echoed again throughout my head, the same sentiment mirrored in Dason's eyes.

He didn't trust her, not yet, but he did care. For now, that was all I needed.

"Am I in the club yet? Because as fascinating as this all is... I... I think I need to lie down." Lorn's sweet, sarcastic voice cut through our standoff.

Immediately our attention flew back to her. One shoulder was pressed against a nearby tree as she let it support her weight, and she rubbed a palm against her forehead.

It took me under a second flat to appear at her side. "What's wrong?"

Lost, sad blue eyes met mine as she tilted her head upward. The bleakness I saw in her gaze was like a punch to the stomach, but it was the dazed look in her eyes that had me immediately worried about her health.

"She must have hit her head." Dason shot me a worried look and then reached for her, helping her steady herself as she straightened from the tree. "Do you think you can walk?" The gentleness he placed into his question shocked me, but if he was willing to play nice now, I wasn't going to look a gift horse in the mouth.

Lorn swayed on her feet as she tried to pull away from Dason's gentle grip to make the rest of the trek to our cabin by herself.

"Contrary to popular belief, current displays notwithstanding, I'm not the kind of girl who needs saving."

It was the last thing she said before her legs gave out under her and she fainted. Reacting with speed and agility, Dason scooped her up before she had a chance to hit the ground.

For one brief, fleeting moment, a look of awe broke across his usually stoic face as he cradled her tightly against the expansive planes of his chest.

Her head was tipped against his shoulder and in a rare display, one corner of Dason's mouth twitched up in a smile. "Maybe just this once, then," he murmured as he lowered his forehead to hers and inhaled deeply.

Just as mine had done, his eyes flashed with the power of the primal spirit that lived inside him.

"Let's take her home." I let my quiet command hang in the air between us, not asking for permission but not challenging Dason and his authority either.

Finally, without further argument, he carried her across the barrier.

SEVEN

LORN

Quiet voices whispered over me as I floated somewhere in the darkness. My head pounded in rhythm with my pulse, and the soft cushions underneath me had me cozying down into their warmth seeking the blissful oblivion I'd been in just moments before.

All I wanted was for the pain in my head and body to cease. The delicious, lingering smell of a home cooked meal slowly pulled me toward the surface causing my stomach to growl. How long had it been since I'd last eaten? And where the hell was I? My surroundings registered one by one. The scratchy feeling of the blanket covering me. The sharp stinging on my leg and palms. The whispering that grew louder. I found myself trying to get my bearings rather than sinking into the sleep I craved.

"You should have seen the amount of power she used. I've never seen anything like it." A guy spoke quietly from some-where nearby, stirring my memory but only leaving me more confused than I already was. There was nothing but buzzing emptiness where there should have been memories. I quickly took stock of everything I could, trying not to tense while I figured out whether or not I was in some kind of danger.

"How did you even know about her?" a second man asked. His voice was harder than the first, deeper and more authoritative. A sense of demand lay behind his question.

"I didn't... Not at first anyway. I was there on a mission for Rook—" the first man began but was cut off abruptly by the second.

"What?!" he hissed angrily. "What were you doing working for the Fae Prince by yourself? And why would he send you to the witches? And for that matter, why is this the first time I'm hearing about such a dangerous mission?" the man nearly growled as he tried to keep his voice low.

"It was something he requested of me personally. Yes, I should have told you, but you would have forbidden me from taking on the assignment. And if you had—need I remind you— she would probably be dead right now!" The argument heated as I strained to listen to their hushed tones. Even though the pounding in my head could rival a drum solo at a rock concert, it wasn't hard to figure out they were talking about me.

"You don't know that I would have..."

"No, he's right." A third person entered the conversation, his demeanor soothing yet strong. "That's exactly how it would have gone down, but we can't change the past, so we should move on from it. You can reprimand him later for his reckless behavior because she's starting to wake up and we don't want her to hear us arguing, do we? It sounds like she's been through enough tonight already. The way I see it, Axel's correct. Every- thing worked out. This time." I heard the edge of warning infuse the man's tone before he continued on, "Axel, we don't do rogue missions. If it's important enough that you want to take on an extra assignment, you bring it before the pack. What you did was heedless and dangerous. We function as a unit which I believe is half of Dason's frustration."

I tried to follow along as the fuzziness in my head started to recede. Axel. Dason. The Solstice. My father. The High Coven. The blurred line between dream and reality that I floated along suddenly snapped into clear, sharp focus and everything came rushing back piece by complicated piece. I felt like my life had just been struck by lightning, and all that was left were charred remains and unrecognizable ash. I relived the entire night in a series of flashbacks and I bit the inside corner of my lip to try and keep myself from reacting to the barrage of memories and emotions that hit me like a hurricane: sudden, unrelenting, and damaging.

I tried to hold my body still, allowing myself time to gather my thoughts. I didn't think I was in danger here, not after the way that Axel and Dason had helped me tonight. I could still remember the warmth and strength of Dason's arms catching me as darkness closed in earlier. This entire night had been one huge clusterfuck, and I wasn't sure what to think about any of it —what I was, everything my father had probably lost just by standing up for me, ending up here surrounded by seemingly helpful strangers. Hell, even the fact that I was still alive. I wasn't sure if I wanted to cry, laugh, or scream.

I tensed as I held back the waves of conflicting emotions, but I had a feeling I wasn't fooling anyone with my sleeping act. The newest male voice, the one I couldn't connect to a name, had said 'pack.' Shifters were known for their perceptiveness and sharp senses. If there were any in the room, they'd be able to hear the rapid beat of my pulse and see the unevenness of my breathing all before I ever opened my eyes.

As if on cue, I was called out.

"Hey there sleeping beauty." Axel's jovial timbre was close, soft, and reassuring, and I released the breath I was holding while letting my lids lift. The gig was up, and as exhausted and emotionally wrecked as I felt, I knew I needed to deal with the aftermath of my disastrous evening head on. I needed answers to my multiplying questions, and I knew that Axel had at least some of them. The way he'd dealt with the beast, the portals, and the bits of magic I'd seen him use... all without a wand... there weren't supernaturals with such abilities.

I'd always assumed I was alone, that my oddities were a curse. Yet he and I were living proof that everything I'd thought was wildly incorrect. There were more kinds of supernaturals in the world than I'd been led to believe.

Apparently, I was one of them.

Eyes open, I blinked as the low light in the room assaulted my vision. With a groan, I pushed myself up from the couch, tossing off the blanket and rearranging my skirt as I sat up fully. Around the room were three men—Axel, Dason, and another— each watching me closely as I got myself together enough to face them. Today had been shit, but shifters could smell fear, so I tried to brick up my mess of emotions and appear strong through the crazy ride this night had taken me on.

Years of built up frustration over never knowing where I came from coupled with all the new holes that had formed in the fabric of my reality tonight left me more determined than ever. I was so over feeling left in the dark about my life and my strange magic, but I started with a more basic—and pressing—question.

"Where am I?" My tone was huskier than usual thanks to my dry mouth, and I swallowed while spots swam in front of my vision before slowly dissipating one by one.

Axel stepped closer, still standing a few feet from the couch I sat upon. "You're at our cabin. We carried you the rest of the way through the woods." His warm brown eyes were both familiar yet foreign, but there was something about Axel that drew me in and made me feel comfortable despite having only met him that morning. "I don't know how much you remember, but you passed out. You had a pretty nasty gash on your leg and we're pretty sure you hit your head when you fell off my bike." Axel drove a hand through his tousled hair. He looked concerned and his eyes scanned over my body searching for visible injuries. My mind was momentarily boggled by the thorough inspection, refusing to focus properly. *Stars, but he's sexy.*

"Well that explains the dizziness and the headache." I gave him a half-hearted smile before another voice pulled my attention to an equally attractive man.

"We didn't want to touch you while you were unconscious, but the cut on your upper leg was bleeding badly," the third man said softly, and I couldn't help but stare. The water around here must be some kind of magickal, because each of the men were ripped, tall, and gorgeous. "We only uncovered enough to clean, heal what we could, and bandage it properly. We worked on some of the smaller, visible cuts on your arms as well. Those healed easily, but your leg and your hands may need more attention if you don't want any scaring." The unnamed man moved closer to me and held out a large white mug filled to the brim. "With your concussion, we'd like someone more skilled in healing to take a look at you. Our friend should be home soon and can check on those injuries, if you're amenable?"

"Okay." I blinked up at him and tried to make my brain follow what he was saying. I felt sluggish and slightly twitterpated. Mentally, I shook myself and it seemed to break the spell and clear some of the fog. I reached for the mug and wrapped my sore palms around it. The slice from the dagger stung upon impact, but at least it had been healed enough to have closed over and was no longer actively bleeding. "That would be great, thank you..."

"I'm Chayton," he filled in the blank for me and I loved his unique name instantly. Somehow, it just fit.

Dipping my head, I inhaled the steam rising from the mug. The sweet smell of the tea had nothing on the scent coming from the guy who'd handed it to me. Chayton's warm redolence reminded me of fresh air, sunshine, and sweetgrass, reminiscent of a summer day. My body pulled toward him, so I could breathe in his aroma again.

"I hope the tea is all right. I can make you something else if you have other tastes." There was an amused smile tilting his lips, and I physically forced myself to lean away as a blush crept onto my cheeks.

What is happening to me? Could I be any weirder? I berated myself. Still, the urge to do it again lingered.

"No, no. This is perfect." I rushed to cover up my blunder with a sheepish wince of a smile that the handsome man returned, his lips curving into an easy grin all his own. The expression was natural on Chayton's features complete with small laugh lines around his eyes. Any remaining hope I had that my odd behavior had gone unnoticed vanished at the self-assured spark in his gaze. Thick, straight eyebrows framed dark chocolate colored eyes that were alive with interest as Chayton let his gaze sweep over my body, drinking me in the way I was him. He had a square chin covered in a shadow of stubble, a straight nose, and smooth looking, golden skin. Long black hair was gathered behind his head in a braid that cascaded down his back. I had the insane urge to undo his hairstyle and run my fingers through the silky length, but I refrained, tightening my grip on my mug instead.

Hands free, Chayton tucked them into the pockets of the

black athletic pants he wore, and they tugged enticingly lower on his cut figure. Behind his white tee-shirt, the corded muscles of his large arms and chest were accentuated, all angling down to a narrower waist. The man was a god.

I pried my attention away from the intense way he was looking at me. Turning back to Axel, I tucked loose strands of hair behind my ear, suddenly aware of the mess I'd become. The elaborate half-up, half-down hairstyle the salon had perfected earlier in the afternoon lay in tatters around my shoulders.

"Thank you for saving me." I put as much feeling behind the gratitude as I could, but the sentiment felt insignificant compared to everything he'd done for me today. Without his help, I was sure I would have been dead by now. Hell, I'd over-heard him say as much already. The seriousness of the night was not lost on me.

"I'm not sure how much you remember, but you saved your-self tonight. I just provided the means to get away in time." His lips tipped up in a proud smirk that only left me more confused.

"You're both lucky to still be alive," Dason quipped from the far side of the room where he stood watching.

I had a million question as I let my gaze fly to his. In the lighting of the cabin I could finally make out all of Dason's features. I'd been able to tell that the man was tall, broad, and intimidating in the moonlight that spilled through the forest, but now his muscles were more than visible behind the confines of the shirt he wore, lending me a new respect for his physique. The light blue color contrasted nicely with his tan skin, and there was something about the way he rolled up the sleeves of his button down, exposing his strong forearms, that was sexy as hell. His eyes were pools of molten steel, the color dark, dangerous, and alluring. I found myself locking gazes with his.

Unable to look away, I held his stare, and the moment bled into something intense, verging on the edge of uncomfortable. The power and strength of his magic filled the room with an air of authority that left little doubt as to who he was. The leader. Alpha.

I didn't know much about shifters, but I knew enough to understand that holding eye contact with an alpha was considered rude and disrespectful. I was blatantly challenging him, and yet every fiber of my being focused harder.

Crossing his arms in front of his chest his muscles flexed with the motion, and my body begged me to pay attention to the sex appeal of the intimidating move, but I refused to break the staring contest we had going. With a slight tilt of his head, he studied me intently. A stormy mask of expression was firmly in place, and I couldn't read anything he was thinking. Then, after what felt like the longest minute of my life, his lips twitched just slightly at the corners. That tiny break in Dason's outward macho facade softened the rough edges of his rugged appearance.

Without speaking a word, he nodded his head once at me. The tilt of his square chin ended the confrontation, and I was finally capable of breathing again. I forced myself to take shallow breaths—rather than the deep lungfuls of air I longed to inhale—in an attempt to portray a calmness I didn't feel.

The other two men in the room ping-ponged their attention back and forth between Dason and me and the little show we'd just put on. While I wasn't positive, I was pretty sure I'd just passed a test and won over the alpha's approval. At least enough that he didn't deem me an immediate threat and was going to allow me to stay. For now.

Until he realized just how wrong he was.

I squeezed the smooth mug in my hands until I worried it

would break, while the creepiest red eyes I'd ever seen flashed through my memories.

I would never forget those eyes for as long as I lived. I shuddered a breath and faced Axel, ready to discuss the important topics I needed to cover.

Without hesitating any longer, I started my line of questioning.

"That beast came straight from my nightmares. What the fuck was that thing?" Axel's expression closed off, like he was thinking through what to tell me—or measuring how much my feminine sensibilities could handle. I narrowed my eyes at him. "The truth. All of it." I paused, realizing I sounded like Dason, and softened my approach. "Please, I need to know."

Exhaling a breath, he closed the remaining few feet between us and took a seat on the coffee table that sat in front of the couch. He dropped his elbows onto splayed knees and folded his hands between his legs, fully centering his attention on me. The build-up was making me nervous, and my heart raced adding another wave of dizziness to accompany my pounding headache.

"That 'thing' was a class three demon; a powerful shade." His eyes flicked over to Dason meaningfully before settling back on me.

"A demon?" That one word made my chest tighten and sent my mind racing. "That can't be right. There haven't been demons on this side of the veil in longer than I've been alive."

Dason nearly snorted from the far end of the room.

"Trust me," Axel said confidently, "demons have been around this entire time."

"Where are you getting your information from?" I scooted forward on the couch—truly on the edge of my seat. I needed to know how legit their intel was. My dreams. The way I'd summoned that... thing. I couldn't even think the word. This was bad. So incredibly bad. That dark omen I'd felt earlier in the evening pressed in around me.

"We don't really need any intel. We've been dealing with them ourselves for years," Axel answered.

"That's insane." I looked at him like this was all some elaborate joke, but when he remained serious instead of giving up the ruse, I sobered. "And I... summoned that... the demon?" I had to drag the words out of my throat, and I bit the inside corner of my lip—hard—while I waited for confirmation.

It was his turn to appear unbelieving. "You're kidding, right?" He paused, but after a beat, he grew more sincere, realizing just how serious I was. His brows pulled together. "Oh shit. No. Of course you didn't." His hand reached up to cup my cheek, but I flinched backward, and he stopped with his arm outstretched in midair.

People touching me... me touching people... neither option was a good idea until I figured out what had happened at the Solstice.

My hesitation didn't seem to hinder Axel, however, and, going slowly, he persisted until his skin made contact with mine, his thumb brushing along the edge of my mouth adding a slight pressure that dislodged my lip from my teeth. Blood spilled onto my tongue from my newest wound and his nostrils flared as he inhaled deeply.

"You were in no way responsible for the demon, Lorn." The sentiment was gentle, and exactly what I needed to hear.

"You're positive? How can you be sure?" I wanted to cringe at the hint of desperation in my voice, but my biggest fear from the entire evening hadn't been the threat from the High Coven but what I was capable of.

"Because you're a skinwalker. We don't summon demons,

we vanquish them." His chin lifted slightly, and a smug smirk tugged at his lips.

Skinwalker. There was that word again.

I closed my eyes and swallowed past the knot in my throat. All I could think about was how much I didn't understand. Nothing in my life made any freaking sense.

I felt like Alice tumbling down that damn rabbit hole, and I didn't know my ass from my elbow.

"Are you all right?" Chayton broke through my spiral and I blinked my eyes open, focusing on the empathetic look he sent me. Blowing out a breath, I nodded and straightened my posture, so I didn't appear quite so deflated.

One breath at a time, Lorn.

"Tonight has been... I'm not even sure I have any words." My throat felt raw from swallowing massive amounts of emotions. "It's a lot to take in. I honestly thought I was going to be marked as a chaos witch, and that was bad enough." My fears over becoming Remilda felt eons away. It was almost laughable. Almost.

I rubbed a hand across my forehead trying to ward off my growing headache.

"I know you've been through a lot, just know you're safe here." Axel dipped his head, catching my gaze and making sure I saw the honesty he was reflecting. "And being a skinwalker is kind of badass." He grinned at me, trying to lighten the mood. "Way better than life as a chaos witch." His smile was infectious, and a disbelieving laugh bubbled out of me breaking all the tension I'd internalized and coiled tightly.

"On that note, what the ever-loving hell is a skinwalker?"

EIGHT

LORN

I looked around the room and took a sip of tea while the guys eyed each other, seeing who wanted to take on the responsibility of answering my question.

"The correct term is shadow touched. That's what our kind prefer to be called." Dason settled back against the wall where the kitchen met the living room, far enough away to survey everything without being directly involved in our conversation.

"Shadow touched," I whispered, rolling the term around on my tongue to process it.

Two words seemed to be all he planned to contribute, but they may have been the most important ones. They were skinwalkers—shadow touched—and so was I. After a beat, I focused my attention back on the others, my eyebrows raised expectantly.

"We're our own race of supernaturals—albeit a rare one," Chayton picked up the conversation.

"So, we're not witches even though we have magic and not shifters even though you call yourselves 'pack,'" I mused more to myself than to them.

Chayton chuckled lightly. "You don't miss much, do you? We do share traits with other types of supes but we're very much our own group. Our lore can be traced back to Native American cultures. Each one of us has some amount of Native American heritage in our bloodline, mostly Navajo." Chayton leaned a hip against the opposite arm of the sofa I sat upon. I studied the men again, noting how each of them could definitely come from Native American descent, before turning my reflections inward. I'd never known anything about my parents or my background, but my dark hair and tan skin could easily fit the heritage.

I latched onto the information like a leech hungry for blood.

"The legends say we started out as medicine men... and women, as the case may be." Chayton paused and nodded at me before moving on. I tried to remain calm about what he was telling me, but deep down I was hanging onto every word he said like a stage five clinger, desperately searching for some sort of connection. "Originally, our people were healers. Navajo medicine is almost like a form of shamanism; their healing practices are tied deeply to spiritual and supernatural forces that rely on balance and harmony." Pulling his hands from his pockets, he crossed one over is abdomen while using the other to motion as he kept talking. "In order to facilitate healing, medicine men learned about both good and evil magic but used only the good to heal others. As the legend goes, most healers could handle the responsibility of only channeling the good magic, but there were those who were said to become corrupt, choosing dark magic over light. In the Navajo culture, they called those who practiced dark magic 'yee naaldlooshii' which over time has been translated and become 'skinwalkers.' They consider us a type of witch and believe we tap into the dark magic to harm, curse, and kill. The lore says we're evil. Research skinwalkers and you will see how much our kind are feared, instantly associated with darkness and thought to be malevolent, dangerous creatures. The truth, however, is different from anything you'll find online, in any book, or even passed down through tales and stories."

Every molecule inside of me was focused on his lilting tenor, absorbing everything. I was trying to hold out judgment until he finished his story, but my heart was beating a million miles inside my chest and my stomach churned at the idea of being some evil creature.

"We are touched by both good and evil magic—that much is true—but we hold the balance of it firmly in our grasp. Our magic…" He held out his hand and summoned forth a swirling burst of magic in his palm, twisting it into a tornado like effect and letting it linger before recalling it into his body, "…is formed from good, a gift from the spirits that we can wield. It's the same magic that you possess but I'm guessing have never—if rarely—used."

"Yes." I was nearly breathless as I drank in the display. Seeing others with the ability to harness the same type of magic that lived in me felt like a lifeline, and I'd been drowning for too long.

"On the other hand," he grew more serious, "we've also been touched with dark magic."

The color drained from my face and the magick within roared to life, responding to my fear. I willed it to stay inside, but I felt a small bit escape, blowing my hair back as it radiated outward, thankfully disappearing without any further effect. I knew my slip up hadn't gone unnoticed, the guys had all eyed each other at the burst, but I was too wrapped up in my own thoughts to worry about theirs.

I actually had access to dark magic. Exactly what Kingston had accused me of. It felt like the bottom had dropped out of my life.

"Just because we're shadow touched doesn't mean that we're evil. Hear Chayton out." Axel reached for me again, squeezing my knee reassuringly. His hand was large on my leg and I could feel the warmth from his fingers through the layers of crumpled tulle that separated us. That small touch grounded me, and I took a shaky breath.

"All right, I can do that." I fidgeted with the mug, taking another drink—mostly to buy myself some time—before signaling I was ready to hear more. I wasn't, not by a long shot, but I needed all the information before I let myself properly freak the fuck out.

"Like Axel said, being touched by dark magic doesn't make us inherently evil, but it does give us abilities that many other supernaturals don't have. We see things from the underworld— from beyond the veil," Chayton explained.

"But the other witches at the Solstice could see the demon as well… How does that work if we're the ones touched by dark magic?"

Chayton looked at me approvingly. "There are some other supernaturals that have the ability to see creatures from the underworld. Witches and warlocks have the ability. So do the vampires, given that they live half in this life and half in the next. There are some strong fae with the ability to magick them- selves the sight as needed. However, species such as shifters and gargoyles can't see anything that crosses the veil. But shadow touched are the only ones who control their existence on this plane."

Axel jumped into the conversation. "That's what I meant when I said we vanquish demons. There aren't many of our kind left, and our group is one of the most sought-after teams of shadow touched in the country. We work for the vampires and the fae, taking care of demons that are summoned into our world, among other tasks." There was a sense of pride radiating from Axel as he filled me in. I could tell the work he did meant a great deal to him, and I was honestly impressed. They faced monsters, like the ones from my dreams, in real life. Suddenly my nightmares made a whole lot more sense adding another layer of validity to their story. One by one, the puzzle pieces of my life were coming together. I didn't have the whole picture yet, but the frame—the foundation—was there.

"Other tasks." Dason's low rumble from the other side of the room brought me back to the conversation. "Like breaking and entering?" he snarked, and Axel shot him a glare.

Chayton dismissed them, clearly used to their antics. "We send the demons that are summoned back across the veil where they belong. We're the only supernaturals who possess the ability. We're connected to the great spirits above and the dark spirits below. As someone who is shadow touched, Lorn, you have access to more magic than you can possibly understand. Our kind? We're much more powerful than your average witch. It's one of the reasons they hate us so much…" He trailed off, watching my face closely for my reaction.

"That's why the High Coven wanted to kill me tonight?" I didn't miss the way the men around me stiffened. The danger I'd been under had been very real, and while everything had happened so fast earlier, the reality of how very close I'd come to death was a heavy weight in the pit of my stomach.

"The witches and warlocks have been hunting and killing our kind for generations." Dason's mouth was turned downward, his expression hard. The mood in the house grew thick and brooding.

"I had no idea…" Having grown up with the witches and

warlocks I felt the need to defend myself and those who'd raised me, but any protest I was going to launch about the covens died on my tongue. I'd experienced their cruelty plenty in my lifetime. I knew how hateful some of them were over anything different or unusual. Other than my father and Emmaline, I'd had no one in my corner tonight. Kingston and his followers had hated me instantly all because of a label I hadn't even understood. At the same time, I didn't think it was fair to judge an entire race off of the actions of some. Half of the witches and warlocks in attendance tonight had abandoned the fight, not getting involved on either side. Exhausted, I tabled the thoughts for later. My mind was already at capacity and my tiredness was fighting hard to stake its claim.

"We aren't blaming you." Axel came to my defense before standing and crossing his own arms, narrowing his eyes on Dason. "She's not a threat."

"I know. Not directly, anyway." Dason sounded as tired as I felt, and he pinched the bridge of his nose.

I stood from the couch and held up my hands, celebrating when I felt steady rather than lightheaded. "I'm sorry but this is all a lot to process, and the last thing I want to do is start arguments between you. It's obvious that I have a lot to learn." Balancing all the new information I'd already received with wanting to get answers to the million questions I had piling up was overwhelming. Part of me wanted to walk out the front door and leave this all behind until I could deal with everything I'd already learned. Then I remembered I literally had nowhere to go.

Chayton must have read the distress on my face because he quickly chimed in, taking the thoughts right from my head and verbalizing them for me. "I know you have a lot of questions, Lorn. I want to answer them all for you, and I promise that we will, but the things we need to teach you and the things you need to learn are going to take longer than one night. Kota should be home shortly to do a better job at healing your remaining injuries. Why don't we get you settled in and pick back up tomorrow? Stay here tonight."

I knew he was telling me more than asking me to stay. We all knew the truth. I had nowhere else to go. I was stranded with nothing and probably being hunted as we spoke. My fondness for Chayton grew. He was making this so easy on me, effectively taking the awkwardness out of the whole situation. Still, a part of me felt uneasy about imposing on their hospitality.

"Thank you." I looked to the other two men as well. "All of you. You didn't have to take me in, but you have. I know the witches and warlocks are a danger to you and I have no idea if they'll be looking for me or not, but if I had to hedge a guess, I'd say they probably are. If you'd rather I go elsewhere, I'll figure it out. I don't want to cause you any more trouble than I already have."

The three guys all shifted in their stances, and Chayton and Axel looked intensely to Dason. Tension pulled at my brows as I watched the scene. There was a sudden, uncomfortable air in the room and I wondered what was going on. It seemed like they wanted to say more but held themselves back, looking to their alpha for approval.

Dason simply held his ground on whatever silent conversation they were having amongst themselves before finally leaving his post against the wall. "You're always welcome here, Lorn. If you need anything, just let us know. Axel will show you to the room you'll be staying in and get you set up with some clothing and towels. Take all the time you need getting cleaned up, and by the time you're finished Chayton will have some food ready for you." He nodded to each of his friends in turn before he focused on me again. "Tomorrow is a new day, and we'll handle it as such. You have a lot to learn. I don't want to overwhelm you, but the faster you embrace this new life the better. It's never been safe for shadow touched like us, and I'd like to see that you can protect yourself. You've obviously got talent and strength from what Axel tells me. I think we should start assessing where your strengths lie."

"If you're amenable." Chayton crossed his arms over his chest, mimicking Dason's posture. While he was addressing me, he didn't take his eyes off his leader.

Dason pursed his lips slightly, refusing to look at his pack-mate. "If you're amenable," he grumbled out.

I nodded, and Chayton's lips quirked up on one side, basking in the small victory of forcing his alpha to show some manners.

Tonight had been overwhelming and daunting but seeing their pack interactions was refreshing. Even though they didn't always get along, there was a true sense of family within this house, and outside of Emmaline, I'd never been involved with a comradery like this one.

It made me feel hopeful and yet more alone than I had all night. All I'd ever wanted was to fit in, to know who I was, and to finally feel like I belonged. These men seemed to have all of that in spades.

I'd lost everything tonight. I no longer had a coven. I wouldn't be matched—perhaps a silver lining to the shit show that my life had turned into as I'd never been crazy about the idea of an arranged marriage. I had no specialty. I might never be able to talk to my father again.

It was too much and I retreated backward toward the stairs, disengaging before my feelings consumed me and I cracked. I was trying to be strong, but I felt my control slipping, and I didn't want to break in front of these men. Especially not Dason. First impressions told me he was someone who didn't take well to weakness.

Following Axel upstairs, I went through the motions of the quick tour he gave me before shutting myself in the bathroom. At the solid click of the lock, I sagged against the wooden door. Fear and then my need for information had acted as tourniquet, covering the inflicted wounds and staunching the bleeding, but now that I was alone I was falling apart. A tear escaped, and I walked to the sink to stare at my reflection in the mirror. I'd done the same thing mere hours before as I prepared for the Solstice, but now everything in my life had shifted.

The person staring back at me already felt entirely different, and I didn't recognize her or her life at all.

NINE

LORN

Hot water soaked into my sore muscles and I sank deeper into the spacious tub.

The water slid over my skin like silk and I finally relaxed, enjoying the luxury of the bath. After scrubbing myself twice in the shower I'd finally felt clean. The salty tears that mixed with the spray had also helped, and I was feeling better. A little, anyway.

From where I lounged, I looked over the room, taking in the manly decor. A mix of cool greys and browns created an earthy atmosphere that complemented the wood lining the ceiling and back wall. Rustic mirrors hung over a double vanity cluttered with razors, men's deodorant, and toothbrushes. I counted them, wondering how many men actually occupied this cabin, if you could even call it that. I hadn't seen the outside yet, but the inside was beautiful and hardly what I pictured when I thought of a cabin in the woods.

On the opposite wall of the bathroom was the large shower I'd already used, complete with beautiful glass doors and a wall made of rock inside. However, it was the humongous soaking tub that was the true feature of the room. With plenty of space to fit at least two people comfortably, it sat below a tall, clear window that looked out over large trees silhouetted by moonlight. I imagined the view must be spectacular during the daylight hours.

Having spent my entire childhood playing outdoors, the forest had always been a favorite place of mine. I wasn't sure how long I'd be staying, but if I ever got the chance, I wanted to take this tub for a spin around sunset just to enjoy the scenery outside of this window.

Not for the first time, I wondered where I was. Axel had used a portal to jump locations—something only a powerful supernatural could achieve—and I didn't know where we'd landed. The trees here were much larger around and the air was cooler and lacking the humidity of my southern hometown of Lennet Falls, North Carolina—a witchy town about an hour from the city of Winston-Salem. My father was the coven leader for the entire region and it was the only place I'd ever really been.

Thoughts of him made me want to cry, but I'd already poured all my emotions down the drain and all I felt now was a spent kind of emptiness. Tomorrow I'd pick myself back up and keep going, but tonight I reserved for wallowing. Only a pint of mint chocolate chip ice cream could make this evening more complete, but I accepted the large bathtub as a close second as far as consolation was concerned.

Tonight had sucked. Royally, horrendously sucked, but after a good cry I realized that there was nothing I could do about all that had happened except to move forward.

Truth? I wasn't a witch—not in the traditional sense, anyway —and while I was still processing that fact I had to admit I wasn't terribly upset by the news. How could I be when I'd never felt truly accepted by the covens? Before the entire night went to crap, I'd been preparing to live life on the edge of their society as an outcast. I just hadn't realized how *much* of an outcast I'd turn out to be.

Silver linings? Deep inside of me the dying embers of hope had sparked to life. For the first time in ages, I felt closer to figuring out who I was, where I'd come from, and who my birth parents were. There was no way that I'd give up a chance to finally get some answers to the questions that had plagued me my whole life. Without even making a fully conscious decision, I knew I was staying here—wherever here was—until I had the clarity I needed.

The worst part, other than having a death warrant placed on my head, was being cut off from my father and Emmaline. I didn't even know how to cope with that reality, and my heart was grieving. So much had happened and all I wanted to do was pick up my non-existent cell phone to call Em so we could hash all this out together. We shared nearly everything. She was my sounding board and my best friend, and I already missed her cool practicality and ability to get straight to the heart of a matter.

My father was the same way. In his own quiet manner, he'd help me see all the sides of a situation and would give me space to come to my own conclusions. I missed that support and the love I always felt radiating from him. He'd given everything up for me tonight to make sure I survived, and I was determined not to let him down. Being a skinwalker severed all ties to my past, but I was already resolute. My father and Emmaline had never abandoned me, and I wouldn't give them up so easily. The High Coven and their rules and prejudices be damned.

I just had to figure out what to do next. The need to get a message to them burned through me. I wanted to let them know that I was all right and beg for information on how they were and what was happening. It was killing me not to know, but it was also an extremely reckless want. After a very long internal debate, I growled in frustration and dunked my head under the water. There were a million things that could go wrong with the plan, the least being that my magic never worked right and the worst being that if I actually succeeded, then there was a good possibility any message I sent could be tracked. I couldn't put these guys, who had done nothing but help me, at greater risk.

Besides, I hadn't endured everything tonight to die by stupidity now. Common sense and my greater self-preservation wouldn't allow my broken heart to make such important decisions.

Breaking the surface, I ran my hands over my face and hair, brushing away the rivulets of water just as the door banged open.

Startled, I stared wide-eyed at the intruder and slunk down into the tub hiding my naked breasts below the thin cover of bubbles that floated on the surface.

"What the—" The man's gaze flew wide and roamed over me quickly before sliding down the length of the tub and back. Inhaling deeply, his eyes darkened, and a rumble broke the quiet stillness of the bathroom. Entranced, I studied the stranger back, completely shocked at how similar he looked to Axel. Their bone structure and build were exactly the same. The only noticeable differences between the two men were that the newcomer had longer hair, which was piled at the back of his head in a messy bun, and his nose was straighter than Axel's, who looked like he'd broken his in the past and hadn't set it correctly before it healed.

Before I knew what was happening, a low, growl-like vibration sounded from him, and he took a confident step further into the room. I wasn't sure if it was a trick of the bathroom lighting as he moved, but the dark pools of his eyes seemed to flash yellow before returning to their normal color.

"Um… excuse me?" I rose an eyebrow at him, ready to call for help if he moved much closer.

In the next instant, shock covered his face and he coughed to cover the audible rumble in his chest, cutting it off as abruptly as it had started.

"Fuck." He shook his head and turned around, nearly running into the vanity in his haste. "Sorry!" He fled the bathroom, shutting the door in his wake.

Sliding up in the tub, I sat a little straighter and stared at the wooden door wide-eyed and just as shaken as the stranger.

Without warning it opened one more time and the man, who I assumed to be Kota, reappeared. Eyebrows drawn together, he looked at me like I was a complicated math problem he couldn't figure out. It seemed I wasn't the only one in this house with a lack of answers tonight. Sheer confusion contorted his features and he looked at me like I was a figment of his imagination.

"Can I help you?" The break in the silence had his attention flying back to my face from where it had lingered on the tub's waterline.

"Kota, what the hell are you doing?" Axel called after his brother seconds before appearing in the doorframe.

My eyebrows shot up at the party gathering outside the door, and I crossed my arms over my breasts and drew my knees up. The water still hid me, but the bubbles were already starting to disappear, and I didn't trust them with my modesty.

"Don't you know it's rude to gawk at pretty girls? Especially naked ones?" Axel peered into the bathroom and shot me a secretive wink that had me raising an eyebrow at him. I didn't know him well, but he was definitely up to something.

"I was… What the hell… Who is this?" Kota fumbled for words, and his entire expression shut down, growing as hard as stone. He glared at his brother with skepticism and I got the distinct impression that Axel was known for messing with his twin. Having seen them together, it was obvious they were almost identical.

"This is Lorn, the girl we called you about." Axel slapped his brother on the shoulder, giving him a shit-eating grin.

Throwing his hand out, Kota pointed in my direction. "That is not a girl. I was expecting some kid, not a beautiful, naked woman in our bathroom." His face reddened as he chastised Axel. Drawing a deep breath, his eyes flicked back to me. "Especially not our—"

"Let's give the lady some privacy so she can finish up her bath." Axel reached out and clasped his brother's shoulder tugging him from the entryway. "Lorn, Chayton is almost done making some food for you and I just changed the sheets on your bed. I left some clothing out too. Take your pick of anything you'd like and help yourself to whatever you need. There's an extra toothbrush under the sink you can have. Kota will meet you soon to take a look at your injuries."

"Just make sure to knock next time." I gave Kota a teasing smile trying to ease the tension in the small space. I hoped the lightheartedness after all of Axel's obvious taunting would help soften the hard lines that had formed on his face, but he simply closed the door without a backward glance.

"You didn't even knock? What kind of brute are you?" Axel's impish tone floated through the door, much to his brother's chagrin.

"I didn't know she was in there! Besides, we all share one bathroom, and you're usually the one hogging it!"

"Dude, privacy. Say it with me this time…" Axel enunciated the word again.

"You know what… just start talking. What the hell happened tonight, because shit clearly…"

I listened to the retreating sound of the two brothers' hushed conversation. It was clear they were close but ribbed on each other like the siblings they were. In some ways they reminded me of Em and me and our endless joking. A pang of homesickness shot through my chest.

Climbing from the tub, I set the drain and dried off, wrapping myself in a fluffy blue towel. Without toiletries, I ran my fingers through my hair, trying to comb the length. The strands brushed down past my shoulder blades in unruly waves that I knew would look like a tangled mess come morning without a brush to tame them. Looking under the sink, I found the new toothbrush and clung to it like it was gold. Sadly, it was the only thing I could call my own other than the fancy black underwear I'd had on under my dress.

I was living the big life.

Hesitating for a moment, I reached for the deodorant and chose one that smelled incredible. I wiped off the top and used it, throwing caution to the wind and hoping the guys weren't too stingy with my borrowing their toiletries. I made a mental note to solve this problem right after I figured out my clothing situation. Using the guys' things wasn't exactly my first choice, but since I had nothing to my name it was a sacrifice I was willing to bend my normal rules for.

Being stranded with nothing left me feeling bereft. It reminded me too much of a nightmare I used to have as a child where my adopted parents had decided they didn't want me anymore. I'd been abandoned in the dark, all alone, without even my favorite teddy bear. Avalon had never been notably caring, but the dreams had started after one particularly bad day when I'd angered her. All these years later and I couldn't even remember what I'd done to earn her disapproval, but I never forgot the cold look she'd sent me nor her grumbled retorts about never wanting me. It wasn't a secret that she'd fought against Cardoc taking me in as a baby.

As I'd grown up, I realized that I represented everything she never wanted. She'd had to share her life, her house, and Cardoc's affection with me, and my presence had left her bitter. While Cardoc had easily stepped into the role of father, Avalon had never mastered being my mother. It hadn't helped that she'd never been able to have a child of her own. Each failed attempt had left her resenting me all the more. I'd always felt guilty that she'd never been able to conceive, but it also wasn't an excuse for all her hostility.

Stepping out of the past, I glanced into the mirror again, and this time I felt a little better. My cheeks had regained some of their color and my hair was back to being dirt and leaf free. I felt clean and smelled good. Life was looking up one small thing at a time.

Securing the towel around my body, I peeked into the empty hallway and quickly padded to Axel's room when I saw the coast was clear. He'd sweetly given up his space and his bed for me. It was just one more thing he'd done today to help, and I vowed I'd find a way to repay him for all his kindness.

His room wasn't anything like I'd expected. Instead of the mess I'd assumed most men's bedrooms were, things were generally tidy. A few articles of clothing lay strewn across an armchair in the corner, but the bed was fresh and the walls held large black and white landscapes framed and displayed at intervals on dark blue walls. I took a minute to wander and appreciate each one. Whoever the artist was had done a masterful job of capturing the essence of the forest. It made me feel comfortable in the unfamiliar space.

A soft knock thudded on the door and I clutched the towel tightly before responding. Kota stood on the other side, tapping his hand against his thigh.

"Hi." I tried to smile at him again, glad to see the stony expression he'd worn earlier had eased some.

"I came to heal the rest of your injuries." He blew out a breath he seemed to be holding and motioned to the door. "Do you mind if I come in?"

Looking down at myself, I decided I was covered enough for now and stepped back giving him permission to enter.

He stepped inside and closed the door over without clicking it shut, and I immediately appreciated the gesture. So far—bathroom incident notwithstanding—these guys had done whatever they could to welcome me and make sure I was comfortable in their home.

"I heard you hit your head pretty hard," he mused after walking into the room, keeping a number of feet between us.

"I fell off of Axel's motorcycle and the ground wasn't as forgiving as I'd hoped it would be." I shrugged, and he shook his head at me.

"Looks like I'll be having a talk with my brother about his driving."

"It wasn't his fault. We were in a pretty precarious situation." The last thing I wanted was to start up another bickering match between the two brothers.

"Yeah, I heard... demons, witches, and warlocks." Ice dripped from the last word. There was no love lost between him and the supernaturals who had raised me. I chose to keep my mouth shut. "And yet it does no good to save you from all that shit only to kill you by motorcycle." Clearing his throat, he pointed to the bed. "Let me take a look."

I gritted my teeth to hold in anything snarky I'd say in response to his commanding tone and moved toward the bed. Sitting down, I took a minute to tuck the towel just right assuring it would stay closed when I let go of the fabric. I took stock of my injuries and held a palm out first.

Kota dragged his brother's computer chair over and sat in front of me before leaning over my hand. He ran a finger over the puckered pink flesh of my cut and the blister like marks that surrounded it, and his eyes sought out mine.

"What's this one from?" he asked quietly, clearly having settled into his role as healer. He was more clinical but the edge he'd had just minutes ago was gone.

"Dagger." The word was a whisper into the space between us. "And a magickal burn." His gaze shot up to my face.

"They cut you?" I was surprised his breath didn't cloud around us given the coldness that had seeped into it. Kota had an uncanny ability to change his moods in zero to sixty, and it was starting to give me whiplash.

"It was voluntary. Part of the ceremony I was in. Don't worry about it." I tried to pull my hand back. It wouldn't be the first scar I had. Maybe it was fitting that I had a lasting outward sign of the day my life changed forever. There must be something poetic in that.

His hand gripped mine and he pulled it back into his line of sight. "I'm going to heal it. I just wanted to know," he said, dropping the attitude he'd had. "Relax for me." His focus flicked to my face briefly before returning to his job. "Have you ever been healed before?"

"We have some people in the covens adept at healing, but it

might be different. They use potions and spell work mostly. I have a feeling your abilities are more magickal."

His lips tilted to the side and the look that crossed his face was so reminiscent of Axel. The two of them may be scary identical but I could already tell that they were very different people. However, the gleam in his brown eyes made me do a double take.

"Everything about us is more magickal, sweetheart." Without warning or giving me a chance to respond, he fired up his powers. Heat tingled across my palm and my attention dropped to watch what he was doing. Warmth crept into my skin from the soft blue glow that emanated from his hand. Tracing one finger along the injury, I watched in awe as the skin knit back together. When he was done, there was nothing but smooth, perfect, unscarred flesh.

"That was amazing!" I breathed.

"That was nothing," he scoffed, but I caught the flash of pride that shone in his eyes before he hid it away behind his unreadable mask. He repeated the treatment on my other palm, and then reached up and placed a hand on either side of my head. Even sitting down, he was taller than I was, and I shut my eyes to keep myself from staring at his lips. "I'm going to check out that concussion that Dason and Axel are so worried about. You might feel some pressure. Internal injuries heal different than external ones."

I murmured my consent absentmindedly. Kota was inches away, and his scent washed over me with his nearness. That same outdoorsy essence that Axel had was present—all mossy forests—but the rest was distinctly cinnamon. I breathed him in while his fingers threaded into my hair. The same heat I'd experienced earlier flared, and then the pressure set in. My head felt like it was in a vice, but soon the lingering effects of my headache miraculously disappeared. A few more moments of holding still and Kota was done. Without a sound, he pulled back an inch taking the pressure of his healing powers with him. His hands found my shoulder and then slowly dragged down my arms inch by inch. A breath rushed from my lips and I tipped my head back, enjoying the touch. Warmth blazed a trail in his path and even though my eyes were closed I could feel his focus on me like a caress. Chill bumps rose on my skin as it cooled. The combination of warm and cold was a heady mixture.

Teasing fingertips reached my hands tracing their way down each of my fingers before deviating to the tops of my thighs. Continuing his trek, he met the edge of the towel where more bare skin awaited him.

Before long, his hand came to rest over the wound on my outer thigh. I barely recognized the soreness as he pressed his palm over the area. Heat seared into the cut, and the sting it caused had me crying out. My eyes flew open, spell broken, and I watched his blue magic swirl into my leg. I couldn't see the healing, but I could feel the pull and tug as the skin and muscle regenerated. The sharp, uncomfortable pain was short lived, but it left my chest heaving as I breathed through the discomfort the healing had caused.

When it was all over, he skimmed his fingers to my knees and rolled his chair away until he was no longer touching me. He sat across from me, tucking a loose strand of hair behind his ear. The moment hung heavily in the room as we both stared at each other, until Kota finally cleared his throat again and broke the tense, terse silence.

"Next time, you should shift. You'll heal faster and save yourself a lot of time, pain, and possible scarring. Especially if

I'm not available right away. There's no reason for you to be hurting any longer than necessary."

"Excuse me?" I was sure I heard him wrong and I shook my head emphatically. "I can't shift."

His forehead creased. "What the hell are you talking about?"

I arched a brow at him, matching his obvious frustration. "Why do you think I can shift?"

"The guys seriously didn't talk to you about this?"

"Definitely the fuck not. I'm a skinwalker—er, shadow touched—not a shifter." I knew Chayton had said we shared traits with other supernatural groups, but this went beyond what I'd thought he'd meant. Now my mind was spinning with even more questions.

Kota clenched his jaw and scrubbed a hand along the back of his neck tipping his head to the ceiling and letting out a groan that was somewhere between irked and put out. "My pack-mates are idiots."

"Hold up a minute." I stood from the bed and glared down at him. "Are you saying I can shift?" I knew my voice was rising in pitch as well as volume, and the door pushed open admitting Chayton.

"It's another facet of our shadow touched magick. We have the ability to take on animal spirits and shift our forms." Chayton carried a laden tray into the room and, as hungry as I was, I ignored it in favor of this new, mind-blowing information.

"Each of you can shift into animals? As in plural?" I gaped at them both.

"It's got more of a learning curve than that, but essentially, yes." Chayton set the tray on the bed, and even though I was in a towel, his eyes stayed above the fabric line respectfully.

I eyed the pile of clothing Axel had set out for me longingly.

I needed the cover and protection of the extra fabric. Vulnerability was not a feeling I enjoyed, and right now I was totally out of my depth. "This is all a lot to swallow," I said.

"What's a lot to swallow? Am I missing the fun already?" Axel walked into the room wearing his signature cocky smirk and shot me a playful wink, but he settled immediately upon seeing my face. I was sure I wasn't hiding my feelings nor my disbelief well.

"Class, Brother," Kota growled.

"Are you all right?" Axel ignored his brother and moved to my side, his joking exterior replaced by his caring one.

"We weren't hiding anything from you, Lorn. There's just so much to teach you. It's rare that a walker grows up outside the fold," Chayton soothed.

"And if they do, they usually don't survive this long," Kota interjected. "Which is why you need to learn to shift. It can make all the difference between living to see another day or dying a slow, painful death at the hands of a demon or the kind that raised you."

"Nice. Way to scare her," Axel hissed at his brother.

"Well someone needs to give the girl the reality of her situation." Kota stood and faced Axel, anger arching off of him.

"I thought you said she was a woman." Axel threw Kota's earlier words back at him. "She already had a healthy dose of reality tonight when the entire eastern half of the US covens tried to kill her in her own backyard!" he ranted. "What we need to do is build her up and teach her."

"Guys!" Chayton chided at the same time Dason appeared and bellowed, "Enough."

"Everyone out," Dason ordered, pointing to the door.

Kota was the first to leave, not even sparing me a backward

glance or a goodbye, and Axel, who passed me an apologetic look, followed his brother.

After a beat, Chayton spoke. "I brought you an assortment of foods because I wasn't sure what you liked to eat. Hopefully something I made will suit you before you crash for the night." Chayton's posture was relaxed and unassuming, almost like he was trying to make me more comfortable through his body language. He was sweet and caring and I thanked him when he reached out and squeezed my arm, warmth buzzing over my bicep. "Get some rest and we'll talk more in the morning."

I murmured a thank you and goodnight as Chayton headed out of the room, sending me one last encouraging smile before he disappeared from sight.

"Look, I'm sorry about them. They can be a bit... much." Dason scratched absently at the back of his neck seeming out of his element.

Overwhelmed, I wanted to laugh. It was true, they were, but so was he. So was all of this.

"It's all right. I'm just at capacity I think." I squirmed, feeling less comfortable being nearly naked around Dason than I had been around the others.

"You let me know if any of them become a problem and I'll deal with them." His stare was intense.

"Thanks, but I think I can handle them." I stood a little straighter against the alpha power that radiated off of Dason.

"If anyone can, it's probably you." I barely heard what he'd said but I didn't get the chance to respond before he shook his head and walked out the door without any further explanation.

"Eat and get some sleep." Everything that came out of Dason's mouth sounded like an order. I almost questioned him just to see what his response would be, but exhaustion pressed in and I decided to rein in my retort instead of possibly pissing off the one guy who had final say on where I slept tonight. The bed behind me was calling my name too much for me to get mouthy.

"Goodnight," I called as he left, watching him head down the hallway to where Chayton was waiting for him. The two entered into a quiet conversation that they took downstairs.

Finally alone, I sent thanks to the universe that the bedroom door had a lock and quickly slipped into the oversized tee-shirt that Axel left out for me. Deciding to save the pants for tomorrow, I crawled between the fresh sheets and sat in the middle of the queen-sized bed. The way the mattress dipped underneath me almost made me moan out loud, but it was the food that had me groaning in gratitude as I downed an entire gourmet sandwich and a glass of milk in milliseconds. After the night I'd had, this felt like bliss.

Turning off the lights, I settled into the pillows, closed my eyes, and settled into a sleepy daze faster than I thought was possible. A vortex of memories flew past my mind's eye in a colorful display of horrifying images that made up my night, and in less time than it took to draw a deep breath, it was over. The distinct tingle of magick was left floating through my head, but I didn't have a chance to dwell on it as darkness closed in around me greeting me like an old friend as it dragged me under and offered me peace.

TEN

CHAYTON

Noon day sunlight shone through the kitchen windows while I stood at the stove and turned over the eggs I was scrambling in the frying pan. I'd felt the pull of Lorn from the moment we'd bonded and had known when she'd woken up. The buzz of her energy was like a direct line that spanned between us, and the new connection awed me. I'd never expected to feel anything like this in my lifetime, but I was already addicted.

I added some cheese and spices to the eggs, plated them, and set everything in front of one of the seats at the kitchen island. I tried not chuckle to myself over Lorn's stalling capabilities, while I grabbed the orange juice from the fridge and poured her a glass, adding it to her spot. Out of the personalities in our pack I was the caretaker, and I wanted to make sure everything was perfect for whenever she decided to join me.

Her hesitation was sweet. I knew she must be nervous, especially in the light of a new day. Waking up in a strange house full of men she didn't know was hopefully well outside of her wheelhouse.

The images from her nightmares still floated through my mind, but I didn't regret taking them from her last night to help her sleep. However, I was pretty sure that the flashes I got of her in danger would stay with me for a long time. Knowing that she was my mate and I could have lost her before I'd even found her had fear settling uncomfortably in my heart. Even knowing all of that, I wouldn't have changed what she'd been through last night because it had brought her to us. Sometimes hardships were necessary, and fate, while unpredictable, had a plan.

A shadow touched female. I could barely believe it.

When Dason had carried her through the door last night, I'd been shocked. The power of her scent had ripped apart my entire world and reconstructed it in a matter of minutes. I'd never felt more complete. Everything that had ever come before Lorn felt pale and insignificant in comparison.

Unlike Dason, I was open and excited about the gift that Lorn was to our pack. His hesitation had been concerning, but I also knew my best friend. He needed time to adjust and accept our new future.

Our conversation from the night before had been echoing through my head all morning.

* * *

"*The universe decides to send her to us now? After all this time?*" *Dason stalked toward the fridge and yanked it open, procuring two beers. Passing one to me, he popped the top with his bare hand and tipped the cool glass bottle back to take a swig.*

"*The universe doesn't operate on our time schedule, Dase.*" *I set the beer on the kitchen island, leaning against it and crossing my arms. "Besides, she's young and obviously our fates needed to align before she could appear in our lives."*

"She's young all right. She's practically a child!" He scrubbed a hand down his face and let out a frustrated growl.

"Trust me, she's not a child. Yes, she's young, but she is a woman."

"How old do you think she is?" The distress on his face was something he didn't show often, but our close friendship allowed him to drop his carefully placed guard.

"We'll have to ask her…"

Cutting me off, Dason leveled me with a look that said he didn't want any placating bullshit. He wanted an answer. I blew out a breath and went over the observations I'd made, before finally giving him my best estimate. "She's at least eighteen if she was participating in the Solstice, but probably older. Maybe twenty?" I hedged a guess.

"You really think she's twenty?" Hope was alive in his tone. At twenty-eight, the age gap between the two of them would be significant, but it wasn't some unheard-of novelty to mate a younger woman in the shifter communities. Don't even get me started on vampires. Their lifespans were unreal.

"She's old enough to have been engaged. It's common knowledge that all the witches and warlocks participating in the ceremony get matched up at the Solstice." I watched Dason closely, and his behavior didn't disappoint. The menacing growl he let out was telling. He hated the idea of another male's claim on her as much as I did. The thought pierced me in the stomach like a jagged edged dagger. I didn't even know Lorn, and already a jealous and possessive part of me awoke.

"Mara." The woman's name on his lips had me sighing.

"I know." I hung my head. "We have to tell her. I feel guilty having to renege on the promises we've made, but I know she'll

understand once she hears about Lorn. We all knew the implications of finding a true mate, even though the odds were slim."

"She's going to be upset."

"I don't think there's anything we can do to prevent that, but I also don't believe she's the type of person to hold our promises against us. I'm just glad fate intervened before we sealed the mating. It's not like we knew this would happen." Reaching for my beer, I opened it and took a healthy drink. I'd never been a huge fan of claiming a mate that didn't call to me, but at twenty-five, I wasn't that far behind Dason in age and I felt the overwhelming urge to settle down just as he did. Taking any mate was better than never having one, and Mara was a sweet, caring, independent woman. We could have done a lot worse for ourselves. While it wouldn't have been a true mating—the connection weak in comparison to what I now felt toward Lorn—I'd grown to care for Mara, and I knew Dason's feelings had surpassed my own where she was concerned.

"What if she's not right for us?" Dason slouched against the wall, rested his head against it, and looked at the ceiling. His beer, which was almost empty, hung clutched in his hand at his side.

"You already know what I think about the stupidity of that question. If anyone's not right for us, Dase, it's Mara. Lorn not being exactly what we need isn't a possibility, and you know it. And who knows what that looks like? There are a lot of personalities in our small pack and it's going to take a very special woman to deal with all of us. I choose to trust fate." My voice was sharp and it snapped him back to alertness. "I know you have feelings for Mara, but you can't let them interfere with the relationship that just fell into our laps. Lorn is the one that we've been waiting for. Don't judge her before you've even gotten to know her."

Straightening from his position, he downed the last few sips of beer and threw the bottle into the recycling container we kept under the sink.

"It's late. I'm heading up," Dason said while he walked to the stairs, ending the argument before it even got started.

I stared after him as he left and shook my head, but I'd caught his barely perceptible nod. That small movement was all he'd give me for now, but it was enough to let me know he'd heard what I'd said.

* * *

Between Lorn's nightmares, my excitement of her appearance, and my worry over Dason, I'd barely slept. I respected Dason as my alpha and I cared about him as the life-long friend he'd always been, but I wouldn't let him get in his own way this time. He was a great leader, but he also had his flaws, like his stubborn streak and inability to accept change. I just had to hope that he'd come around in his own time and realize how blessed we were. Shadow touched matings were incredibly rare. Once the others in our community caught wind of ours, there was bound to be a celebration… and an influx of men hoping they were also part of her bond. I pushed the worry to the back of my mind as I heard an upstairs door creak open.

Soft footsteps padded down the stairs as Lorn finally emerged from her room.

"Good morning." The smile that found its way onto my lips was natural, effortless, and all for her. However, it faltered as she paused at the bottom of the steps, propped her hands on her hips, and raised an eyebrow.

"One of you magicked me last night." She cocked her head

and studied my reaction with a hard expression in place. It was clear that she wasn't happy, but I hoped she wasn't too mad.

I chose to look contrite, and I cleared my throat and held up my hands in surrender. "I did. I'm sorry, Lorn. I probably should have asked, but with the way the night went down, I just wanted to make things a little easier on you. I figured you'd probably have a restless night of sleep without a little help."

"It's not okay to magick me without my permission." Her stare leveled me.

"I swear I was just trying to help. The magick acted like a dreamcatcher, keeping the nightmares away so you could get some sleep, but you have my word that it won't happen again."

She nodded and softened, dropping her hands from her hips and moving into the kitchen. "I get that you were just trying to help but next time... just ask me, okay?"

My hand flew over my heart. "You have my word."

Any remaining hostility she was holding disappeared with the deep breath she released and then she was looking at me with sincerity. "Thank you all for giving me a place to stay last night."

"You'll always be welcome here, Lorn. You're one of us now. You always have been, you just didn't know it." I wanted to reach out to her and pull her into a hug, to tell her that she'd never have to be alone, but I kept my hands to myself and watched her instead.

Heavy emotion shone behind her eyes. I had just enough time to catch it before she hung her head and her hair fell into her face acting like a curtain that shielded her from view.

"Something smells amazing." Lorn changed the subject as she took a deep inhale and moved toward the plate of food she spotted sitting out for her, all while she fidgeted with the hem of the large tee-shirt she wore. Even in the baggy sweatpants that she'd had to roll a few times at the waist to keep secure she was beautiful.

"I made you breakfast." Pulling the seat back from the island, I waited for her to hop up before I scooted it in.

"Dinner last night and breakfast this morning? A girl could get used to this," she joked, breaking the heavy atmosphere we'd been in just seconds before. I took my cue from Lorn and followed her into lighter topics with a chuckle. It warmed my heart to know that my actions were making her happy.

"Then I'll have to keep up the treatment." I grinned and returned to the other side of the island. "I'm not sure what you typically eat in the morning, so I opted for the safe choices of pancakes, scrambled eggs, sausage, bacon, and orange juice."

She peered wide-eyed at all the food. "Hell, I'm used to just eating cereal. This is all for me?"

"Sure is. Help yourself and don't wait on my account. Eat up. I've already had mine and the others ate before they left this morning."

I watched as she slid a bite between her bow shaped lips and hummed in satisfaction.

"I'm sorry I slept so late." She glanced at the wooden clock hanging on the wall of the kitchen noting the hour. "Although I guess that's really your fault." She smirked, and I gave her a cheeky grin. "Anyway, I should have asked if I needed to be up at any certain time. Where are the others?"

"Hunting," I said vaguely.

"Like, for deer?"

I shook my head and held her gaze. "For a class three demon shade." I wouldn't lie to her. Demon hunting was our reality, and as much as I hated the idea of her in harm's way, from what I'd heard of her powers thus far, I was sure we wouldn't be able to keep her from tagging along—or even joining in—for long. Not after she got the knack of her magick.

Choking on a gulp of orange juice, she coughed and cleared her throat. "They went after the demon? Are they crazy? That thing was powerful and dangerous!"

"I know. So are we. It's three against one; you don't have to worry." Lorn seemed like she wanted to argue but ended up forking more food into her mouth to keep quiet. I chuckled, braced my hips against the counter opposite her, and hooked my thumbs into the front pockets of my jeans. "I know you don't know me yet and that's something I want to change. Lesson one: you never have to hold your tongue with me. I'll always want to know what's going through that beautiful mind of yours."

Her gaze flew to my face and I watched her cheeks take on an attractive rosy hue. I decided then and there that I wanted to put that color into her complexion every single day.

I was a goner, but a damn happy one. I usually wasn't thrilled to be left out of a good fight, which the demon shade was sure to provide for my packmates but getting to spend time with Lorn and get to know her was well worth sitting on the sidelines.

"All right," she consented. "I don't understand. How are the demons crossing the veil? And why are shadow touched the ones who need to vanquish them? For that matter, are shadow touched stronger than other supernaturals? Because I've seen some very powerful warlocks before. And what about injuries? I don't know much about demons, but I know enough to know that a demon inflicted wound means death. How can you stand there so calmly as your friends go to battle with one?"

Lorn's questions circled us right back to where we'd been and all I could do was stare at her with increasing pride. Already I could tell my mate had a curious mind that was not only observant but smart. The fact that she didn't sit passively by and let life run over her but instead took it by the balls and demanded answers had my grin growing wider on my face.

"That's a lot of questions, but I did promise you answers, so let me see if I can help offer some clarity. Each group of supernaturals has their own specialties where they excel. I'm sure you know better than I do about the different magickal affinities that witches and warlocks can have and how they form covens that contain people from each of the different specialties. The more balanced the coven the more powerful it becomes. They practice what we call 'confined magick' which means they need their wands, potions, and spells to use it. I'm not saying that it's not powerful magick, because it is, but it does have its limitations.

"Then we have the fae who are immortal and have power over perception, like their glamours. Most of their magick relates to their sensitivity over the energies that run through the realms and their ability to wield it, but they also have strong empathic talents that allow them to read people. It's because of this that there are so many warnings about their kind as they're easily able to bend and manipulate people and situations to their will."

"Right," she said with a nod. "Vampires have their super-speed, strength, heightened senses, and insanely long lives."

"Don't forget their mind control and other mental capabilities," I chimed in. "And then there are the shifters. Obviously being able to shift forms is their most powerful asset, but they also have increased senses, speed, and are unparalleled trackers. Their strength in both forms is unmatched. My point is that each supernatural race has their own advantages.

"Shadow touched are the same. We have the ability to transform into any animal we desire. As you can imagine, that makes us versatile in many fields of work in the supernatural world. We're stealthy, can heal ourselves and others, and we have an added bonus of being able to speak telepathically when we're shifted. Like I'd said last night, we contain both light and dark magic, and that gives us unique talents like the sight—what allows us to see creatures from the underworld—access to the veil, and powerful, untethered magic. So while I wouldn't discount the other races and say were superior, we do have skill sets that makes us different—hated by some, valued by others.

"The reason we take on the demons versus other supernatural groups? That has to do with our connection to the veil. We're the only supes who can cross beings from the living realm to the underworld and being shadow touched gives us immunity to the lethal venom demons carry. Other supernaturals can't survive a demon wound like we can. As long as we have the ability to heal ourselves, we survive. It's dangerous work but we've become very proficient at what we do. It's why we're highly sought after by the fae and the vampires to handle any demon problems they encounter in their cities."

She leaned forward instinctively, food forgotten. "We're linked to the underworld and our job is to literally battle demons back to the other side of the veil..." the words fell from her mouth in shock.

"It pays well." My attempt to break the tension didn't seem to work. She gaped at me, blinking through the silence. "It's what we do. We police the human and supernatural world to keep balance between the realms. It's an important job, and one only we can do. Demons can't be allowed into our world. They're banished to the underworld for a reason."

"Why do the witches and warlocks hate us if we serve such an important role?" Her voice was nearly a whisper, but I caught her question. Her gaze dropped back to her plate, and she pushed the food around with the tongs of her fork. Knowing what she did about our feelings toward the people she'd lived with her whole life, I assumed she was hesitant to ask the question.

"We honestly don't know, but we have our theories." I tried to keep my tone casual, but her attention snapped up to my face and her eyes narrowed. For a few moments she studied me, and then dawning broke across her features as she landed on her conclusion.

"You think they're behind the summonings, don't you." It wasn't a question, so I didn't treat it like one.

"I won't deny that it's crossed our minds more than once. The fact that one turned up last night at your Solstice is just one more concerning bit of evidence." The last thing I wanted to do was argue with her and start off our relationship on the wrong foot, so I shut up. Giving her more information was a call that Dason would need to make, anyway. It was just one more reason I didn't envy his job as alpha.

"I don't know a single witch or warlock that dabbles in that kind of dark magick," she defended.

"I'm glad to hear it, but there are evil doers in every race of people, Lorn."

She pursed her lips, but then her face softened, and she huffed a breath. "I know, and I can't account for all of them. I can just account for the people I am—was—closest to."

Her entire countenance fell as the struggle of her night returned and appeared to crash over her head. My packmates and I had a lot of work to do to make sure that Lorn felt at home here, and it still might not be enough to fill the hole that losing her friends and family had left in her heart. It was one more topic I added to my list of things to talk with Dason about. If there were people she was close to that she didn't want to lose contact with then somehow we'd have to find a way to keep them in her life—at least in some capacity. This was all new territory for us. I couldn't think of a single case where a skinwalker had been raised outside of one of our communities. We were all treading in new, unknown waters.

Before I could say anything or try to offer any comfort, Lorn visibly brushed off her melancholy and changed the subject, her casual demeanor returning. "So, what are we doing today while we wait around for Dason, Axel, and Kota to arrive home *unharmed?*" She threw that last bit of sass over the glass of OJ she brought back to her lips.

"Well my little skinwalker," I said with a smirk. "I thought we'd take our little powwow outside and see just how powerful you really are. From what I've heard, you disarmed an entire fleet of magick users last night. An impressive feat."

She laughed, and I reveled in the sparkle that entered her cornflower blue eyes. "More like desperate plea to the universe for survival, but if you want to give me the credit, I'll take it. Truly, I'm not sure what the hell I did last night. It all just kind of happened."

"That's what training is for. It's time to hone your skills and finally let that magick you've been suppressing free." Walking around the kitchen island, I let my gaze roam up and down her baggy, ill-fitting clothing with a look of disapproval. "But first, we need to get you something that fits, or you'll end up with Axel's pants around your ankles."

Not that I'd mind the view. I kept that to myself and held out my hand, letting my magick flare to life in my palm. "May I?"

ELEVEN

LORN

H*oly hormones, batman.* I stared at Chayton's slanted smile and nearly melted at how handsome he was. I'd never been surrounded by such sexy men before, or had their attention solely on me. Sure, there'd been plenty of good-looking warlocks when I was in the academy, but something about these men called to me in a way others never had. I'd praised myself so far for not making a complete fool of myself in front of them, but now Chayton stood close to me in all his gorgeous glory, and I had to remind myself to speak.

What the hell had he asked me?

Looking down I noticed his red, glowing palm and I bolted from my seat, backing up with my palms outstretched. "What the fuck? I thought we were on the same side!"

His magick immediately disappeared and his face scrunched up in confusion, which helped ease the shock I felt. A little, anyway. My quick movements seemed to have taken him by surprise, but years of ingrained trust issues had me keeping my hands where they were, ready to block any impending attack.

My magick was quick to respond, building in my hands and spreading up my arms.

"I was offering to make you some clothing, and it's best if I touch you so I can magick the correct measurements. What made you freak out?" He looked sincerely lost as he tried to reason out my reaction. I let out a sigh of relief. Taking a chance, I lowered my hands and tried to make my posture look less defensive.

"The red color. With witches, it's deadly. I was surrounded by it last night before I de-wanded people."

He winced. "I'm sorry. I didn't know. Red is simply my magick's color. Kind of like how Kota's is blue. We each have a stronger skill than the others in our pack, and it tends to color our magick." He cocked his head and held his hands out gently, not making any drastic moves. "Here, I'll give you an example." Facing his hands toward each other, he let his magick come to life again. It spanned the space between his palms and I watched as he began crafting something out of the red glow. Before I knew it, the burst of color was gone, and in its place was a black t-shirt. "It might not be a perfect fit, but here you go." He tossed the material at me.

Unfolding it, I smiled at him. "#badass?"

He grinned cheekily, and the expression lit up his entire face. "Just calling it as I've heard it."

Laughing, I stepped closer and let Chayton use his magick to fashion me a pair of jean shorts, converse shoes, and some undergarments. A blush infused my cheeks when he handed me a lace-covered red bra and a pair of matching bikini underwear.

"When you're ready to learn more about yourself, Lorn, come and find me."

The searing look Chayton gave me before he sauntered out of the house followed me all the way to the bathroom as I stripped and changed into the perfectly tailored clothing. I knew he was talking about meeting him outside when I was ready to start my training, but there was a note when he spoke and a spark in his eyes that let me know there was a double innuendo in his words.

Why was I attracted to all these men, especially when romance should be the furthest thing from my mind? I'd just escaped a lifelong commitment I hadn't wanted, and now I had the opportunity to figure out who I was and where I'd come from.

That's all I should be focused on.

I gave myself that pep talk all the way outside, but as soon as I stepped onto the wooden front porch and closed the cabin door behind me, all my thoughts fled.

Large trees surrounded the house, three times the size of the ones back home. Their red-brown bark was rich in color and each tree was a tall, silent giant. Everything surrounding the cabin was green, mossy, and fresh, and I simply stood there breathing in the clean, cool forest air that played over my skin. The seventy-degree weather was a refreshing contrast to the staggering, humid upper eighties we'd been experiencing back in North Carolina.

When I'd had my fill, I scanned the yard and my gaze landed on Chayton, who made an equally stunning picture against the forest backdrop. He was wearing a pair of athletic pants, which should be illegal for the way they showed off his ass and a tight, black sleeveless shirt that left the corded muscles of his arms on display. Two long braids hung down on either side of his head, framing his strong jawline and dark eyes. I jogged down the steps and walked across the yard to where he was standing, attempting not to drool while I tried to keep calm.

"Where are we?" I forced my voice into something that hopefully sounded normal and not awestruck.

He's just a guy, I told myself, and then internally rolled my eyes. *A freakin' hot one.* I ripped my gaze away to look to the surrounding scenery, instead of moving closer to him the way I wanted to.

"Washington State, or more specifically, we are in Olympic National Park. We live on the outskirts of the Kwoli packs' territory," he answered, but his eyes were drinking me in, sinking down my body in appreciation.

My lips curved upward when I noticed his attention, but then what he'd said registered and my mouth nearly dropped open. I had to remind myself to keep it closed it. "I've never been outside of North Carolina before!"

"That's the beauty of portal jumping... you can go anywhere you want. If your magick is as strong as I believe it is, then it's a skill you'll learn soon enough, but we need to conquer the basics first."

My eyes sparkled at the idea of my first training session. "Well, Yoda, I'm your faithful student. So," I held up my hands and wiggled my fingers, "how do we do this?"

* * *

"Try again," Chayton chided, as he waved a finger at the shimmering air in front of me.

"You know, when you said you were going to train me, this isn't exactly what I had in mind," I grumbled playfully, but held out my pointer finger and with sweeping motions, drew a fluid symbol into the air in front of me. A glowing trail was left in the wake of my movements, and my nose scrunched up in concentration as I focused on the task at hand.

"I know you want to get to the good stuff, but you have to build your foundation first. The magick you learned from the witches is massively different than ours."

Blowing out a breath, I dropped my hand away from my drawing and raised my eyebrows at Chayton, waiting for his scrutiny or praise.

"Almost," he smiled and stepped behind me. His sweet scent floated over me and his body warmed my back as he stepped into my personal space. "You're almost there, but the symbols have slight nuances that you'll need to pay attention to." Chayton set the fingertips of one hand lightly on my shoulder, and then they were moving, tracing down my arm in a gentle caress that left my skin tingling and body aware of every touch. Trailing his fingers to my hand, he guided my arm back up and held on to my wrist. My back brushed against his chest as we moved together and redrew the symbol. "The curves need to be deeper," his voice was like smooth chocolate to my ears, "and you missed this extra line." He walked me through what I needed to work on, but I didn't miss the way his voice dropped into a husky tenor, nor the way his nose skimmed against my hair.

I let my eyes run over the rune, memorizing the curves and intricacies as Chayton and I froze in the moment. Our bodies brushed together with each breath, and he slowly lowered my arm and inched closer, nuzzling his nose against the top of my head. I turned my face toward him, glancing at him over my shoulder, and then closed my eyes to just enjoy the moment. Being this close to him had a strange sense of… home. Being in Chayton's arms felt good. Right. And I couldn't explain it.

His hands landed gently on the curve of my waist and he gave my hips a little squeeze. "Your turn," he murmured in my ear. I nodded, a little dazed, and pulled my focus back to what

Chayton had been teaching me. I let a miniscule amount of magick escape my finger and drew the symbol again, this time on my own. When I finished, I looked back at Chayton hopefully.

"Well done! See, you're getting the hang of this." He beamed at me, and the look transformed his entire face, making my heart skip a beat. His thumbs rubbed small circles on my lower back just before he reluctantly released me and walked around to my front. "Learning the runes is just as important as accessing the magick you have within you. While the magick holds the power, it's the runes that shape and command it." He spoke with his hands as he continued, "Think of it this way… you can go into battle with brute strength, but if you're equipped with weapons, your odds of winning increase, right?"

I nodded, following his logic. "So you're saying our magick is like brute strength and the runes are like weapons?" I surmised.

"Exactly. You're a quick learner." Reaching for the book he'd been teaching me from, he closed it and held it out for me to take. "If you start studying, you'll have the basic runes memorized in no time. Each day we'll add a few more to your training."

I gratefully accepted the book, marveling at the buttery soft feel of the brown leather. It was obviously old, yet well cared for. "I'll take good care of this," I promised.

Chayton gave me an approving smile, and I could tell that he appreciated my reverence.

"That book's been in my family for a long time now," he informed me, "but what's mine is yours. We're a pack."

I cocked my head to the side, studying him. "Am I part of the pack now?" I wasn't sure how that all worked, and while it felt like another sudden, life-altering change, there was an unexplainable piece of me that surprisingly yearned to be part of their group.

Chayton watched me intently and I squirmed under his attention as embarrassment stole its way through me.

What the hell were you thinking asking that question? Gods, what is wrong with you? You've only known these guys for a few hours at most. I bit my tongue, wishing I could draw the words back in and lock them away.

Eating crow, I felt my cheeks warm. I waved a hand in the air as if to erase the words floating between us from existence. "Nope. Back up. Rewind and ignore that." I spun on my heels and walked toward the front porch, where I set the book down on the weathered wood, freeing my hands so I could continue training. Shaking my head, I mumbled more to myself than to Chayton, "I obviously misinterpreted what you said."

"Lorn."

A strong hand landed on my shoulder, startling me and making me jump a little before I relaxed into Chayton's touch again. I'd been so lost in my own head that I hadn't heard him follow me. That, or he was extremely quiet on his feet. Spinning me around gently, I found myself face to chest with the man, and I let my eyes roam up and over his strong shoulders and neck, scanning his handsome features until I finally made eye contact.

"That's not a question I can fully answer, since I'm not the alpha of our pack. There is a hierarchy that I have to obey and follow, but what I *can* tell you is that you *belong* here. I'm sure this is all a crazy whirlwind for you, and you must be feeling completely off-kilter, but I trust in fate… and I hope you will too. None of what's happened over the last twenty-four hours was a mistake, even if it was hard to live through." Chayton rubbed his thumbs back and forth over the tops of my shoulders, teasing my exposed skin lightly but reas-suringly.

My focus flicked back and forth between his eyes, and then I did something that may have been the stupidest thing of all. I stepped into him, wrapping my hands around his middle, choosing to trust him and take him at his word. The warmth of his body enveloped me, chasing away the slight coolness I felt from the balmy climate.

Everything about Chayton was calming and comforting. I hadn't spent much time with these guys yet, but it was already obvious to me that they each brought something different to the table. Chayton was the pillar and the glue. He supported the pack and bound them all together. His inner strength was like a magnet that drew me to him and I closed my eyes, leaning against his chest and breathing in his sweetgrass scent, while I took the hug I'd so desperately needed since last night.

When his arms came around my shoulders, he squeezed me closer, cocooning me in the best hug I'd ever had in my life.

"Stars, you're good at this." My words were garbled into his body, but I was too content to move. I'd never been hugged so fully and if I was being honest, being pressed up against a sexy as sin man was just as mind-blowingly amazing as the hug itself. When the moment was over, however, I pulled back and smiled sheepishly up at Chayton. "Thank you."

He flashed a perfect set of white teeth at me and chucked me under my chin. "Anytime you need a hug, my arms will always be open, *nizhóní*."

"What does that word mean?" I asked, enjoying the way Chayton ran his thumb lightly over my chin before his touch disappeared.

Smiling cheekily at me, he waggled his eyebrows. "I think that's an answer you'll have to earn. Come on," he walked backward and rubbed his hands together, "I think it's time for some magick, don't you?"

A grin broke out across my lips. "You mean study time is over?" I propped my hands on my hips, refusing to move until he promised me the fun stuff. We'd been learning runes for the entire afternoon, and I was ready to move onto something more physical, rather than mentally, challenging.

"I think it's time to release some of that magick you've got bottled up."

"Finally!" The little squeal that escaped was pathetic and girly, but I didn't care. I was going to purposefully use the magick I'd been hiding all these years. While I was still a little terrified of what I was capable of, I was also excited to find out. I just hoped my curiosity wouldn't get me or anyone else killed in the process.

I jogged to Chayton's side and followed his instructions.

"Close your eyes and breathe deeply. Your magick should feel like an electric current running throughout your body. Do you feel that?"

The timbre of his voice was soothing as I exhaled and latched onto the buzzing magick that thrummed just under my skin. Its presence was strong and more forceful than what I'd describe as an electric current, but maybe that was because I was so used to stifling it. Magick rushed to my fingertips, flooding up my arms as I followed Chayton's instructions on channeling the flowing vibration.

"You don't need runes to use your magick. You have control over it to an extent. Remember that runes are for molding your magick into extra skills, like becoming invisible, increasing strength, or creating weapons or other objects, but for now, let's just focus on letting your magick out and controlling the flow of it."

Opening my eyes, I bit my lip in concentration as I focused on the far end of the yard where Chayton had set up a target.

"Most of the time, our magick is offensive in nature. First and foremost, it's there to protect us, so in its most basic form, it will seem destructive. However, last night your magick worked both offensively with the fire you created, and defensively when you de-wanded a hundred warlocks and witches. So, you're a bit of a mystery. I'm not sure which side will come more naturally to you." Chayton looked contemplative as he crossed his arms over his chest.

I sighed playfully. "Story of my life. I've always been a mystery... even to myself."

"Well then, I look forward to figuring you out." His gaze scanned down my body and then back up again, and I felt my magick thrum wildly as my heart rate picked up. "You look amazing, by the way."

Warmth suffused my body and I smiled shyly at Chayton. "Thank you." I wasn't sure a man had ever paid me a compliment and meant it the way I knew Chayton did. I'd never really dated before, with the exception of my cheating ex, and after the way things had ended between us, I didn't believe anything he'd told me was true.

"When you're ready, aim for the farthest target. Your magick may not make it that far, but I have a feeling the energy you contain is rather powerful, so I wanted to aim big for your first shot. Try and control the stream of magick, hitting only the target and not the surrounding area."

Tucking my hair behind me ear, I lifted a hand with my palm facing the target, and felt my magick awaken in a rush. "Actually... you... uh... may want to step back a little," I warned, as my magick grew to unbearable levels inside of me. I felt it prickling against my skin from the inside out in an uncomfortable way, which had me shifting on my feet and growing more serious about this training session. Apparently, my magick was more than ready to break free now that I'd finally acknowledged its presence rather than suppressing it. "Chayton, you need to move." The urgency in my voice must have prompted him into action, because he was suddenly by my side and a step behind me.

"Lorn..." Chayton was talking in the background, but I didn't hear what he was saying as my magick grew to painful levels.

Breathing rapidly, I threw my other hand up as well, aiming at the target. "I'm not sure I can control it." Magick saturated my arms and weighed down my feet, filling me up so fully that I felt like I might explode.

I threw my head back on a scream as a burst of purple swiftly shot from my hands in a never-ending stream. Violet glowed behind my eyelids as magick surged out of me and the force of the blast threw me off my feet, knocking me backward. Air surrounded me, and I was weightless before gravity, like the evil bitch it was, took hold and slammed me into the unforgiving ground.

My eyes flew open on a breathless gasp and I stared up at the cloudy, white sky peeking through the green foliage above. Black dots swam in my vision and I groaned. The pain radiating in my head was a sure sign I was still alive, but I couldn't move. My entire body felt weighted and my ears rang with a high-pitched, annoying sound that only stopped when a much more chilling intonation invaded my mind.

"We see you." The rising and falling tonality of the voice was sickly and terrifying, and my nails dug into the cool earth beneath my fingers as I fought to gain control of my body. Somewhere in the background, I could hear Chayton frantically calling my name, but he sounded distant. I desperately looked around for him, but thick, black smoke crept into my vision, engulfing me and obscuring my view of the world around me. I tried not to breathe it in as I fought against the rising, all-consuming panic. The hair on my arms stood on end as the smoke settled over my body, and my head spun from the lack of oxygen.

"You hide from us no longer, Little Keeper," the voice hissed, sounding like a snake in my head. My lungs burned sharply, and when the choice became life or suffocation, I finally relented and inhaled deeply. The dark smoke felt like razors tearing at the inner lining of my throat, and I threw my head back on a scream that came out eerily silent.

I tried to kick my feet and legs, desperate to find purchase and pry myself off the ground, but I simply writhed against the forest floor in my onyx cloud of agony. Blackness covered my vision and I felt hot tears sliding down my cheeks. And then, I fell.

The world felt like it dropped from beneath me and I gasped as I lost the last of my bearings. My sight returned in flashes—stark black trees, the sharp prongs of a gate jutting like spears into a bloodred sky. The evil sonance of a million jeering creatures made my stomach wretch.

"We are coming for you. Your days are limited."

Just as fast as the black smoke had ascended, it was ripped from my lungs as it disappeared, giving me back my sight and leaving me broken on the forest floor.

"Lorn!" The sound of another voice initially made me flinch, but once it registered as Chayton's, I scrambled to stand and landed in his arms as he scooped me up. "Thank fuck!" he cursed hoarsely as he held me close, only setting me down to inspect me for injuries. "The black magick... I couldn't get to you!" His voice was edged with panic as he guided me gently to the steps of the front porch. I sat down slowly, still feeling dizzy from my initial fall. "What the hell just happened?" I felt his hands heat as they roamed lightly over my body, healing my various scrapes and cuts, but my true wounds weren't the physical kind.

Black magick? Is that what it was? I shivered involuntarily as the images and threats played over and over again inside of my head. I felt like a shell of myself, iced over on the inside.

My throat was scratchy and raw as I tried to talk, and eventually, Chayton shushed me. His hands cupped the sides of my throat and heated in the telltale sign of healing magick, but after trying to fix the damage for a few minutes, I was still only able to rasp rather than talk.

"What the hell?" Chayton let out another rare curse, as his eyes flew over me in concern. "That seems to be the most my magick can heal." I could read the frustration in his body language and the resignation on his face. "We're going to need Kota to fix that for you." Chayton's brows pulled together in serious concern as he hopped up off the stairs. Rough wood branded my palms as I gripped the porch step tightly to keep myself from going after him, not wanting to be left alone, but luckily he only took a few steps before facing me again. With one last lingering look, Chayton's form contorted and disappeared in a shimmer of red magick, and in his place stood a beautiful grey wolf.

TWELVE

LORN

"Seriously man? Did you break her already? We just got her!" Axel called, teasing a wolfish Chayton as he jogged through the iridescent blue portal, seeming a little worse for wear. Dark red blood stained his white t-shirt, although it looked like he was trying to cover it up by wearing a black leather jacket.

Relief coursed through me when Kota stepped through next, followed by the largest wolf I'd ever seen in my life, who I assumed was Dason. Each of them sported telltale signs of a fight, each stained red, but they were alive.

A faded, cracked landscape was just visible beyond the portal before it shut and disappeared.

I gaped at all of them.

Just as fast as he'd shifted, Chayton was back in his human form, fully clothed and glancing at me with concern written all over his face. I stared at him in complete shock and confusion, which he seemed to be able to read even though I couldn't physically speak. I'd never seen anyone shift before, and while it was magickal, it was also mind-blowing. "I had to transform in

order to communicate with Dason. I reached out to him telepathically, which is only something we can do in our animal
forms and the only way I'm able to access him across realms.
He usually fights in a primal form. It was our best chance at
getting Kota back here to heal you."

I nodded. Axel's face turned from energetic happiness to
stormy worry, and he let his eyes roam over me, looking for
apparent injuries as he headed toward me.

"I'm okay," I tried to reassure him, but it came out a
breathy, nearly silent mess.

Axel tensed and jogged faster until he was standing in front
of me. "What's wrong with her?" I knew he aimed his question
at Chayton, but I tipped my head back and patted the front of
my neck with a shaky hand, and then shook my head, indicating
I couldn't talk. "If we're playing charades, the only thing I got
from that was something resembling 'The Little Mermaid,' but
somehow I doubt you traded your voice to a sea witch for a
chance at true love, sweetheart."

I loved that he let his Disney show, and I gave him a small
grin. Leave it to Axel to diffuse a difficult situation and make
me feel a little better in one fell swoop. He stopped in front of
me and squatted down, placing his hands on my bare knees
before he glanced over his shoulder, and looked pointedly to
Chayton for answers. Chayton didn't appear like he was in a
hurry, however, as he waited for the others to approach.

While we waited for the rest of the pack to join us, I
welcomed Axel's touch and let it thaw some of the ice I still felt
in my veins from the threat. I hated to admit it, but I didn't want
to be alone. The soothing touch that first Chayton, and now
Axel, were offering helped. I'd take any small measure of peace
without hesitation after the hell I'd just been through.

I was briefly aware of a long, low growl coming from Dason as he and Kota drew near.

"What happened here?" Kota looked to Chayton, anxious to learn what had occurred.

"I couldn't reach her. I healed what I could, but we need more. I have no idea what happened," Chayton began to fill the guys in. I tried to focus, but a pounding started in my head as a bouquet of scents bombarded me.

"What do you mean you couldn't reach her?" Axel let me go and stood, before propping his hands on his hips while he tried to understand what had gone down earlier.

"You were right when you said Lorn had an insane amount of power." Chayton let a hint of pride escape. "The problem is that as soon as she tapped into her magick, it flooded her and she lost control of it. The next thing I know, she's flying backward and hitting the ground hard enough to knock a full-grown football player out."

Kota moved in front of me, bringing another wash of scent, but it was unique to him. He smelled of fresh forest, and cinnamon spice. Underlying each of the males individual scents was something distinctly coppery.

"I already healed most of her injuries, but she can't talk. Her throat... you should feel it Kota. It's raw and torn. Her voice box... I couldn't fix it. My magick wasn't enough. That's why I reached out to Dason. We needed your skillset."

Taking his brother's place, Kota squatted down in front of me and held his hands up to cup my neck, but he paused and looked at me in question before making skin to skin contact.

Fire licked down my spine as I breathed in all their fragrances again, and it was all I could do to shake my head at Kota. He couldn't touch me. Not when their aroma was this intoxicating and heady. I couldn't think clearly. My head was reeling when he pulled back, looking confused and... hurt?

I tried to shake myself out of it, but my fall had either given me a wicked concussion, or the aroma surrounding me was melting my brain. All my thoughts fled as a litany of animalistic sounds echoed through my mind in a melodic song.

Kota stood suddenly and looked down at his bloodied clothes, and then I saw him talking to the others, waving his hand toward me as he spoke. I couldn't hear a word he said past the primal song drowning out his voice and the rest of the world.

My grip on the porch intensified as a sense of rightness welded to my soul. My magick surged through my veins and tingles shot down my arms and legs, settling low in my belly. Whatever was happening to me felt amazing and I bit my lip against the sudden, assaulting pleasure that arose out of nowhere. The weight in my abdomen grew heavy, causing me to squirm against the hard, wooden planks where I sat.

"Holy fuck!" I exclaimed, in a hoarse whisper that I hoped the others didn't hear. My breathing became rapid and I felt myself grow wet. Unable to stop myself, I squeezed my thighs together to provide the blissful pressure my body begged for. I'd never felt so turned on in my life, and I tried to fight back the waves of rising rapture, fully aware that I wasn't alone in my room but outside with the guys instead.

Then my world shattered and realigned while my magick writhed. I tipped my head back and closed my eyes, riding out the sensations on a breathy moan I couldn't contain.

My nipples stood at attention behind my bra, and each heaving breath rubbed them deliciously against the fabric, causing zings of pleasure that had my pussy clenching frustratingly around nothing.

Even with my eyes closed, I was newly and keenly aware of each of the men standing only feet from me. My eyes flew open when I realized that all conversation had stopped. They were staring. At me.

An array of hunger, eagerness, shock, and intensity were reflected back at me. The pure sexiness of the god-like men had my ovaries standing at attention, ready to roll over and beg. I stood and fought against the magnetic pull of Chayton, Kota, Axel, and Dason.

Their undivided focus acted like a bucket of cold water against my overheated libido, and whatever strange occurrence had just happened faded slowly into the background, leaving me with the utterly humiliating repercussions.

"Shit," I rasped and pressed my hands to my warm, flushed cheeks. Taking a minute for myself, I did a mental check as I paced away from the guys along the front porch, which spanned the entire front of the cabin. This morning couldn't have been more bizarre. Between the creepy as hell threat, and then almost orgasming in front of four guys I barely knew, this morning topped my long list of 'oddest days ever,' which was a hard feat to accomplish given how many freakish days I'd had in my life thus far. Turning back to the guys, I mouthed, "What was that?" in the loudest whisper I could manage.

"Lorn," Axel broke the silence. He placed his foot on the bottom step of the stairs like he was going to join me at the top, but he seemed to think better of it and paused. I was grateful for the mere feet that separated us. A husky edge infused his tone and his normally dark eyes were even darker when they settled on my face. "It's okay. We can explain."

I drew in a shaky breath to stave off my freak out, and looked to each of the guys in turn, waiting for answers. My whole life felt like it was spent just waiting for answers.

In the blink of an eye, grey magick sparkled over the remaining wolf, and then I was staring at a human Dason. He took a second to clear the gravel from his throat, and then he dealt the winning blow with the most shocking answer I never could have imagined. "We're your mates, Lorn, and that... response... you just had was the bond sealing on your side."

Mates? I blinked at them as my mind stuttered to a stop. *Holy hell in a handbasket.*

I opened and closed my mouth a few times then gave up, remembering I couldn't reply anyway and unsure of what I would say if I could. In one of my less than stellar moments, I tucked tail and disappeared inside, letting the screen door swing shut with a bang behind me.

THIRTEEN

CHAYTON

"Shit," Axel murmured what we were all thinking as the door closed, obscuring Lorn's beautiful curves as she disappeared inside.

For a beat, we all just stood there in silence, breathing in the lingering fragrance of Lorn's arousal tinting the air.

Clearing his throat, Kota was the first to move as he turned and adjusted himself as discreetly as possible. It was a problem we all seemed to be struggling with.

Dason scrubbed a hand down his face and began pacing in a rage. "You forced my hand, Axel. I told you to wait before charging back through the portal."

"Why wait?" Axel rolled his shoulders back, standing straighter in the wake of his alpha's wrath.

"Axel…" Kota shot a warning look at his brother that said 'tread carefully,' but Dason's ire had already risen.

"So we could have cleaned up our blood, changed, and avoided that." Dason angrily jutted a hand toward the porch where Lorn had been just moments ago.

Mimicking his movement, Axel growled back, "That was inevitable. She's our mate, and now she's bonded to us!"

Dason vibrated with fury as he held out his hands like he wanted to strangle Axel before striding away, and running those same hands over his dark, short, curly hair.

"Stop." I jumped in the middle of their argument. "It was bound to happen sooner rather than later. The question was simply when."

"Why are you fighting this so hard?" Axel's exasperation came through loud and clear.

"Did you ever think that she's been through enough in the last twenty-four hours and that waiting to solidify the mating bond may have been for Lorn's best interest?" Dason pivoted to face us, the stony expression still jagged on his features.

"Honestly, no," Axel retorted, throwing his arms out to the side and then letting them drop. "She's strong, and this will let her know she's not alone. Haven't you felt her homesickness and sadness since last night?" he inquired, glancing around at us. "She belongs here, and I want her to know it."

Generally as the peacekeeper of the group, I could see both viewpoints of the argument, but I had to side with Axel on this one. "She asked if she was a part of our pack during training earlier. You should have seen her face, Dason, when I couldn't outright answer her with the truth. Axel's right. She needs to know that she belongs somewhere. Her entire life has turned upside down. I don't see the harm in getting all the big changes over with at once and letting everything settle. She needs to find her new normal, and that's here with us." I crossed my arms, ready for a fight, but Dason simply pinched the bridge of his nose in his typical stressed mannerism.

"This isn't about Lorn," Axel growled out, throwing down

yet another challenge. "This is about Mara, isn't it? Are you hung up on her?"

"You don't know what you're talking about." Dason's tone was as cold and hard as steel.

"And yet you're not denying it either." Axel's sharp eyes were locked on Dason, not giving him an inch. "Mara's not shadow touched, Dason. She could never have been our true mate."

Feeling the anger boiling between the two of them, I stepped forward and blocked the glaring contest that was about to ensue. It was one thing for Lorn to stare down Dason last night, but it was entirely different for Axel to challenge his alpha in the same manner, and with everything going on, we didn't need the added complication of a fight between these two. "That's enough," I stated and turned a hard stare on Axel. "Take a walk." Axel took a harsh breath and turned, prying his gaze and bristling demeanor from Dason as he turned and made a wide circle around our group, not going far while he cooled down.

"We do need to talk about the whole Mara thing," Kota finally interjected.

"I'm not denying that fact." Dason turned steely eyes on Kota.

"We have much bigger issues than Mara or the mate bond right now." My muscles were tense with the worry that had been eating away at me since my training session with Lorn.

Finally calmer, Axel rejoined us. "How the hell did you break her voice?"

"I can feel the rawness of her throat through the bond." Kota rubbed a hand across the front of his own neck in sympathy and each of us took a moment to check in on Lorn.

A mixture of fear, confusion, anger, and embarrassment washed over her in crescendoing waves. The roughness of her throat was a constant ache I wanted to see healed. I hadn't cared about someone on this level outside of my packmates in a very long time, and even then, this was a different kind of concern. One bred out of an intense connection and an all-consuming awareness that Lorn was mine to protect and cherish. I knew each one of us wanted to go tend to Lorn, but we could also feel her need for a little space and privacy as she worked through the cacophony of chaos she'd been through in the last hour alone.

A frustrated sound escaped when the memory from earlier hit me full force, and I leaned against the pillar of the porch, feeling helpless as I relived the terrifying experience so I could relay it all to my pack. "I'm not entirely sure what happened," I admitted, "but she's stronger than any of us know."

"I told you. What she was capable of last night was incredible." Axel's eyes sparked with interest at our mate's abilities.

"Her magick is boundless," I murmured, and the quietness of my voice showed my reverence of her talent. "When she released it though, she had no control over it. Incredible amounts of magick poured out of her and crashed into our barriers. The whole area shook and trembled from the force of it. It literally erupted out of her and tossed her off her feet." My eyes flicked to Dason's, making sure he noted just how much power it would take to rock our defenses. His eyes were intense as he stared back at me, and I was confident he understood my message loud and clear.

"The vision of Lorn being thrown through the air is going to be permanently tattooed on my brain. The adrenaline alone..." I trailed off, swallowed, and redirected around the roughness suddenly constricting my throat at the danger Lorn had been in not four feet from me. "I tried to reach her. I should have been able to make it. At least to soften the blow of her landing. To help her." Moving, I sat on the top step of the porch and pressed my palms into my eyes like I could wipe away the image of Lorn hitting the ground. The impact had been damaging. My lingering panic formed a lump in my chest that made it hard to breathe. "This black magick rose up out of nowhere before Lorn even made contact with the forest floor. It acted like an impenetrable blockade." Uncovering my face, I glanced up to meet three other sets of intense, worried eyes as my packmates listened to my story. The feelings of regret and helplessness were living things inside of me. "I couldn't reach her."

My ribs were bruised from the proof of my effort. I'd called for her over and over again, trying to claw my way through the onyx ether surrounding her, but instead I'd been subjected to watching my mate writhe on the ground in a silent scream that had my heart freezing to ice inside my chest.

I relayed everything back to the others and ended by lifting the edge of my shirt up, showing the discolored marks on my abdomen and chest from where I'd fought to muscle my way past the dark magick that had covered Lorn.

Their eyes were all fixed on me as they processed what I'd just told them.

Fear flitted over Dason's expression before he schooled his features. "You don't mean actual black magick."

I gave one sharp nod. "It had a dark and desolate feeling to it. It harmed both Lorn and myself. I'm not sure what else it could have been."

"This isn't good," Axel muttered. He was wound tightly, vibrating from the stress of his feelings. I knew how much this news would affect the twins. After the loss of their younger brother it was hard for them to let others in, and now they had Lorn. Nothing compared to the soul deep level in which we'd bonded to her, and the thought of losing her after finally finding her was unimaginable.

Threats against Lorn were now threats against us, and I'd be damned if I let anything happen to her.

"What does this mean?" Kota asked bitterly. "Do you think the witches and warlocks taught her black magick?" His voice betrayed his anger and he nearly spit the question.

"No." I stood from the stairs and tucked my hands into the pockets of my pants. "You're way off base, Kota. Don't let your hatred of the species harden your opinion of your mate. She wasn't practicing black magick. It was attacking her."

"It had to be someone sending a threat," Axel surmised as he looked to each of us.

"Nothing should have been able to penetrate the wards." Dason's voice was more animalistic than human.

"That doesn't change the fact that something did," Kota countered, his frustration apparent.

"I think it's time we got our mate's side of the story before we jump to conclusions and decide how we need to proceed," Dason suggested as his gaze wandered to me, and I nodded my agreement. As his beta, I was his right-hand guy and it was my job to not only back him up, offer council, and support his decisions, but to be a sounding board for complicated situations. Everything that had happened with Lorn definitely qualified.

"Just make sure you tread carefully." I tuned into the link I shared with Lorn and picked up on her jumbled, emotional state. "She just found out we're her mates. She's still processing."

"I was raised by women. I think I can handle my mate," Dason stated curtly. We all tried to keep a straight face, but a minute later Axel broke down and started chuckling.

"Can we take bets on this?" Axel prompted, digging his wallet out of his back pocket and thumbing through a few green bills, effectively shattering the tense mood hanging in the air between us.

Even Kota smirked, rolling his shoulders to ease the tightness he carried. "I'd take some of that action."

"Even your grandmother would be worried about you right now," Axel teased and reached for the money Kota held out, a crisp fifty, before waving the bills while he grinned at Dason.

"Put that away," Dason growled and rolled his eyes, but I caught the tilt at the corner of his mouth. Deep down, he didn't mind being the brunt of the packs' joke to make things easier in a tough time.

"You guys ready?" I asked, standing from my seat on the porch. We'd powwowed long enough, and I was anxious to get inside and ease the stress I felt radiating through the connection from our mate.

Tucking his wallet away, Axel jogged up the steps and reached for the door. "It's now or never, gentlemen. Let's go get our girl."

FOURTEEN

LORN

The kitchen was open and airy, with plenty of space for multiple people to move around without being in each other's way. Late afternoon light streamed through the window above the sink, brightening my workspace. The flooring was inlaid grey stone and the cabinets were oak in color, matching the log wall interior. Digging through the fridge, I grabbed a variety of ingredients and lined them up across the slate grey countertops. I needed a menial task to keep my hands busy and my brain numb. Anything to bury my mortification and the news I'd just received.

After such a tumultuous day I was starving, and I was pretty sure the guys would be as well. Nothing probably worked up an appetite more than battling a demon.

Was this really my life? I felt like I was on the edge of hysteria from the whiplash of life altering events that were taking place at such a rapid pace.

Taking a deep breath, I tried to calm the tornado twisting around in my gut.

Mates. I had mates. Three of them.

And someone was trying to kill me.

Your days are numbered, I shivered involuntarily.

Not to mention the cherry on top of the proverbial ice cream sunday of death—I had made enemies with the entire eastern seaboard of witches and warlocks, and they were most likely on the warpath also.

Death. Death from all sides.

And mates.

My mind spun and I gripped the countertop, hanging my head as I collected myself.

One thing at a time, Lorn. You're safe for right now. Didn't you overhear the guys mention something about this place being protected? I told myself, feeling my pulse slow to a reasonable beat that wouldn't kill me from overexertion. *Besides, they're right outside.* I could hear their deep, masculine tones filtering through the thick walls of the cabin.

As much as I wanted to escape to my room and hide from the incredible amount of embarrassment I was going to have to live through when the guys came back inside, I couldn't bring myself to leave them that far behind. Not only did everything inside of me want to be close to them, but I was still thoroughly freaked out from the episode where black, smoky magick tried to strangle me.

My swallow grated my throat, adding insult to injury.

I inhaled deeply as I went back to sorting my assembly line of food. I'd been raised on the idea that large issues couldn't be solved on an empty stomach, and everything that had just gone down had been monumental.

I was digging through the cupboards for plates by the time the door squawked again and the guys piled inside—all in human form. I hadn't even looked up. I didn't need to. I'd known they were coming before the door had made a single, solitary noise. The strangeness of my new connection and cognizance with the guys was unsettling. My nerves tap danced with anxiety as I focused on getting dinner together, trying to ignore the warmth that took up permanent residence in my cheeks.

Four sets of eyes tracked me around the kitchen while I ignored reality in favor of sandwiches.

"Lorn." Dason was the first to speak, which surprised me. "We need to talk about what happened earlier."

I kept my eyes glued to the dinner I was creating. I shouldn't have been surprised that they weren't going to let me live in blissful avoidance. A pardon from this conversation had been too much to hope for.

"Do you think she's in denial?" Axel crossed his arms over his chest as he watched me, angling his comment to his brother.

I pursed my lips, but he was partially right. I wasn't sure I was ready to face them yet. Not after nearly orgasming in front of them. The talk that was coming had awkward written all over it.

Kota rubbed at his jaw and pursed his lips. "Maybe we shouldn't fix her voice until after we explain all of this mating business to her."

A dry laugh escaped Dason, and I finally glanced up at the sound, shocked that it had come from him. I'd only seen him with his serious face on so far. He didn't seem like the kind of guy to express amusement often. "I've found that women rarely enjoy being silenced unless it's for sexual pleasure. If you want to ruin any chance you have with her, you go ahead and refuse to heal her voice until after you've pleaded your case."

I shot each man an unamused look, which I hoped conveyed that I could hear them talking about me. The downstairs was open concept for star's sake, and they were only a few paces away. Truly though, my mind was skipping like a record player over the 'sexual pleasure' part of Dason's comment and my mind ran away with the possibilities. I wasn't sure if the room was growing warmer or if it was just me, but I wanted nothing more than to scoop up a plate from the counter and start fanning myself with it.

Axel seemed to notice my reaction and he chuckled a low sound that made the butterflies in my stomach take flight. "If there's one thing I've learned about our mate," he enunciated the word, "it's that Lorn can handle her curveballs. This is all new, but she's going to be fine."

One corner of my lips tipped up at his faith and confidence in me. It only endeared him to me more. Sighing, I mouthed, "Damn right." It was the metaphorical kick in the lady balls I needed to calm down and face this situation head-on. I might as well get it over with. It wasn't like I truly had anywhere to escape to for long, seeing that I was living under the same roof with the very guys I was evading.

Kota stepped into the kitchen and slowly approached me, then questioned, "Will you let me fix that for you?" He held up his hands, already glowing blue with his healing powers.

Sighing, I nodded and stepped around the kitchen island, meeting him halfway. His hands were cool when they met my skin. The buzz of his healing energy came alive and sunk into my neck. My throat stung as he seared everything back together. A whimper slid past my lips, but just as quickly as the pain started, it receded. He placed his hands on my head next and when he was done, Kota pulled away.

"Are you all right, Lorn?" Chayton inquired, stepping up next to his friend.

I cleared my voice and attempted to speak. It took me two tries and a sip of water, but I finally got the words I'd been trying to say out. "Mayonnaise or mustard?" I asked with a smirk, receiving a guffaw from Axel in the background. Rounding the island, I held up a jar of each for their inspection.

"You don't have to make us dinner." Chayton looked put out, but I simply raised an eyebrow, waiting for the proper response.

Shaking his head in exasperation, he caved and answered, "Mayo for Dason and Kota, mustard for Axel, both for me, please." Men can never ignore their stomachs or the promise of food for long.

"See, that wasn't so hard, was it?" I smiled in victory and went back to my task of piling ingredients together on top of the rectangles of bread. It was the least I could do to return their hospitality. Hell, I was even using their groceries. I needed to find a way to repay them, but earning my keep was a start.

"Lorn. We do need to talk about what happened." Coming around the island I was using as a shield, Chayton grabbed my elbow to slow my movements.

"I know. We will. Just... can we wait until we have food first? Things are always easier to solve on a full stomach." I was stalling, and we all knew it, but they respected my need for time and waited as I went about my work. I set two completed sandwiches on their respective plates and continued on to make the rest.

A few minutes later and I was out of ways to delay the inevitable. The guys all helped carry the food to the table and I joined them, setting a pitcher of lemonade and a few bags of chips in the center of the beautifully carved wooden table. Dason stood behind his seat at the head of the table, and the guys shuffled around the remaining chairs awkwardly. I glanced from man to man as I tried to figure out their seating arrangements.

"Here you go," Chayton offered, pulling out the seat to the right of Dason, and I glanced at him quickly, trying to gauge if he was okay with me sitting so close to him. While Axel and Chayton were comfortable to be around, Dason and Kota had been pricklier.

Noticing my hesitation, Dason narrowed his eyes in challenge, and I stood a little straighter. Glaring in return, I crossed behind him and took the proffered seat. It didn't go beyond my notice that the guys didn't sit until I had.

Grinning, Axel whipped out a brown, worn leather wallet and placed it on the table next to his plate. Drumming his fingers on the top of it, he waggled his eyes at Dason and left it on the table while he rubbed his hands together in anticipation of devouring the massive sandwich I had made for him.

Just like earlier, none of the men ate until I took my first bite.

"This is really good," Axel commented, breaking the growing silence, but I could tangibly feel their increasing tension through my new connections. Everyone except for Chayton. I peered over at him, wondering why I couldn't feel him too.

"Okay." I set my sandwich back on the plate and ran my hands nervously over my thighs. My cheeks betrayed me with their traitorous rosy hue. "This is awkward. And embarrassing."

My focus was locked on the intricate wood grain of the table as I waited with bated breath for someone to speak so I wouldn't have to.

Always my savior apparently, Axel laid it all out for me. "There's nothing to be embarrassed about. We all know how intense the mate bond can be when it first forms."

My attention snapped up at that. Had they gone through something similar as well? How had I missed it? "Excuse me?"

I wheezed and grabbed my glass, sipping the sweetly sour lemonade in hopes that it would clear my throat. "Can you elaborate?"

"You're our mate," Dason replied matter-of-factly, with very little emotion behind his words.

"Yeah, I got that. And you could sound a little happier about that there, alpha," I snarked back, and Chayton smiled while Kota gaped. "I'm a catch." I had no idea what possessed me to say that—I wasn't usually one to toot my own horn and I wasn't even sure I *wanted* to be mated to him—but something deep inside me pushed me to one-up him.

"Damn, I think I love you already," Axel stated, sounding tickled pink.

I expected the entire world to feel off-kilter given how much I'd been through, but the only thing that threw me off was how right everything felt. It was as if my subconscious was already twelve steps ahead and waiting on the rest of me to catch up.

"Mated." I tossed the word out there verbally for the first time and looked around at the guys. No one looked away from me. This was either an elaborately cruel joke, or they were serious. When no one cracked up and started laughing at my expense, I knew I officially had my answer. Well, that and the invisible simmering link of connection I could feel flowing freely between us. That was going to take some getting used to. "Why is Chayton left out?"

It might have been a ridiculous first question. I probably should have asked how, or why, or said something like 'holy hell, all three of you?' but instead I simply addressed the gaping hole I felt where his bond should have been.

"I've already mated you," Chayton, who sat across from me, answered. "So have Axel, Dason, and Kota." He kept his steady gaze locked on me and I knew he was reading my reaction. I stared at him in confusion. "We need to scent our mate's blood before a bond is formed. Axel and Dason scented yours last night when you were injured from the motorcycle and I scented you when they brought you home. Kota caught the aroma of your blood from your clothing last night when he barged into the bathroom. The bond on our side was sealed, but it goes both ways. Today, when these three came back from fighting off the shade, they were each bleeding. That's why you reacted so strongly. Your spirit was bonding with theirs. You haven't been around my blood yet, so our connection, on your side, isn't complete yet."

I adored Chayton for stating my 'reaction' so mildly. I'd nearly come in front of them. Hell, I tried not to wriggle in my seat just remembering the phantom feelings that had crashed over me on the porch.

Four fucking mates. I didn't even know how to process that.

"Great. Now that we have that all cleared up, I need to know what happened to you during training, Lorn," Dason pressed, resting his forearms on the table and folding his hands together while blowing off the biggest news I'd received... in the last twelve hours.

Something about that thought resonated as funny, and I found myself chuckling before I broke into a full-out round of laughter. My eyes watered and my stomach clenched with the ab workout.

It hadn't even been a full day since my life had taken a drastic left turn, and now it was speeding down unfamiliar curvy roads like a teenage girl who just got her license, hair down and belting out some good old-fashioned Backstreet Boys at the top of her lungs as she swerved around the twists and turns, going way faster than the speed limit, completely unaware of what was around the next bend. There were no familiar landmarks or maps to navigate by. My life was insane, reckless, carefree, and unpredictable.

"Shit, guys." The concern in Axel's voice sent me into another round of giggles. "I was joking earlier, but I think we may have actually broken her."

FIFTEEN

LORN

The even ticking of the clock and the rhythmic sound of Axel's breathing were the only sounds occupying the house as I crept downstairs. Light spilled from the fridge as I reached for the milk and quickly poured myself a glass. Putting it away, I slid onto one of the barstools behind the kitchen island. It was after midnight and Dason still wasn't home.

Telling the guys about the threat I'd heard when my magick had blasted me off my feet hadn't exactly gone well. I didn't think they'd be *happy* about the news, but I'd never expected the reaction I'd received—pure anger. Luckily, not aimed at me.

As it turned out, males got very aggressive when their mate was threatened—a concept that still felt surreal in the pandemonium that was my life. After a lengthy, tension-filled discussion, both Kota and Dason had left. It had been over six hours and I was still waiting for the alpha to walk back through the front door.

I replayed the conversation as I listened to the seconds tick by, looking for details I might have missed.

* * *

"**F**uck!" Axel drove a hand into his dark brown hair, tugging on the strands as he paced beside the kitchen table.

"I didn't know about the threatening voice or the vision before. Do you think it could actually be the witches and warlocks?" Chayton was on his feet as well, looking for answers from his alpha. Obviously, they'd been talking about the possibility when they'd been outside earlier. I tried to keep up as I stayed in the background and listened.

"Like you said, they shouldn't be able to bypass the wards." The surety in Axel's voice was comforting, and I hoped he was right. If the witches and warlocks had somehow tracked me down, I wasn't sure any defenses the guys had in place would be enough. They outnumbered us by a ridiculous margin.

"Underestimating them is what took so much from us in the past, brother," Kota chimed in coolly from his place at the table. Leaning back in his chair with his hands folded on top of his head, he was the picture of relaxation with his elbows splayed wide, but his tone contradicted his posture. His words were like an iceberg that sunk Axel's good mood, making the light dim in his chocolate eyes.

It didn't take a genius to know that Kota had delivered the blow on purpose, seeking damage, but what everyone else may not have been privy to was the amount of angry sorrow that flooded through the new connection I had with Kota. The effect left me breathless and I rubbed at my chest, trying to push back the sadness swamping me.

The air became charged with tension as the two brothers stared at each other in silence. I'd never felt more like an outsider than I did in that moment. Clearly, I was missing something big, but now wasn't the time to ask. I filed the ques-

tion away at the top of my list to address at a more appropriate time.

Dason and Chayton eyed each other in a silent conversation before Chayton rubbed at the patch of stubble coating his chin. "We'll recheck the barriers," he finally spoke, and I knew that he and the alpha had come to that decision. "We'll all feel better knowing the wards weren't damaged in any way during the training session."

A loud rumbling growl was the only input Dason added as he all but prowled toward the front door, and then back again. His muscular features bulked up beyond normal. It was clear he didn't like the idea of a threat landing so close to his home and pack. Whether he cared that it was me who had been threatened, I didn't know, and I tried not to analyze it.

"Nothing should be able to take down those wards." Dason's gravelly tone held a note of disbelief.

"You didn't see the strength of her magick." Chayton shook his head like he hadn't believed it either until he'd seen it with his own eyes.

"And now I feel like a freak on display at the circus or something," I chimed in, half joking and half serious. The way they were in awe of a magick I had no control over and didn't understand only made me feel inadequate.

Trying to ease the tension with my comment didn't go over well, and I decided it must be a talent that only a few people, like Axel, actually possessed.

I changed tactics. "If the barriers are fine, what does that mean?" Fear brushed over me as all my worries resurfaced. The timing of the attack, right after I'd released my powers, seemed suspicious to me. I rubbed my thumb across one of my palms, wondering all over again what I could be capable of, and why everyone seemed to want me dead.

Dason sighed and his rigid posture seemed to soften. His gaze landed on me, where I'd planted myself against the wall. The conflicting emotions careening through the depths of his eyes were mesmerizing to watch. "I don't have the answers for you, but we're going to make sure you're safe." I latched on to the promise he was making as he held my gaze longer than was considered casual. My heart caught in my chest, wondering if maybe he cared more than I'd given him credit for.

The screeching of a chair against the hardwood broke the moment we were having. Kota stalked past me and ripped open the fridge, pulling a dark bottle of beer from within. He popped the top with his bare hand before he took a healthy swig and braced his free palm on the counter, staring out the window into the front yard.

"Kota." The way Axel snapped his brother's name was so sharp, I could feel the slashes from across the room.

Kota turned his head, catching Axel in his peripheral vision as he upturned the bottle and took another swallow of the bitter liquid. I wrung my fingers together in nervousness as I glanced back and forth between the brothers. So many unspoken words and emotions filled the kitchen that it made it hard to breathe. Whatever was happening between the two of them, I knew this wasn't their first show down. That much was clear. My heart ached at the pain filtering to me through the link I was still unused to.

The silence grew jagged until Dason crossed his arms and spread his feet in a dominant stance. "Kota," he barked. His alpha power expanded into a thick swell that quickly became suffocating. I fidgeted with my fingers nervously but forced myself not to move into the next room to lessen the effect.

The animalistic noise that ripped from Kota's throat startled me, and I jumped slightly. Kota's entire expression had darkened like a storm cloud obscuring the sun.

"Get a head start on checking the barriers," Dason ordered. "Take the east side. I'll join you soon and start on the west."

I could tell Kota's hackles were up, even though he was in human form. The shiver of power that raced down his spine had him cracking his neck as he fought for control. His eyes flashed yellow when he turned and looked at me, and then the bottle thudded onto the counter with a loud clink before he stormed outside.

A strange tingling awareness invaded my thoughts. He shifted. I had no idea how I knew that but I did. With certainty. A low, snarling roar reverberated into the night, sending the hair on my body into an upward salute as it acknowledged the impending danger of whatever large, cat-like animal I knew Kota had just changed into.

Distance spanned its way between us as he took off into the woods to do his alpha's bidding, taking his thunderous aura with him.

"What was that about?" I whispered to Axel, but he only hung his head and shook it, refusing to answer as he hooked his thumbs into his front jean pockets.

"Not now," he murmured in response when I opened my mouth to ask again. It was a gentle whisper meant to appease, but all it did was make me feel more uncomfortable. He was more somber than I'd seen him yet, and it was just another reminder that while I was physically attracted to these guys—and apparently now mated to them—I didn't truly know them. Clearly, I was missing something, but no one seemed inclined to fill me in. I pursed my lips but fought my instinct to take a step back and distance myself from the rest of their family meeting. I

felt like an outsider, but this was my life they were talking about
—even if it affected all of us—and I'd be damned if I was going
to be left out of the conversation.

"What if it's not the witches and the warlocks?" I ques-
tioned, finally giving voice to my most pressing concern. I could
tell by the skeptical stares thrown my way that they didn't have
many doubts about who was behind the latest threat like I did.

"What makes you ask, Lorn? Because from where I'm
standing, they're our most logical enemy," Dason asked.

"I don't have a good answer for you." I threw my hands out
to the side in a shrug, and then let them fall to my sides against
my outer thighs with a clap. "I just know that the voice sounded
dark. Slithery, almost. It was really unsettling." I wrapped my
arms around myself, gripping my biceps in a self-hug meant to
ward off the unpleasant feelings the memory provoked. "I know
that Kingston, the head of the High Coven, is dangerous, and I
have no doubt that the threat he presents is real, but he's also
old school, traditional, and very straightforward. The black
smoke doesn't seem like his style. It was evil and it made a
statement, if nothing else. If Kingston had been able to reach me
in any capacity, I have no doubt that he'd have killed me
without delay." I paused and worried my lip between my teeth,
wondering if I should bring up my anxiety that whatever
happened earlier was somehow my fault.

"I'll keep that in mind," Dason muttered, taking away my
chance. He stared at me for a moment longer, searching for
something before promptly turning away. "Keep me informed,"
Dason rigidly told Chayton, and then headed for the front of the
house. His hand was braced on the wooden frame of the
screened door when Axel called after his friend.

"Can you keep an eye on him?" It was the first time Axel
had spoken since the incident with his brother earlier.

"I've got him," Dason reassured Axel. It was only three little words, but they held a world of tenderhearted confidence that surprised me. It made me realize how much depth there was to Dason who seemed like mostly growls and commands on the surface.

"What's your game plan and do you need backup?" Chayton, who'd been quietly observing, spoke up.

"I'm going to run the barriers, and then I'm going to schedule a time to meet with Ephrem. They've been kind enough to allow us refuge on their land. The least I can do is let them know about the renewed threat the witches and warlocks pose to us now that we've found Lorn. Hold things down here," Dason ordered over his shoulder.

"Will do," Chayton gave his alpha his word.

Guilt dropped on me like a pile of bricks. I lowered my gaze to the floor, feeling like a burden.

I focused on breathing and waited for the moment I could escape upstairs and replay the last few hours over in my head. I needed to try and find anything I may have missed that could help us figure out what was going on, because the last thing I'd do was become a hindrance and a danger to more people who mattered in my life.

"Lorn." The softness in the way Dason said my name had my gaze flying to his. "You're not a burden." His deepened tone and the confident, serious way he spoke resonated down to my very soul.

I barely drew breath as he pushed his way through the door and disappeared down the porch steps.

Seconds later, I felt the wash of magick zip through my connection with the alpha as he shifted. Each mile of ground he covered stretched the link between us until it was merely a low hum in the background.

* * *

Dason's sentiment remained with me for the rest of the night. Axel had quickly disappeared to the basement, which I hadn't known existed, to work off the angst he was feeling over his brother in their home gym. While Chayton had tried to be sweet and offered to do a movie night, the distraction of the screen didn't dull my spinning thoughts and I pleaded exhaustion after one film. It was clear the tension from dinner had never dissipated and each of us had to deal with it in our own way. I'd spent the evening holed up in Axel's room while I tried to figure out a way to process my own emotions past those of the guys' zipping through the link. Finding a pen and paper, I drew the random images I'd seen during the attack. When they didn't become obviously useful, I reverted to practicing the runes Chayton had taught me, trying to perfect each curve and line.

Every so often I let my gaze wander to the glowing clock that sat on Axel's nightstand. As the minutes and hours ticked by and passed midnight, I allowed myself to worry over Kota and Dason, neither of whom had returned home.

Tossing my rune doodles to the side, I laid down and tried to sleep, but it was no use.

The bond I felt with Kota told me when he drew near the house. The current grew stronger as he became closer. As much as I wanted to check on him when he finally slipped back inside, I left him to his solitude, gripping my pillow in an effort to keep myself planted in bed instead of going to him like I felt drawn to do.

It may have been my womanly intuition, but I had a sinking feeling that whatever was bothering Kota wouldn't be helped by my interference or intervention. Either way, keeping my distance from him had been an exercise in self-control.

After another half hour of lying awake with way too much occupying my mind, I'd crept downstairs in hopes that a glass of milk would soothe me enough so I could finally pass out. Doubtful, but worth trying.

Which brought me to the solitude of the kitchen I sat in now. I took a sip of my cool beverage, feeling the chill trickle into my stomach as I glanced at the clock on the wall again. Three whole excruciatingly slow minutes had passed while I'd reminisced, the time reading just past midnight.

"What are you doing awake?" Kota slid into the kitchen soundlessly, sending me into a momentary freak out.

Jumping out of my seat, I rebounded like a cat who'd just fallen from a tree but landed on her feet. I smoothly held up my glass of milk toward Kota in answer and took another drink. "Milk usually helps me sleep."

"It's better if you warm it up, you know. For sleeping purposes," he said, angling his head toward the microwave as he leaned against the cabinets. His attempt to talk to me felt like a peace offering and I grabbed hold of it like a kid traversing the monkey bars for the first time.

I couldn't help the grin that spread across my face. "That's what I usually do too." Happy memories floated through my mind of the many nights my father and I had met in the kitchen in the middle of the night. That nighttime routine had been a ritual anytime I'd had a nightmare until I'd gone off to the academy, where I'd continued the tradition by myself. "I didn't want to wake up your brother by using the microwave." I peered over my shoulder at the couch where Axel slumbered.

Kota smirked. "My brother could sleep through a hurricane.

Trust me, you're fine. The hum of the microwave isn't going to bother him."

Slipping from the stool, I padded across the kitchen in my bare feet, adjusting the slouchy t-shirt and shorts Chayton had fashioned earlier in the evening and thoughtfully left in Axel's room for me.

I grabbed a second mug, poured another cup of milk, and stuck both into the microwave. As they warmed I stood there and watched, catching the machine before it beeped.

I stepped across from Kota and held out the second cup. "My dad taught me the milk trick when I was a young teenager. It's his tried and true recipe to bring on sleep. I thought you might need a cup after the day you've had."

Kota's gaze settled on me from where he relaxed against the cabinets, with his elbows bent and his hands gripping the countertop. Strands of his hair fell freely from the bun he had piled on top of his head, and they framed his chiseled jawline and dark, intense eyes as he listened. The moment I brought up my dad though, the Adam's apple in his neck bobbed as he swallowed and looked away.

The moment between us broke, and I set the unclaimed mug on the counter next to me. Everything with Kota felt like one step forward and a million steps backward, but as I thought back over the few interactions we'd had together so far, I started connecting the dots.

"You don't like witches or warlocks, do you?" It was probably a stupid question. Of course he didn't. They had hunted his kind—our kind—for generations, but this was different. This went beyond the history of the two species.

I could feel the well of his hatred through our supernatural tie, and it was saturated in heartbreak.

"They took someone from you?" It was the only logical

conclusion I could make given the depth of the sorrow I'd felt earlier. I rubbed absently at my chest and blinked back the tears building behind my eyes as a fresh tsunami of feeling crashed through our bond. His pain had become my pain, and it was overwhelming.

I would've given anything to know where the far-off look in his eyes had taken him in that moment, but he didn't answer me or divulge any information. He simply gazed off into the distance, staring past the fridge into memories I couldn't see. His jaw ticked and the muscles below his skin strained from the way he gritted his teeth. Then he cast his censure back on me.

The weight of it was suffocating.

"Fuck," I mumbled. "I'm so sorry."

"You had nothing to do with it," he responded, but his eyes told a different story.

"Yet you resent me for being raised by them..." I took a wild guess and cocked my head to the side to study his reaction.

His focus slid off my face, looking past me again, a tell that I'd hit the metaphorical nail on the head.

"I'll get past it," he finally said through a tight throat.

"I know you probably don't want to hear this, but they're not all bad." I went out on a limb to support the few people I actually cared about. "I know I'm new to this world, but it doesn't seem fair to condemn an entire race based on the actions of a few," I stated, as softly as I could. As far as I knew, most witches and warlocks weren't murderous killers. "Every species has evil people in it, but I'd like to think that the good ones far outnumber the bad."

His eyes blazed with anger and I was hit with the full force of his bitterness. "You don't understand because you weren't raised shadow touched. You can't possibly fathom what we've been through, how we've had to live in hiding, or how much each one of us has lost. You waltz in here and think you comprehend, but you're clueless."

I bit down any rash repartee I would have made, focusing on the thrumming agony pulsing through our connection. "Then share with me," I challenged him. "Tell me. I can't learn if you keep everything bottled up. I feel your pain and your resentment as if your wounds are fresh."

"Stay out of my head, Lorn." Kota's whisper slashed through the kitchen as he pinned me with a fathomless look.

I recognized his need for privacy, but I didn't know how to control our link. "I'm your mate..." The word came out as a rasp as I used it in context for the first time. "It's the bond." My voice was as low as his, holding a hint of regret for not being able to give him the solitude he craved.

"Don't claim the title unless you plan on filling the role," he countered.

I bristled. "Have I given you the impression that I'm planning on walking away?"

"I don't know. I don't know you."

The sting of his retort ricocheted through my chest, but I knew my reaction was unjustified. I hadn't even begun to process the idea of having a mate, let alone four. Yet his challenging, cavalier attitude had me fighting the urge to rub at my breastbone again to ward off the hurt I couldn't help but feel. The supernatural mating between us made everything more real, despite our lack of time together... I cared about Kota. I cared about all of them. The gravity of the situation hit me in that moment and I inexplicably knew one thing for sure—I couldn't walk away from them, even if I wanted to. And I didn't.

I gripped the handle of the mug containing my cooling, forgotten milk and answered with the only truth I could give him. "I know this might not make a lot of sense to you, but I've been searching my whole life for somewhere to belong—for answers to who I am and where I come from. For the first time, I feel like I'm close. This whole mate thing came out of nowhere, but it *feels* right, Kota... on a mental, physical, and spiritual level. I'm not walking away." Taking a deep breath, I forged forward. "Are you?"

He took a beat to swallow, and then leaned into my space with a contained ferocity that emanated from every line of his body, but I refused to move an inch, letting him crowd into my personal bubble. "I never walk away from a challenge." Heat raced through me from his closeness as his words sunk in. Reaching out, he grasped the mug I'd discarded on the counter before sauntering out of the kitchen with the litheness of a predatory cat.

The edge of the counter dug into my back as I relaxed back into it, my muscles nearly spasming from the intense way I'd been holding them during our confrontation. Slowly, I learned to breathe again. Worrying the inside of my lip, I quickly lost the silent argument I had with myself and decided—like an idiot —to open my mouth one more time.

"Kota," I called after him, speaking into the darkness of the kitchen without turning toward his retreating form. I could feel his presence nearby and knew he'd stopped in his tracks. "Listen, I get not wanting to talk about it. I especially understand your not wanting to talk to *me* about it. And trust me when I say that I know we just met and you haven't known me for very long, but the connection between us, it's visceral. I can feel the chasm of your pain, and it's not healthy to keep it all to yourself. I'm not saying you have to share it with me, but you should share it with somebody. Don't let your grief bury you."

The sharp inhales of his breath were the only sign that he was still there and had heard what I'd said, and I took it as a good sign that there was no anger or frustration sliding through the line between us.

The silence stretched on, nearly becoming awkward before a ringing static permeated my head, making me gasp just before Dason invaded my mind and our private moment.

Everyone up, he commanded loudly, giving me an instant headache.

Axel snorted awake on the couch, groaning from the intrusion to his REM cycle. "Shit, I hate when that happens and I'm asleep," he complained, capturing my attention as he jumped up from the couch wearing nothing but a pair of sexy black boxers that clung to his muscular thighs. Catching sight of Kota and me, he paused with his shirt halfway up his arms. "Everything okay over there?" he asked, clearly reading the tension still floating through the room.

"All good." I faked a smile and set my mug on the counter while Axel finished dressing. "What's with the wakeup call?" Curiosity rang through my question as Chayton jogged down the stairs and strode into the kitchen, fully dressed in all black and ready to take on the night. His hands were already glowing red as he headed toward me.

"Oh, please. Let me!" Axel said excitedly, and I raised my eyebrows at him.

Chayton glanced over at Axel. "You're going to dress her?"

"Abso-fucking-lutely." He grinned, and all my wariness rose to the surface as he rubbed his hands together and moved to my side.

"You're not about to put me in some slutty cat woman outfit, are you?" I held up my hands and warded off Axel and his overeager expression until I had a solemn promise that there would be no tomfoolery.

"I wouldn't trust him, if I were you," Kota piped up. His

tone was roughened from our earlier emotional conversation, but my heart swelled at the olive branch those few, simple words offered. At least he was talking to me. Leave it to Axel to smooth things over, even unknowingly. The man had a gift.

Nothing between Kota and I was fixed, but we were both adulting, putting our drama on hold to deal with more pressing issues.

"I give you my word. It will be appropriate." Axel bowed at the waist like a true gentleman, regaining my attention, and I relented.

His magick tingled over my body at the same time the front door slammed open, admitting Dason.

"Good, you're all ready to go. Axel, bikes—Lorn rides with you."

Outfit finished and promptly forgotten, I watched Axel head outside with haste in his steps. I moved toward Dason, resisting the urge to reach for him and make sure he was all right. The instinct to be touchy feely with my mates was already growing, and I needed to clamp down on the compulsion before I made a fool of myself.

"What's happening?" I distracted myself with my need for information.

Dason's hard gaze pierced through me, and I thought I saw a flash of regret in his eyes, but if it had been there at all, it was gone just as quickly. I held my breath as I waited for the next curveball to be thrown from the alpha's lips, and he didn't disappoint.

"We've been summoned."

SIXTEEN

LORN

The rumble of the motorcycle vibrated through my leather-clad thighs as I clung to Axel with my eyes tightly shut. The pants Axel had fashioned for me were tighter than what I usually wore but seemed to fit the whole 'biker girl' look I had going on. Magick washed over my skin in a refreshing wave as we crossed through the portal, landing safely on the other side —thankfully with me still firmly planted in my seat this time. Breathing a sigh of relief, I let go of my fear and opened my eyelids as the wind from our forward motion fluttered over my skin.

Shadowed forms of Dason, Kota, and Chayton—each on their own motorcycles—greeted me as we speed up and followed them out of the dark alleyway they'd chosen as our entry point. Throwing out a hand as he rounded the corner, Dason recalled his magick and shut the portal, leaving no trace of anything otherworldly behind.

The guys expertly steered into traffic, commanding space on the busy roads of whatever city they'd brought me to. Lights reflected off of every surface as we headed downtown, traversing the boulevards and buildings that spread out in every direction. The vast cityscapes morphed into increasingly taller structures the farther we traveled. By the time I spotted a few palm trees in the median between lanes, my curiosity had gotten the better of me.

I shifted closer, pressing fully against Axel's back, and leaned into him hoping he'd be able to make out the question I yelled into the wind. "Where are we?"

"Los Angeles," Axel replied over his shoulder, and while I couldn't see much of his face because of the helmet he was wearing, I picked up on his excitement through the link spanning between us.

"You're kidding me!" I grinned behind my own helmet. "I've always wanted to come here!" The city had been on my bucket list of places to visit since I'd hit puberty and fallen in love with boy bands, movies, and music.

"It's an amazing place! You'll love it here!"

"I've always wanted to see the Pacific," I shouted over the wind that whipped at our conversation.

"You're on the West Coast now, baby," he flirted. "I'll make sure you get to see it." I felt his promise and tightened my grip on his body into a hug of gratitude. The white fabric of his t-shirt rippled against my hands while I held onto him and took in the sensory overload of L.A.

Wrapped up in the feel of the warm breeze, the outdoorsy scent of the man between my spread thighs, and the pleasant reverberations of the growling engine that fueled our ride, I almost missed the creeping sense of dread that inched over my skin.

Do you feel that? Dason's tenor pierced into my brain. I held on to Axel tighter and gritted my teeth against the physical pain his intrusion caused.

It gets easier. Axel tossed the errant thought my way and then redirected to answer his alpha. *It feels—*

Sinister, I cut him off, testing the telepathy thing for the first time.

Adjusting his grip on the handle of the bike, Axel glanced down through the visor of his helmet. His left hand was adorned with a ring I hadn't noticed before, and I stared in awe at the changing color of the center stone. Blood-red crawled along the surface until the entire gem looked like a glowing ruby where it had been a mellow blue before.

What's happening? The creepiness in the air only grew as we swerved lanes and sped through the downtown district, following Dason's lead.

Demon. Chayton's tone—even mentally—was darker than I'd ever heard it.

A powerful one. Axel's muscles grew tense under my grip, and I sat up straighter, peering around for the danger pressing in on us.

We're almost there. Do you think we can make it? Kota shifted in his seat, looking more alert and aware than he had a few moments earlier. The mood of the entire group had changed.

No, and Rook wouldn't want us to leave this beast free in his city, either. You know once he catches wind of it, he'd just call us out to deal with it. A distinct growl coated Dason's words, making them animalistic and raw.

I must have dug my nails into Axel's chest and abdominals in reaction, because Axel soothed, *Dason has to shift in order to communicate with us telepathically. Over the years he's learned how to partial shift so we can communicate silently when necessary, but his primal spirit is very close to the surface.*

Got it. I leaned to the side with Axel as he turned down

another street, and the hair on my arms rose under the leather jacket I wore. Wherever we were going, it was closer to the danger that shimmied down my spine.

You realize I hate this right? She's out here with us with one training session under her belt. Chayton's motorcycle flanked Dason's on the right, but he hung back just slightly, clearly providing backup. Kota took up the left side while Axel pulled up behind Dason, completing their diamond formation. *It's too soon.*

Can't change it now. The roar ripped through my mind. I wondered if anyone knew how hard these partial shifts were on their alpha. The urge to go full-on predator was riding him hard, his need to shift sliding unguarded through the bond.

Don't worry about me. Just focus on what you need to do. I tried to reassure the guys, even though they were content talking around me as if I wasn't there. All my dreams of demons over the years came rushing back, but I blocked them and swallowed down the bile that tried to escape my throat. They didn't need to be worried about me when they had a battle coming, so I faked a braveness that was only partially there.

Show no fear. Mentally, I played my favorite kickass playlist through my head to psych myself up. I wasn't a weakling. I could face this with them. Hell, it was going to be my damn job once I'd been trained enough. Talk about one hell of a 'specialty.'

The guys pulled the bikes to a stop around the corner of a populated, busy street, and dismounted. I followed suit and swung off the back of the bike, using Axel to keep myself steady until my legs became stable again.

He turned toward me and wrapped an arm around my waist. "Are you okay?" he asked, keeping his voice down so just the two of us could hear it.

I gazed up into his dark brown eyes and smiled. "I'm good. Just not used to such a long ride."

Smirking at my words, Axel shot me a wink. "Don't worry babe, I can break you in to long rides in no time."

"I have a feeling you meant that to sound dirty." I arched an eyebrow at him.

Axel's arm tightened, and he pulled me close. Leaning down, he brushed his mouth seductively against the shell of my ear. "Maybe I did."

I couldn't help the grin that stayed on my lips, even given the tense situation we were in. Axel's charm was magnetic. I was a moth to his flame, and somehow, I wasn't afraid of getting burned. Axel always seemed to be right there to help and protect me. He was like my own personal knight in shining armor, and it led me to an unequivocal conclusion. I trusted him. Even now, as a new wave of danger crept along my skin.

Picking up on the same danger I was, Kota tensed and eyed me over his shoulder, before heading toward Dason, and directing his thoughts mentally. *We should send her to Rook with Axel. He can make sure she gets there safely. I agree with Chayton. I don't like her being out here.* The guys edge closer to the entrance of the alley while Axel and I hung back. Using his body, he ushered me closer to the wall of the building that rose up on our right to try and keep me away from the action.

Safety in numbers, Dason said as he peered around the corner. I could feel his hesitancy to send me away, but I didn't have long to ponder why. A string of expletives came next, and I tensed before slipping closer to the back of the group ahead of us, with Axel bringing up the rear.

What do you see? Chayton was all business. The way he held himself made him look like a badass fighter ready to pound the living daylights out of some guy in a boxing ring.

Dason spun back toward us, out of sight of the street beyond. *Class four shade in a feeding frenzy and a bunch of floaters.*

The curses around me had me looking from guy to guy.

So... what does that mean? I asked, while the guys shrugged out of their jackets, hooked them over their bikes, and then fired up their magic.

It means you are to stay here, glued to Axel's side. Dason's order was accompanied by a hard stare that told me he meant business.

Unsure of what prompted me to do it, I nodded and mouthed, "Yes, sir," then I brought my hand to my forehead and gave it a sharp tug downward in a salute, which I knew Dason would not appreciate.

Reaching up, the alpha ran a partially shifted, furry claw-tipped hand over his short hair. *Axel, take care of her and keep her out of trouble.*

Sure thing boss, he agreed with a smirking chuckle.

Chayton, Dason prompted.

I'm on it. Red magick flared to life, building into a swell, which Chayton released. His power rose and spread outward like a large blanket.

"Can't the humans see that?" I whispered to Axel.

"Chayton's perfected this enchantment, so it's not visible to the mundanes." We both watched it bubble over a large section of the downtown area we were in. Without even having to ask, Axel continued and explained, "Chayton is the most skilled at protection, and right now that's manifesting as persuasion." He nodded toward the ward-like covering. "Nothing close to what the Fae can accomplish, but enough to encourage the mundanes to vacate the area or head indoors. Makes luring the demon easier if we don't have to worry about human casualties."

"So each of you has an important role on the team. Kota's the healer. Chayton's the protector. What are you?" I mused and glanced at his handsome face. I wouldn't deny that my curiosity was piqued in regard to my mates.

Axel smiled and braced an arm on the wall next to me, before leaning casually into my space and making me aware of every breath between us. "I'm a tracker," he murmured quietly into the evening air. He never looked away. My body was keenly in tune with his and I unconsciously swayed toward him. Flashes of color on the building's wall caught my attention before I pressed my body against his, and I shook myself out of the spell that was Axel's sex appeal, returning to my senses and the happenings of the world around me.

The guys worked together like a well-oiled machine, and I stared as they drew runes onto their skin. Their individual magickal colors lit the night and I watched in fascination as the glowing symbols sunk into their forearms and disappeared. Then they did the same, slipping around the corner and out of sight.

I crept surreptitiously closer to the corner against Axel's protests and snuck a glance around the bend.

There, in the middle of the street, was a humongous demon. Horns jutted from its head, curving upward in sharp points that seemed to flip off the sky. It stood on two stocky legs that supported its mass. Just like the other demon, this one was made of the same smoky, swirling, cloudlike substance with curved claws on its hands and feet—part substance and part ether. Around the area, at least a dozen shadowed, wispy forms made their way up and down the sidewalk, twisting around the humans and flying in and out of the doors, unimpeded by earth side materials like wood and steel.

Opening its mouth, the class four shade drew a deep breath,

pulling golden, glowing energy from the people standing unaware around it on the sidewalk, talking outside one of the many clubs and bars that lined the street.

"Oh my gods." My shocked whisper broke the night and I watched, horrified, when the demon took another inhale, breathing in the essence and energy of its prey. The humans swayed on their feet, bracing themselves against the building for balance as if they were drunk or high. "Dason said feeding. It's eating their energy?" I spun on Axel with a disbelieving expression covering my face.

"One of the many reasons we fight so hard against the demons, Lorn. Once they're on our plane of existence, they have to feed off something in order to sustain themselves. The mundanes' life force is an easy target." A somber Axel took his own gander around the corner, scrubbing at his face as he turned back to face me. "This is going to be a nasty fight. That thing is fucking huge."

"What happens? To the mundanes, I mean." My arms circled my body and I rubbed at the chill that had nothing to do with the weather in L.A.

"If they're lucky, they'll survive. The enchantment is already working and people are heading out of the area."

As if to illustrate his point, a group of chatty humans strode by the entrance of the wide alley we were in, heading away from the upcoming fight. Looking around the corner again, I saw that many of the bystanders were going into the bars or clubs, leaving the street emptier than it had been a moment ago.

"And if they're not so lucky?" I asked, barely above a whisper.

"The mundanes can't process things like magick, supernaturals, or demons. Their brains will logic out a way to explain the occurrence of finding a group of dead partygoers. Drugs, usually. Class two or three demons don't feed off of larger groups but pick off their prey one by one. Sometimes the police will suspect a serial killer. It's rare that we fight anything above a class three. The stronger the demon, the more they need to eat to sustain themselves on this plane." Axel leaned a shoulder against the wall, effectively blocking my view.

"How many classes are there?"

"Five. One for every point of the pentagram."

"And you've never taken on a class four before?" I wanted to bite my nails as my anxiety built.

"We have…" Axel trailed off, and I knew there was more to the story.

"Spill it." I couldn't get over the churning in my gut. I knew these guys were fighters. Good ones. But they were now *my* fighters, and that just served to fuel my worry. I didn't even know them well, but in that moment I knew if I lost one of them, I would feel it in my very soul. That was the power of the mating bond. I shifted on my feet at the realization of just how deeply mating had affected me already, and what it meant for my future. For all our futures.

Burying the thought for another day, I tuned back into Axel as he started divulging more information.

"The higher the class, the harder they are to beat. They're more powerful. Class one shades—the floaters—are generally harmless to us. They're temptations. Think of them like the seven deadly sins. Instead of feeding off of mundanes' life sources, they feed off of the debauchery and sinful nature they can persuade people to commit. Class two's, unfortunately, have the ability to possess others. They're tricky bastards, but no match against our pack. Aptly, we call them the possessors. Class three shades, however, are stronger, more powerful, and malicious, as you saw the other night. They're larger and scarier. Their powers are deception, lies, and nightmares. They're also skilled fighters, making them hard, but not impossible, to send back across the veil. A class four, like this one," Axel hitched a thumb over his shoulder, "is a warrior. They're summoned for a purpose and put up one hell of a fight. They're trained and dangerous."

My heart thumped harder in my chest, which forced me to breathe harder. The guys were out there with a fucking class four demon, and I was standing around doing nothing *and* taking away a valuable member of their team in the process. "That doesn't make me feel better," I growled.

"I'm always going to be honest with you, even if the truth isn't pretty." Axel crossed his arms over his chest, and added, "I got the impression that you're not the kind of girl who wants things sugarcoated. Am I wrong?"

I stalked a few steps away from Axel before spinning on my heel and facing him, some of the wind going out of my sails. "No. You're right."

His mouth quirked to the side but quickly straightened when a deadly sounding roar shot into the night. I rushed past Axel to peer around the corner again, but he caught my arm before I made it more than a step past him and spun me, placing my back against the concrete wall that made up the base of the building we were standing by.

"Don't. They have this under control." He moved closer and braced a hand on either side of me, his palms flat against the rough concrete. He'd effectively boxed me in with his body, trapping me right where I was standing. My eyes flicked to his face, trying to read whether he believed his own sentiment or not. "You don't believe me, but all you have to do is check the bonds."

My eyebrows furrowed as I studied him. "You can feel the

connection?" It made sense that the link would be two-sided. I just felt dumb for not considering the possibility sooner.

"Yeah, sure can. That sizzling magick that binds us together." He shifted an inch closer. "I can feel your worry and anxiety." He tipped his head to the side and his dark hair fell across his forehead, brushing against his brow. He pressed closer and inhaled deeply before saying, "I know you care already."

"I can't explain it. I don't know you and yet you're mine," I declared, verbally putting my feelings into the universe. Returning his gesture, I breathed in his scent, taking comfort in the familiarity of it.

Axel drew back, and I watched as his eyes flashed yellow before he closed them tightly, swallowing against the rumble that began in his chest. "Say it again."

"I can't explain it..." I started, confused.

"No." He focused intently on me, and I was struck by the golden color that swirled through his chocolate colored eyes. "Call me yours again."

The raspy quality of his voice did funny things to my stomach as he leaned forward an inch, our breath mingling together.

"Mine." It sounded breathier than I'd meant it, but I figured it only added to the surreal sentiment.

Axel groaned and pressed into my space, tilting his head to the side of mine as he skimmed his nose over the sensitive skin of my neck. Tingles raced through me and my breath hitched from the sensations. He drew my fragrance into his lungs again like an addict who couldn't get enough.

The possessiveness of his action, mixed with the intensity of the fight that had started just down the road, created a mixture of desire and apprehension that wrung me dry from the sheer intensity of clashing feelings bombarding me from all sides. I could feel the exertion of the others through the link as they battled, and my muscles tensed while my magick filled my fingers, hands, and arms, ready to be released.

Please, be careful. I sent the thought toward Dason, hoping it would reach him and the others.

Feeling completely jazzed and ready to jump out of my skin from the amount of magick simmering inside of me, I distracted myself by bringing my arms up and gripping the sides of Axel's leather jacket, simply for something to do with my hands.

Axel pulled from my grasp just enough to gaze down at me. "Fuck, you're powerful. I can't believe I can feel that. It's… trippy." He smirked.

I opened my mouth to respond but all that exited was a silent, pained scream as agony tore through my body. My back arched into Axel at the same time a wicked roar rattled through my head. My scalp scraped against the concrete behind me as I threw my head back and rode out the suffering. The bond between Kota and me shook, and by the time I was able to right myself to coherency, Axel was pacing wildly in front of me with a hand dug into his hair.

"Kota." I tried to speak past the gravel in my throat. "Go, Axel!" I practically yelled at him, waving toward the opening of the alley.

Axel looked completely torn. "You're my mate, Lorn. It's my responsibility to take care of you. If anything happened…"

"He's your brother. Your twin. And I don't need a fucking babysitter," I insisted urgently, trying not to fidget on my feet. The demon roared again, and Axel looked wide-eyed over his shoulder. "Please! Go!" I begged.

Resolution covered Axel's features and his warrior mode switched on. "Jacket off," he ordered, shrugging out of his own as well.

Not wasting any time, I followed orders, but I couldn't resist asking, "Why?"

Taking the leather from my hands, Axel tossed the jackets haphazardly toward the bikes and gripped my wrist, pulling my arm straight out in front of me. "I've never done this before for someone else," he mumbled to himself. "Let's hope this works."

Orange glowed from his fingertip as he drew a rune on my skin. The flowing lines pulsed and burned into my skin, sinking below the surface before fading from view. Axel quickly repeated the process one more time as he drew a second rune.

"Stay here," he commanded, apparently happy with his work. Surprising me, he grasped my face between his hands and before I knew what was happening, he'd covered my mouth with his. Our lips met in a quick dance that left me wanting more when he pulled away. His thumb brushed over my bottom lip in a soft caress, and then he was gone. I was reeling as he jogged to the corner, drew runes on his own forearms, and disappeared from sight.

Stunned, I pressed my fingertips against the pressure I still felt on my lips and stared down the empty alleyway until another roar rent the air.

Then, like an idiot or an avenging angel, I disobeyed orders and followed Axel.

SEVENTEEN

LORN

As it turned out, dreams of demons were vastly different from the real thing. The stench of the creature alone was enough to make me want to gag, but I stuck to the shadows and willed my stomach to settle as I crept closer to the battle taking place in the middle of the posh, downtown district, which had no idea that evil had descended upon it.

Looking around, I quickly spotted Kota on the ground, leaning against a sleek, glass building with dark tinted windows. Blood covered the hand he had clutched to his leg, which was clearly decimated if the bloody slashes and ripped fabric of his dark wash jeans were any indication.

Rage rose inside of me at the sight of him, injured and in pain, and I narrowed my gaze on the creature that was currently fending off attacks from Dason and Chayton. I could just make out the shimmering form of an invisible Axel as he raced across the street to reach his brother.

Dason slipped into his wolf form in seconds, darting deftly through the demon's legs before shifting back into his human form and throwing a blast of grey magick at the beast, making it roar again from the damage. At the same time, Chayton let loose a stream of red, sparking flame-like energy and hit the creature from the front. The coordinated attack seemed to be weakening the demon, but every shot served to anger it and made it more desperate to get in a killing blow on one of the guys.

I watched them fight, my gaze tracking each man as they took turns trying to fend off the creature's attack while repeatedly hitting it with magick. Call it a sixth sense, but I could actually detect the decreasing energy of the beast, like it was some video game boss with a health bar. Each destructive hit the demon took was one step closer to sending it packing to the other side of the veil, where it belonged.

Dason shifted again—into a large, black cat this time—and dodged nimbly past the swing of the demon's arm. Working together with Chayton, the two of them tried to lure the beast out of the main drag and down a wide alley.

My magick burned in my hands and I clenched them into fists, keeping out of sight while I tried to decide what my next move should be. The urge to help nipped at me my heels and I debated how angry Dason would be if I interfered in their fight. He'd be steaming, raging mad.

Another set of hits to the demon and it let out a thunderous roar that left my head spinning and my ears ringing. Circling around to try and claw Chayton, the demon faced me, and I felt the exact moment its deadly, red eyes landed on my form in the shadows. It huffed like a bull and smoke billowed from its nostrils. The world seemed to pause as it locked every ounce of its attention on me, swatting at Dason and Chayton like they were nothing more than pesky flies instead of shadow touched warriors about to send the demon back to its hellish home.

Powerful magick throbbed in my fingertips. I felt overfull,

ready to explode from the pressure of it. Stepping from the shadows I took measured steps into the light, leaving the sidewalk and entering the street. The demon's breaths were audible, ragged rumbles. It tracked my movements.

Lorn! What the fuck are you doing? Dason snarled into my head. Enraged was right. My lips curved up ever so slightly in the corners, but I didn't answer him. No. I stared down the demon, feeling drawn toward it.

Just like every dream I'd ever had, I faced the demon and studied it as its hot, rank breath washed over me. The difference was, it was real this time, which meant it was deadly, but in a way I'd been facing down demons for a long ass time, and somehow that helped keep my legs and arms from shaking.

Babe! Get the hell out of there! Axel commanded, both alarmed and angry.

You were supposed to be watching her! Dason mentally ripped into Axel.

Not the time, Chayton interceded, and drew Dason's attention again as they coordinated a more elaborate attack against the demon now that its focus had deviated from their fight.

Two blasts of magick hit the demon in the back simultaneously. The creature threw its head back, maw open, and roared. Chayton and Dason ran around on opposite sides of the demon, their magick ripping into the creature's body, the ether slicing open as a substance that looked like hot lava poured out from the inflicted wounds.

I heard Chayton's yell of pain seconds before I felt it for myself. Gritting my teeth against the searing burn, I raised my hands. Pounding magick threatened to erupt prematurely as I rushed toward the demon. I saw the exact second that Dason was about to be slashed by a set of wicked, long looking talons, and I let instinct take over in a way it never had before. After what had happened with my magick earlier, I was wary to release it again, but oddly, I also trusted it. It had defended me against death once already, and now I called on it again, putting all of my intent behind my plea for help.

Purple magick left my hands in nearly uncontrollable streams, and I squinted my eyes against the brightness of the blast. My body worked in a coordinated dance that I didn't even know I was capable of as I let my magick slice through the arm of the demon, severing it off just before the claws raked through Dason.

The scream was unlike anything I'd heard escape the beast's mouth yet, and I couldn't contain a cringe as the demon unleashed its fury. I just managed to keep my hands outstretched in defense mode instead of covering my ears against the onslaught of sound. A small feat but one I was proud of.

Dason, who had dropped to the ground as he'd tried to evade the incoming blow, pressed himself up in a pushup and gazed at me with shock, and something deeper written across his face.

Time slowed as we watched each other between breaths, and then he pulled a leg up like a runner at the start of a race and launched himself off the ground as his eyes widened. I heard him yell my name. I watched his lips move, but I didn't register the intensity of the way he threw himself toward me until it was too late. I turned in time to see the demon careening toward me, with its remaining arm raised and ready to deliver a lethal blow. I threw my hands up and my magick reacted to my panic by flying from my fingers, but it was too late to block the attack. Claws raked through my flesh like a knife through butter and I got in one last deep breath before stinging, excruciating torment knocked me flat on the asphalt in a bleeding tangle of limbs. I clutched my stomach, the black t-shirt I wore already soaked and warm with my blood.

The demon dropped over me and I rolled from my side to my back when it roared. If I was going to die, I wanted to see it coming.

Dason was running toward me, dodging the sizzling lava like blood that covered the ground around him while he threw himself into danger. Faintly, in the distance, I could hear him scream my name, but my own breath in my wheezing lungs and the high-pitched static in my ears muted it.

The demon drew back, its mouth open in a hiss that made every hair on my body stand on end, before it lunged for me with death in its eyes. I gasped for air and waited for the moment my life would flash before my eyes. As cliché as that seemed, I truly expected it to happen. The creature's jaws were inches away when it screamed and whipped its head to the side. Out of the shadows came a masked man wearing all black, wielding weapons he launched at the demon, distracting and weakening it.

My magick settled like the eye of a hurricane—the calm before a dangerous storm—and I lifted a shaky hand with nothing but surety.

"*Sayonara*," I gasped and then coughed, and released my hold on the power inside of me.

The dam on my control broke apart, and purple and black magick crackled together, surging uninhibitedly from me directly into the demon's chest in never-ending waves. The class four shade shrieked and cried in the deafening throws of defeat. Three more blasts of magick—one grey and two red—joined my own as Dason, Chayton, and the masked stranger threw their powers into the mix.

And then it was over. We had won.

I collapsed against the black tar of the road and focused on breathing, dragging precious air into my lungs. Each breath hurt like a bitch, and I realized the importance of what Kota had said about learning to shift to heal, and I mentally moved it up my to-do list to the number one spot.

I rolled my head and tried to spot the stranger who'd helped us, just barely making out his figure in the shadows between two buildings. A small blaze of magick flared and lit his face, before the wand in his hand stopped sparking magick. A downward sweep of his hand and the wand was gone. I tried to push myself up, to lift my upper body and support my weight on my elbows, but my ruined torso screamed in protest and I collapsed back down. He took a half step forward as we locked eyes, and then Dason reached my side, pulling my attention away momentarily. His face appeared against the dark, cloudless sky above. High-rises kissed the night behind him.

"Stay still," he ordered, and then I felt his hand land warmly against mine, before moving it off my tattered flesh and replacing it with his.

I sucked air through my teeth at the pain and turned my head away, looking for the stranger again, only this time… he wasn't there.

"You never do what you're told, do you?" Dason shook his head at me, but it was easy to read the worry etched into his expression.

"Maybe I just like to challenge you." I gave him a smirk that I knew didn't reach my eyes and tried to shrug, but it just pulled at the oozing wounds on my abdomen and I groaned and writhed on the ground.

"Defy me is more like it," he grumbled and shook his head. "Try to not to move." Dason flicked his eyes from my stomach to my face, and I saw one corner of his mouth twitch upward. "Please," he added.

I nodded my agreement, unsure if I should mention the man I'd been straining to see to the alpha. If I saw what I thought I saw—a wand in my mysterious stranger's hand—that would mean a warlock came to our aid. With the history between warlocks and shadow touched, I wasn't sure what good could come from opening my mouth. At least not right now when the guys could give chase. The last thing we needed tonight was more spilled blood, especially when the man all but saved me— literally—from the jaws of death.

The choice was taken away from me when Dason's hand grew hot and rendered me speechless. I gritted my teeth and grunted as he used his power to knit my muscle and skin back together. "We're going to need Kota, but he won't be any use to you until he heals himself. He and Chayton are out of sight right now, shifted and healing. It's going to be a little while until either one can lend a hand."

"Mmhmm," I hummed, eyes closed tightly against the pain. When he'd done as much as he could, Dason pulled away and sat back on his heels.

Without another word, I winced and stood, bearing the pain of the minimally healed slashes that cut across my abdomen. Sticky blood wet the black, tight t-shirt I wore, making it cling to my skin.

"Easy." Dason got to his feet and reached for me, but I was already walking forward.

Smoke rose from the burnt pile of ashes that remained on the asphalt. The sulfuric smell of it stung my nose. Dason moved behind me while I bent an elbow and covered my nose and mouth to block the scent.

Angling my head, I inspected the gleaming, phosphorescent

symbol that spread out in a sweeping circle from where the demon fell, at its center, and disintegrated. Slowly, I started to walk the circle, my eyes scanning the lines that converged in the center.

"What are you doing?" Dason watched me with restrained patience.

"The markings…" I pointed to the ground and continued my trek until I was standing with Dason again.

Crossing his arms, Dason looked first to me and then to the ground I was still staring at. "What markings?"

I glanced up at him with surprise. "You don't see those?" I pointed to the glowing symbols.

He studied the ground harder, but the marks were obvious, and it was apparent he wasn't seeing what I was.

Skeptically, he lifted his gaze to mine and raised an eyebrow. "What is it you see?"

"It's a glowing symbol of some sort." I went to step forward but Dason shot an arm out and caught my elbow.

"When a demon falls, it can leave an aura behind, so to speak. A negative, evil energy. It will fade eventually, but this one is fresh." He nodded toward the pile of ash. "It's best to avoid them."

"A demon mark?" I stared at the pavement, trying to decide if it was worth the risk. The compulsion I felt drawing me toward the symbol was enough to have my feet moving forward.

A growl at my insubordination was all the protest Dason threw, but he kept a watchful eye on every move I made, ready to swoop in and save me if something bad happened. My heart warmed at his protectiveness.

Stooping down on a groan, I squatted near the pile of ash and brushed it away with my hand. Just as I thought, there was a symbol below the ash. I let my eyes scan over the whole circle once more, and then ran my finger over the artistic symbol in the center, recording it all to memory so I could redraw it later.

"What is it?" Dason stepped around, still trying to see what I was inspecting.

"I think it's a sigil." I rubbed my hands together to clear them of the black soot, and then pushed my palms against my knees to stand. I turned toward Dason and pursed my lips, debating if he'd believe the theory that was running through my mind. Deciding to trust that he'd take me seriously, I opened my mouth and explained, "My guess is that it's either the sigil of whoever is summoning the demons or a sigil for the demon itself."

EIGHTEEN

LORN

The motorcycles purred to a stop outside of another huge high-rise, which cut across the starless L.A. sky in a tower of sophisticated glass and metal, complete with long balconies that wrapped around the outside. It was the kind of place that screamed luxury. I glanced around our battle worn group, taking in our ratty, bloodstained, and burnt clothing, feeling wholly inadequate to walk through the doors that had "Glamor 610" written in gold lettering across the tinted glass.

The men dismounted, and I released Axel and climbed off the back of his bike, thankful that my stomach was now healed, courtesy of Kota. Once he and Chayton had shifted and knit themselves back together, they'd rejoined our group and taken care of my wounds as well. The only downside of being back to one-hundred-percent was the feel of Dason's vibrating need to scold me for interfering in a demon fight in the first place. The barely controlled lecture was sitting on his tongue, ready to be unleashed as soon as we were home again.

After learning about my newfound ability, the men had been oddly silent on the ride here, and with the tension I could feel in in Axel's body while he drove, I couldn't help but wonder if they'd been talking mentally without me.

My suspicions were confirmed when Axel spoke. "This isn't something we can ignore." He brushed his windswept hair back into place with his fingers and eyed Dason.

"I'm not planning to ignore it."

"Then what the hell is your plan?" Axel narrowed his eyes on the alpha.

"You don't always need to know everything, Axel. You need to learn the art of patience." Dason's exasperation was clear as he fired back a response.

Kota, who was in the middle of resecuring his man bun with a rubber band, laughed. "'Axel' and 'patience' don't really go together there, boss man. You should know that by now."

Dason pinched the bridge of his nose and walked toward the double doors that led inside. As soon as he moved closer, the doors swung open, each manned by a doorman dressed in elaborately tailored suits, complete with sunglasses and earpieces that made them look like secret servicemen instead of glorified door butlers.

Chayton jogged the few extra paces it took to catch up with the alpha and clasped a hand on his shoulder. "I know this is a rare occurrence, but I agree with Axel this time. We don't know a lot about female shadow touched. I think this is something that we need to look into. I've never heard of anyone with this ability before." Chayton was careful how much he said in the public setting, and for that, I was grateful.

Letting out a bothered sigh, Dason grumbled, "I'm planning on it. Do you really think I wouldn't explore this further?" He angled his upper body to glare at his packmates before he headed toward the elevators at the far end of the elegant lobby we had entered. Curved, white couches were settled around the space, and there was a receptionist desk off to the left with a beautiful brunette sitting behind it. She simply waved to Dason and picked up the phone, hitting a short combination of numbers and speaking briefly to whoever picked up the other end of the line.

Wrapping my arms around my middle to try and cover up my bloody clothing, I hurried after the guys and piled into the small cab of the elevator. Dason hit the button for the fifteenth floor and the elevator smoothly kicked into action.

"So... what's the plan?" Axel leaned back against the wall of the elevator and slipped his hands into the pockets of his dark wash jeans.

Dason cracked his neck. "I'm putting a call into Mama Dunne. If anyone has the answers, it's her."

"You're sure about this?" Chayton looked concerned and the expression instantly set me on edge. "You know what she's going to want in return..."

"What?" I eyed each of the guys. "What's she going to want?"

"A promise," Kota answered, bracing his hands against the metal railing that ran along the back of the elevator.

"A promise for..." I trailed off and waited for more than the half answers they were giving me.

"That's the thing. No one knows what she'll ask for. It's why it's risky." Axel's voice echoed in the small, quiet space.

"So, it could be something simple or it could be a big ask," I prompted, trying to get clarity.

"Yes," Dason met my gaze, "but she's also our best chance at receiving answers, and our questions about you and your powers are growing by the hour." He cocked his head and stared at me like he wanted to figure me out.

Well, buddy, that made two of us.

The elevator doors dinged open, emitting music with a deep bass, and I followed the guys into a dark club with pulsing lights and a crowd of dancing, writhing bodies in the center. More elegant white couches were set up around the room, with lounging couples and groups all relaxing with drinks in hand. White would never have been my color of choice. I would never be coordinated, nor clean enough, to keep from somehow staining the pristine upholstery, but everywhere I looked the partygoers seemed to be graceful, almost swanlike, in their movements. I spun in a slow circle, taking it all in. Three of the four walls were made of glass and opened to a wraparound balcony, which sported amazing views of the never-ending sea of lights making up the city. I stared, awestruck at the beauty of everything.

I'd never seen so many gorgeous people in one room before, and it made me overly aware of my bloody, disheveled appearance I caught sight of in one of the many tall mirrors decorating the room. The one thing I knew for sure was that none of these partygoers were mundanes. This was Fae territory. If the name of the building wasn't enough of a clue, the model perfect specimens dotting the room around me, and the subtle buzz of magick in the undercurrent of the room, were enough to clue me in.

"Ah, there you are!" I turned at the sound of the creamy, lyrical, male voice, only to be greeted by the broad shoulders and wide backs of the guys blocking my view. I pursed my lips and crossed my arms at the way they kept me out of sight from whoever greeted our group. "Aren't you a sight!" the man exclaimed, not sounding the least bit surprised.

"Know anything about a class four shade in the area?" Dason ground out, but I didn't pick up any malice coming from him.

The music turned down, and curious eyes watched us from around the room as everyone waited with bated breath. Whatever was going down, it seemed I was missing a key piece of information.

Feeling very much like the third wheel on the most awkward date imaginable, I tried to peer around the guys to get a better view, but it was no use.

"Yes, well, as always, we appreciate you taking care of the problems that plague our city." At once, a round of applause went off with whistles and cheers. When the noise died down, the man called out, "The next drink is on the house, in honor of our guests!" The roar of approval echoed off the walls, and the music picked back up as waitresses started handing out drinks from the bar that was stationed along the only solid wall in the room.

The guys all shifted around me as the man—who we'd apparently come to see—stepped around our group, finally spotting me amidst the guys. "Interesting. So very interesting," he said, but simply motioned for us to follow him back into an elevator. The awkwardly silent ride took us up to the very top floor of the high-rise.

The doors swung open, admitting us into a modern, crisp penthouse. Every inch of the space looked immaculate, and I almost didn't dare step foot on the sparkling wooden floors for fear of contaminating the space with the filth covering me. I needed a long, hot shower to get the dirt, soot, and blood off of my skin.

Taking the chance, I trailed the others into the space, while the man we followed waved away the servants stationed around the room. No one spoke as we waited for them to disappear, giving us the privacy the man demanded. Using the time, I assessed the Fae before me.

The man was at least a head taller than me. He had a runner's body, toned and muscular, but lean and his clothing looked casually expensive. His white, flowing tunic had a deep V-neck, showing off the smooth contours of his chest, while his shirtsleeves were rolled up to his elbows. He had the grace of a bird, but the strength of a lion, and he exuded an air of power so effortlessly, that I knew he'd been born to it. A pair of brown, tailored pants made from some sort of exotic material, an expensive golden watch, and suede loafers that covered his bare feet, completed his outfit. His perfectly coiffed, nearly white hair was swept messily away from his face and loosely woven into a wide braid that cascaded down his back, wafting with every movement he made.

Gliding naturally across the floor, he stopped and turned with the precision of a practiced dancer, and his glacial blue eyes landed on me. "If I had realized the missing shadow touched was a woman, I would have asked for much more than the Tavia Glass." he commented, breaking the silence and tsking his tongue with a shake of his head.

"You're just lucky she's still alive," Axel replied, narrowing his eyes on the blond.

The anger filling the room seemed to take the man's cockiness down a level. "I didn't realize she was in danger. If I had, you know I would have given you the coordinates of the skinwalker's location without delay. What exactly happened?"

Axel filled in the Fae, explaining about the events of Solstice while I watched his reactions play across his features, judging his honesty and trying to pinpoint if I could trust him or not. So far, he seemed to be genuine, if not operatic.

Dason stepped forward when Axel was done, his rugged voice low when he said, "You crossed a line by targeting a member of my pack behind my back." He tipped his chin up, apparently having no problem confronting the man whom everyone seemed to revere downstairs.

I held my breath, my gaze ping-ponging back and forth between the two vastly different men. Where the blond was polished and refined, Dason was rugged and manly.

"Yes, well, I had my reasons." The man sighed and walked over to a small cart near the couch, which held various decanters full of amber liquid. He poured one and offered it to Dason, downing the contents himself when Dason refused. He refilled the glass before turning back to our group. "I don't suppose you were successful in your mission?" he asked.

"Of course I was." Axel smirked.

The blond swirled the liquid in his glass and arched an eyebrow at Axel, clearly waiting for him to present his haul. "One of the reasons I summoned you tonight, albeit not the main one, was to obtain the Tavia Glass. Do you purposefully keep it from me?"

"You didn't hold up your end of the deal, Rook." Axel crossed his arms and stared down the Fae, who sighed and glanced down into the swishing liquid. "I found the shadow touched on my own."

"I don't suppose you're feeling generous? You were in the right place at the right time thanks to my *request*." The blond continued to twirl his glass while he tried to reason his way into receiving the article he wanted.

"Not today," Dason interjected, before Axel could answer.

"What Axel took wasn't his to take." I stepped forward, feeling the need to defend what had been stolen from my father. I wasn't sure what the Tavia Glass was, but I wouldn't let Axel simply hand it over. Him and I were going to need to have words, and soon, about his thievery, even if it was what essentially led to our meeting and all the corresponding events that happened after.

"Lorn…" Axel started to explain but swallowed whatever else he was going to say when Dason shot him a hard glance that clearly said, 'not now.'

The corner of the blond's mouth tipped up, and he turned to me. "Us imbeciles have been rude this whole time, haven't we? I'm Rook, Prince of the Fae." He bowed slightly at the waist in introduction. "And you are?" He straightened, keeping his eyes locked on mine.

"None of your business," Dason stated before I could answer, crossing his arms.

"Nonsense, we've been friends forever, Das. I made a mistake, and for that I am deeply sorry. Won't happen again… and all that," he groveled, throwing his free hand over his heart in a solemn, overexaggerated promise.

Defying Dason's desire to keep me in the background, I took another step forward. The guys needed to learn that I wasn't a sheep, and they couldn't simply order me around. While my mind wasn't made up about Rook and whether he could be trusted, my feminine instincts told me he was essentially good, and I trusted that gut feeling now. Smiling, I offered Rook my name, unsure if I should bow or curtsey or just stand still. "I'm Lorn, Your Highness." I chose to go simple with a royal title instead.

The guys all groaned while Rook laughed, looking positively over the moon.

"Oh, I like her already!" When he grinned, it was stunning.

"Don't start with all that title shit," Kota grumbled. "It just gives his already inflated ego a boost."

"He's right. It probably does." Rook's eyes sparkled. "Dason and I have been friends for much too long to use formal titles. That extends to his pack as well." He cocked his head and studied me through narrowed lids. "And you, my dear, are most definitely pack, are you not?"

"I..." I glanced to Dason. "It's still being worked out."

Rook tsked again. "Ridiculous. I can see it as clear as day now that I'm paying attention." He turned his focus to Axel, before continuing, "I think my finding your mate should be enough to earn me the Tavia Glass, don't you think?"

"Need I remind you, you didn't find her, I did. You just sent me on a dangerous mission and endangered Lorn's life in the process by withholding valuable information for your own greed," Axel argued.

"Ouch!" Rook feigned being shot in the chest before straightening, but his countenance remained jovial. "Unknowingly!" Rook shook a finger in the air. "Unknowingly endangered... I didn't even realize the Solstice was schedule, let alone what would occur."

"Enough!" I propped my hands on my hips. "What happened at the Solstice is no one's fault. Rook has made his point. He didn't know," I cast a glance in his direction, "or so he says. There's really no use in going around and around about something that none of us can change. The fact is, it happened, and luckily I'm still alive and finally learning about what I am." I angled my stance toward Rook. "No harm done, but I agree with Dason, you're not getting the Tavia Glass." I faced down the Fae Prince, unmoving in my decision. For a few moments, the air in the room grew tense while Rook appraised me with flashing golden eyes.

Then Rook inclined his head toward me in a bowing nod. "I will respect that, for now, in the hopes that I can earn the artifact I seek, and with time, I hope to one day earn your trust as well." Rook waited until I'd nodded my assent, and then turned to

Axel, Dason, and the others, while I released the small breath
I'd been holding as discreetly as possible. Rook continued,
"And I truly apologize. I didn't know Lorn was in danger at the
time."

"But you do now?" Chayton moved a step closer to Dason,
separating himself from the rest of us as he took his place on his
alpha's right-hand side, having seemingly picked up on the
nuances of what Rook had said.

"I always said it was Chayton who should be your beta, Das.
Such a good choice. He doesn't miss much." Rook took a sip of
his alcohol and hummed in blissful approval like he was a
connoisseur of hard liquor.

"What did you actually summon us here for?" Dason
demanded. "When you called, you said nothing about a shade.
Was the Tavia Glass your only purpose?"

"No. I didn't know the shade was going to appear in my city
when I summoned you. Although there is that saying, kill two
birds with one stone... a rather distasteful statement though,
now that I think about it." Rook wrinkled his nose as he thought
it over. "Alas, you are correct, as per usual." He shook his head,
clearing his expression, only to focus on Dason and let it bleed
into something more serious. "Other than hoping to acquire the
Tavia Glass, I summoned you because of the girl." He nodded
his head toward me, and my stomach dropped while my hands
turned cold at his announcement.

"What about her?" Kota spoke up, surprising me with the
hostility coating his tone. He clenched his teeth, making his jaw
sharp enough to cut diamonds.

"She's in danger. More than you may know. It's what
prompted me to call for you. I wanted you to know."

"So, you knew she was a woman?" Axel challenged, trying
to call Rook out on his lie.

"No. Not when I sent you for the Tavia Glass. I honestly had no idea. Who could have guessed there was a female shadow touched out there? There've been only men for the last twenty years. But afterward, yes. I did learn of her existence. I'm not sure who is searching for her," Rook's icy gaze met Dason's, "but we've all been warned against harboring her."

Dason's jaw ticked repeatedly. "Who's 'we?'"

"Alistair, leader of the vampires, and I have both been warned, as the rulers of the largest branches of supernaturals in the country. I'm sure the leaders of the gargoyles and the alphas of the shifter packs across the United States will be next."

Growls rippled through the room.

"Do you know who's behind the threats?" I chimed in, worry turning my stomach sour.

"You can see for yourself." Walking across the room, he picked up a piece of thick white paper and delivered it to Dason. I moved closer and let my eyes scan the ominous missive. "That was quickly followed with more menacing messages, and then a class four shade shows up in my territory." The playfulness fled Rook as he spoke and I saw the prince behind the mask.

"That's not a coincidence," Dason commented, glancing up at Rook, and the two had a silent conversation.

"No it's not." Rook took the paper back and tossed it onto the coffee table behind him. "I don't scare easily. If you ever need anything, you know whom to come to. Our friendship runs thicker than blood." The two men clasped wrists.

"Thank you for the intel," Dason replied, and then turned and waved us toward the elevator. "I appreciate the risk you've taken."

"And will continue to take. I meant what I said, I would never sell you out. You know this. You're welcome here anytime. Our numbers are strong, and we stand behind our own.

You know you and yours are included in that, Dason." Rook hooked his hands behind his back and nodded sharply at the alpha.

The two shared a heavy look. "I do know it. I just wish I could reciprocate the gesture."

"You do. Every time you protect my city and my lands. This is just one small way that *I* can repay *you*." Rook bowed his head to Dason. "On that note," Rook snapped his fingers, "Renick!"

A male, who was clearly a servant, stepped forth and held out a cloth sack to Rook, who took it and handed it to Dason. The jingle of metal on metal could be heard as the satchel was jostled from man to man.

"A little something for you." Rook smiled, his playful nature reasserting itself. "For your services."

"You make me sound like a whore," Dason said with a laugh, but took the proffered money.

"No, definitely not. A classy escort, if nothing else." Rook sighed dramatically and then cast his gaze on me again. "Ah, how I will miss our fun, Das. I don't suppose you'd be up for sharing her with your dear old friend?"

Animalistic snarls and hisses had me jumping in place as the guys' eyes flashed yellow with their primal spirits, and I reached out with both hands to soothe Axel and Kota who were closest to me. "He's joking," I soothed, trying to calm them down—even though I wasn't sure Rook was, in fact, joking—and keep the peace. This guy was offering us sanctuary if we were to need it, and he'd already taken a huge risk by informing us of the threat.

Rook looked positively giddy at their reaction. "I'll take that as a no." He grinned.

"You're an ass," Dason muttered, rolling his eyes at his

friend, heading toward the elevator, and hitting the button to open the door.

"A loveable one," Rook teased, and then his smile sobered. "Dason, take this as well. It's the last reason I summoned you here. I didn't trust anyone to deliver it. I wanted to hand it to you personally." Reaching into his pocket, he produced a smooth, perfectly round stone that sparkled lightly, holding it out for Dason to take.

"A communication stone?" Dason said with a hint of awe. "I thought these were rare." He glanced up at his friend.

"Extremely. There are only a few in the mortal plane, although we have plenty back in the Fae Realm. They're not easy to smuggle outside of our lands, but there are certain advantages to being a prince." Rook shrugged one shoulder and bounced the hand holding the stone, waiting expectantly for Dason to accept it. "Say what you will, but I have a feeling things will only grow more dangerous from this point forward. If the threats are real, which I believe they are, I'd like a way for us to communicate if all else fails. Please. Take it and take care of yourselves."

"Always." Dason palmed the stone and tucked it safely away. "Thank you, friend." The two men shared a brief hug, slapping each other on the back, before Dason turned and entered the cab of the elevator. We all trudged in after him.

I watched Rook as the elevator slid closed, catching the look of concern that flashed across his face, and when the metal doors met and we started our downward descent, I saw the same concern mirrored in the reflection of the girl staring back at me. Myself.

NINETEEN

DASON

My muscles strained as I lifted the axe one more time and swung it down, splitting the log I was aiming for with a satisfying whack. Putting my weight behind it, I muscled the sharp tool free from the thick log, only to line up another one and repeat the motion, swing after swing, numbing the thoughts with the rhythmic action that offered peace—however momentary. Seeing Rook tonight and hearing of the increased threat against Lorn had done nothing but raise my ire, leaving me restless and unable to sleep. Ever since that girl had burst into my life, things had grown more complicated, and I wasn't sure what to think about that.

Tonight had been too close of a call on so many levels. Injuries were common in our line of work, we all knew that, but the images of Kota, and then Chayton, being injured by a class four shade would stay with me for a long time. Yet it was the heart-stopping memories of Lorn that plagued me the most. My heart had damn near exploded out of my chest when I saw the shade bearing down on her, about to rip her throat out. Even now, my stomach churned and bile scalded the back of my throat as my mind ran away with all the what-if scenarios.

What if she'd been injured? What if she'd been fucking gutted—dead, right before my eyes?

I paused my work, swallowed hard, and swiped a hand across my sweaty forehead. Gritting my teeth, I tossed the axe to the ground in sheer frustration. I didn't even know the girl and yet she fucking meant everything to me already.

Chopping wood had lost its calming effect, and I propped my hands on my hips, tipped my face skyward, and closed my eyes against the growing headache that seemed to add insult to injury. I worked on calming down and pushing the multitude of possible outcomes away. Rainy mist filled the air, instantly cooling my overheated skin while I stood under the covering of the trees, leaves, and clouds above that nearly blocked out the midnight sky.

I'd almost lost some of my team tonight. Some of my family. My fucking...

I halted the word, unwilling to give it life by conjuring it into my thoughts, but the primal spirit inside me, one that was unwilling to be tamed, whispered the truth of what Lorn was to me over and over again, making it hard to ignore the insistent four-letter word.

Mate.

Deep down I knew what she was... what she meant. My pack was ready to accept her with open arms, so why the hell was I having a hard time?

I blew out a breath and ran a hand over my short, curly, dark hair while I listened to the sounds of the forest, trying to knock myself back into the numb state I'd managed to obtain earlier. The sound of frogs and insects created their own melody in the woods, and they mixed with the late night noises of nocturnal creatures scampering about in the foliage, both on the ground and in the trees. Normally, my primal side would try to surge forward, ready and willing to work off some steam by hunting, but tonight all it wanted to do was stay close to the house and guard what was ours. Another change I appeared to have no control over.

The familiar creak of the front door pierced through the peacefulness and I snapped to attention, watching as Lorn left the house.

"What the hell?" I murmured into the darkness and started toward her. Without fully knowing our grounds, she wouldn't know I was outside given her vantage point. I didn't try to keep quiet as I broke into the clearing where the house sat, hoping the extra noise would draw her attention. When she didn't turn toward me, I called out, "Couldn't sleep either?" Hoping I wouldn't scare the girl witless.

Still no response. *Seriously? Was she ignoring me?*

She walked down the stairs robotically, her movements were stilted, and my hackles rose as I rounded on her.

"Lorn?" My voice was a mixture of hesitance and curiosity, and I dipped my head to get a better view of her face. Honestly, she didn't look fully awake. The only response I received in return was a cute little hum, before she stepped around me and headed into the woods.

"Really?" I rolled my eyes upward, talking to the moon, the sky, the spirits... whoever the hell would listen. Scrubbing a hand over my face, I followed after her, mumbling about sleep-walking and troublesome women the whole way.

I trailed after her, grumbling to myself, until I felt the first tingle of her magick shoot through our connection. It grew more intense as I quickly rounded the set of trees that had hidden her from my view, just in time to see Lorn throw her head back with a cry of pain as a swirl of purple magick covered her from head to toe.

Her clothing disintegrated into small, nearly indiscernible pieces, and then standing in the same spot where my mate had once been was a sleek, midnight black wolf. Shaking out her lustrous coat, she threw her head back and howled into the starless sky. She cocked her head to glance over her shoulder, and the she-wolf appraised me with stark blue eyes that seemed to see straight into my soul, and then she loped off, increasing her speed until she was nothing but a dark blur in the shadowed forest.

Cursing, I magicked my clothing away and let my shift take me, choosing to go into my basic wolf form so I wouldn't startle her animal when I caught up to her. Animal instincts were tricky beasts, and it stood to reason that animals were more comfortable with their own kind.

My paws dug into the soft dirt of the forest floor as I ran, and the stretch of sinew over bone felt better with every stride. My primal spirit surged inside of me and I let a howl escape into the trees. The resounding sound that Lorn echoed back at me made my wolf happy, and I pushed myself faster. It didn't take long for me to catch up to her, even though she was fast—especially for a shadow touched who hadn't been shifting for long. The way she'd destroyed her clothes and the pain of her shift told me how inexperienced she was. Fuck, from the conversation I'd overheard the other night, it hadn't sounded as if she'd even known she could shift. More questions piled up in my mind I wanted answers to, but I filed them all away for later as I saw Lorn heading for the barrier.

Growling out a warning to her, I pressed my thoughts into her head. *Don't go past the wards.* The command in my tone was enough to tell her that I wasn't fucking around.

Her eyes flashed over her shoulder as she threw me a look and then forged forward, her eyes locked on something beyond the protective barrier. Her white fangs glinted in the moonlight as she let out a menacing growl, coming to a stop and pacing along the line of the wards. Thick, dark hair stood on end along her neck and back, and her hackles were raised in agitation and danger. I felt her need to continue past the barrier, but somehow, I also knew she wouldn't disobey me. Whether that was because I was technically her alpha or because she sensed the risk, I wasn't sure.

Her sense of foreboding washed through the link between us as she stopped her pacing and shifted on her feet, her claws scratching into the dirt under her paws. Striding forward, I checked the woods, trying to see whatever it was that had her on alert, but nothing was out of place or threatening. For a few precious minutes, all we did was stay locked in the odd standoff we had going, with her watching the forest beyond our protected territory and me watching her the entire time—neither of us moved. Finally, her posture changed and she took off into the forest again. I trailed her, deciding to hang back and keep a close eye on her as she ran herself to her limit. We flew through the dense trees, disturbing the undergrowth and sending small critters scattering to safety as we passed. Each time she increased her speed, I matched the change, keeping her in my sights until she drew to a stop, with her tongue lolling as she panted hard. With a small whimper, a flare of purple magick went up like smoke, engulfing Lorn until she was back in her human skin, slipping to the forest floor as if she'd fainted. Startled and so fucking confused, I rushed to her side, letting my shift fill my body in a burst of magick until I was human as well.

I stared down at the creamy, light tan color of Lorn's naked skin. The curve of her ass was perfectly on display as she lay sprawled out on the forest floor, and I swallowed hard from the sight of her. Shaking off my reaction and uncaring of my own nudity, I stooped down to make sure she was still breathing and relatively unharmed. Driving a hand through my hair, I let out a groan that was a combination of frustration and lust at seeing Lorn this way.

Fighting the urge to reach out and smooth a hand down the soft lines of her back, I quickly stood, conjured my clothing, and slipped them on before letting my magick heat my palms while I created a blanket to wrap Lorn in. I was willing to do anything I could to provide her with the modesty she was due, no matter how much I longed to study her body. I wouldn't take any liberties without her permission—although what I'd already caught sight of was seared in my mind.

I reminded myself of her young age and how wrong my lust was as I carefully wrapped her in the blanket. I kept my eyes averted and scooped her into my arms. The fact that she didn't so much as stir had worry clawing my chest. Lorn's slight form pressed up against my body, causing a strange contented rumble to build in my chest—her presence was soothing—and I didn't bother to hide it as I took Lorn home. I listened to the faint sound of her steady pulse as I carried her through the front door of the cabin and up the stairs to the room Axel had lent Lorn. His scent, which usually permeated the room, was already starting to mix with the sweet fragrance of hers, and for the first time in my life I was jealous of him. The need to have Lorn's scent marking my room—my territory—became a hot and wild need I had to suppress as I laid her down in his bed, covering her gently with the sheet and blanket. Her dark hair fanned out around her beautiful face, and she looked peaceful. It was only when I heard her contented sigh and saw the way she snuggled into the warmth of the mattress below her that I tore myself away.

I shut the door behind me, satisfied that she was home safely and tucked into bed. Something about the entire evening —from her odd sleepwalking, to her shift, to the way she'd released her hold on her magick, and essentially passed out— was off, and it was time to get answers.

There was only one place, one person, who I trusted implicitly that I could turn to for help—even at this late hour.

Pushing a hand into my hair, I huffed out a sigh, then jogged down the stairs as silently as I could, left the house, warded it with magic that would let me know if Lorn left while I was gone, and took off into the night.

* * *

Lights gleamed from the front windows of the small cabin and I shook my head. My lips curved into a smile as I climbed up the familiar steps, before opening the door that was always unlocked.

"You always know when I'm coming." My deep tenor filled the small space as my gaze landed on the small woman rocking away in her favorite chair in the living room. "It's like you have a sixth sense."

"When it comes to you, you know I do." My grandmother grinned and set aside her book on the small, rustic table next to her rocking chair. "I had a feeling you would be here tonight. It's the only reason I'm up so late." She proceeded to get out of her chair and came over to give me a kiss. In her older age, her posture had stooped, and she was a full head and a half shorter than I was. Leaning down, I kissed her cheek, and my heart became lighter just by being in her presence. Then she headed into the kitchen, retrieved a bowl from the fridge, and popped it in the microwave, before grabbing a bottle of beer and plunking it on the kitchen table for me. "Sit down." With a wave of her hand she motioned me toward my typical seat at her table, her tone gentle yet firm. She was the only person in the world who could, or would even attempt, to order me around. And I let her.

Huffing out a sigh, I realized Lorn was now the second person in the world who could do the same. While she hadn't tested that skill to the fullest yet, I had no fucking doubt she would. With the way she already liked to push my buttons, I knew that girl would keep me on my toes.

I obeyed my grandmother's commanding request, and the wooden legs of the chair scraped lightly against the thick, plank flooring of the cabin as I took a seat. Two minutes later, a bowl of her famous stew was steaming in front of my face, making my mouth water from the aroma of vegetables and thick chunks of meat. Grinning at her, I gave her my thanks and dove in, humming my approval as the flavors hit my tongue.

My grandmother let me eat in peace, but the second I was scraping the bottom of the bowl, she leaned back in her chair and crossed her arms over her chest, narrowing her eagle-eyed stare on my face. "I know you, Dason. Something is bothering my boy. What's got you running around with your boxers twisted tight this far past midnight?" My grandmother raised her eyebrows at me, planning to get her answers.

Her white hair was a testament to her wizened age, but there was nothing frail about the woman who sat across from me. Strength radiated from her and her brown eyes sparkled in the low lamplight.

It took me a while to fill her in, and when I was done, nothing but the light chime of an old clock could be heard in the room.

"You found your mate," she breathed, her hand fluttering to her heart. A watery sheen glimmered in her eyes and it was easy to tell how happy she was at hearing the news.

"I did." I drove a hand through my hair. "More like she fell into my life, but—" I shrugged, and a smirk found my lips, while I shook my head over the whirlwind finding Lorn had been for my packmates and me. These last few days had been more insane than usual, and that said something when you hunted demons for a living. "Anyway, I was hoping, as our unofficial historian, that you might have heard about some of these strange occurrences before, or maybe even had a book in your shop that might be able to lend me some insight, because I'm lost when it comes to this girl." I tipped my beer back, taking a healthy swig to punctuate my statement. If anyone in my life could help solve the mystery of Lorn, it would be my grandmother. Not only was she well versed in our histories, but she ran a combination bookstore and library on the Kwoli pack's territory that contained the only accurate information on shadow touched I knew about. The wealth of her knowledge on supernatural topics was endless, but I had a feeling Lorn's situation may surpass even my grandmother's expertise.

"There's nothing in the shop that I can think of off the top of my head, but there may be something in the histories we keep in the library section. It's been so many years since I read them. We'd be better off asking Mara, since she's recently been going through them," my grandmother paused, cocking her head as she studied me, "but I have a feeling that you haven't told Mara any of this yet." Guilt ate away at my stomach and must have shown on my face, because my grandmother nodded. "I assumed as much. You're going to have to tell the poor girl."

I groaned and hung my head, not looking forward to that

inevitable conversation. "I know, I'm just... this is all..." I let words trail off.

"It's sudden." The soft skin of my grandmother's wrinkled hand rubbed over my arm in comfort. "Finding one's mate is always sudden and unexpected, because we never know when or where it will happen. Yet, it's also one of life's greatest gifts. You, more than most, should know this." Compassion lit her eyes and my tortured gaze met hers as memories of my past—of my mother and father—washed over me in waves. Clearing my throat, I glanced away and covered my emotions with another draw of beer, locking them away as I swallowed down the cool liquid. I missed them more than I'd ever admit, and pain stabbed through my heart whenever I thought of them.

"I'll talk to her, I promise." My voice sounded like I'd swallowed gravel, and I cleared my throat again.

My grandmother patted my arm and leaned way, gathering the cup of tea she'd brewed while I'd eaten earlier, and let the mug warm her hands even though it was anything but cold in the cabin this time of year. "I wish I could be of more help," she shook her head, "but I can't guarantee I'll have any books that will point you in the right direction. From the sounds of it, my best guess would be that Lorn has had her powers for quite a while and has been at odds with her magick and her primal spirit. They're not communicating. She may not even know how to."

"We just started training her in the ways of her magick."

"Sounds like you need to add shifting to that list, and the sooner the better."

I completely agreed and made a mental note to talk to the guys about it when I returned home.

"There is someone who you could call," my grandmother hedged.

"It's in my plans. I just hoped I could avoid it." I rocked back in my chair, swirling the remaining beer in the bottle, and watching it swish against the dark brown glass before finishing it off.

"Agatha is your best bet for answers to unusual problems. It's why she has such a reputation. Besides, she's an old family friend. You shouldn't have anything to fear. I'm sure she'll want to help you in any way she can." My grandmother smiled reassuringly, but I didn't share her enthusiasm or her optimism. Agatha—Mama Dunne—was a piece of work, and I wasn't keen on involving her unless we absolutely had to. Unfortunately, we were at that point.

My grandmother got up and placed our dishes in the sink. Taking the cue, I scooted my chair backward and stood. "I'll call her in the morning. Thank you for the help. If you find anything at the shop, anything at all you think may help, just let me know and me or one of the guys will swing by to grab it."

"Stay here tonight, Dason. It's already after two in the morning. Your old bedroom is already all set and there are fresh towels in the bathroom," she offered with a smile, rinsing out our dishes while I eyed the door. A large part of me wanted to get home to Lorn, but I also knew how much my grandmother loved the company. She'd been lonely since I'd moved out a few years back, so whenever I could, I tried to swing in and keep her company. Closing my eyes, I mentally checked on the ward that was tied to the magic that lived inside of me. With no sign that Lorn had left the house again, and the peace I felt emanating through the link I now shared with her, I figured she was still asleep and safe. Glancing at the clock and the hopeful sparkle in my grandmother's eyes, I acquiesced.

After making me promise to bring Lorn by to meet her soon, we both headed to bed. The rest of the night was fitful, and I tossed and turned, finally rising a mere three hours later to grab a shower, followed by a cup of coffee. Every part of me itched to head home, back to the guys... but mostly back to Lorn—although I hated to admit that, even to myself. The physical distance between us was uncomfortable, and I gritted my teeth against the invisible tether, unsure whether I liked it or hated it. Probably a bit of both.

I'd just finished stirring milk into the mug, prepared to down the caffeine and head home, when the front door slipped open just after six.

"Dason!" Mara's feminine voice floated toward me with a hint of surprise.

Shit. It'd been days since I'd reached out to her, even before Lorn entered my life, and I winced before turning around and trying to offer her a smile.

"Hi." It was a lame response, but it the best I could do given the way my heart constricted in my chest. Mara was a sweet girl and a good friend. We'd grown up together, which only complicated the workings of our semi-romantic relationship.

Her brown eyes sparkled up at me and she smiled as she sauntered forward, setting the basket she carried down on the counter. Walking over to me, she placed her palm flat on my chest and leaned up to give me a kiss. I didn't stop her when her lips brushed against mine, but now that I was mated, revulsion turned my stomach at the affection of another woman and I visibly tensed, torn by my reaction.

By definition, Mara fit every checkbox I was looking for in a woman, except that she wasn't mine. She respected me, listened when I spoke, gave me space when I needed it, and generally cared for the guys and me. She was a caretaker and I knew I could count on her. Mara was dependable and steady. She was always a friend and over the years, she'd grown to be more. Lorn, on the other hand, was headstrong and young. I either wanted to kiss her or growl at the way she challenged me. I never knew what to expect from her next, and she was far too alluring for her own damn good. I hated the way I wanted Lorn when I had what I'd always planned for standing right in front of me.

"I've missed you!" Mara exclaimed when she leaned back. "I haven't heard from any of you all week!" she scolded, smacking me lightly. It was unlike us to go so long without having at least a phone conversation if not a visit. Hell, she lived right next door to my grandmother in the small cabin she'd had built behind her parents' place. Having stayed at my grandmother's last night, I should have been more prepared to run into her.

Pulling away from me with a sweet smile on her lips, Mara reached for the coffee pot and retrieved a mug of her own, setting herself to the task of creating her drink, oblivious to my discomfort. "Lucky for you boys, I've been busy categorizing the history books. Did you know your grandmother has an entire collection in the attic that has never seen the light of day? I'm slowly going through them, but it's rather tedious work," she rambled, and I immediately zeroed in on the topic.

"You have unseen history books somewhere?" My mind instantly went to Lorn and the mystery she presented. "Anything interesting?" I asked, trying to dig for more information.

"So far it's mostly a history of births and deaths, some random facts. Some of the content repeats what we already have in the library, but I'm still reading through the stack." She shrugged and sipped her sweetened coffee—three scoops of sugar and a splash of milk, just like she'd always taken it. Mara was familiar and comfortable, and I tried to let myself sink into the natural flow we'd always had between us, but the buzzing connection I held with Lorn was a constant reminder that things had changed, and nothing would be the same again.

I sighed quietly. Reaching for any mundane topic of conversation to give myself time to organize my thoughts—unwilling to dive head first into the inevitable discussion that was coming —I eyed the basket Mara had plunked on the counter. "What's that?" I motioned with my mug toward the basket.

"I brought your grandmother some muffins." Mara moved the basket and retrieved one of the baked goods, bringing it over to me. "Blueberry, your favorite." She beamed and sashayed back to grab one for herself, her voluptuous hips swinging enticingly as she moved. "I also have chocolate chip and a few cinnamon ones in here for Axel, Chayton, and Kota. I was going to bring them by this morning." Anxiety shot through me at the idea of Lorn finding out about Mara and I gritted my teeth, wishing I could rub away my impending headache. Oblivious to my internal turmoil, Mara continued, "I also brought Grams some herbs. She's been incessant about needing more for the elaborate dinner she's been planning for our mating ceremony." Mara finished fussing with the basket and sent me a sweet smile, her eyes sparkling.

Guilt sparked in my gut and spread until it was a rapid wildfire.

Propping one curvy hip against the counter, she sipped at her drink and hummed in happiness, completely unaware of the storm I was experiencing inside.

Skipping over the topic of our mating, I tried to stick to safer subjects. "Thank you for taking such good care of her. You know I'd like to be here more often, but the job—" Mara pressed a slim finger against my lips, shushing me.

"I know, Dase. You don't need to explain. Your grams means the world to you, but she's important to me too. I've always known what your job and your life entailed, and my role in it. I'm happy to help her. Besides, she's really taken me under her wing and taught me the ins and outs of her business. I'm enjoying running the bookstore and library with her. Someday, it'll me mine." She smiled, truly happy with the work she was doing. Mara had always enjoyed reading, so when my grandmother had chosen to mentor her, she'd jumped at the opportunity. While Mara wasn't shadow touched, she did share my Native American bloodline, and after my parents had passed when I was eight and my grandmother had taken me in, we'd grown up together as neighbors, friends, and now more.

"Well, thank you anyway. I just want you to know how helpful it's been to have you keeping extra tabs on her." I rubbed a hand along the back of my neck as the awkwardness of the situation grew, unbeknownst to Mara.

Slipping closer once more, Mara gripped my t-shirt and pulled herself toward my unmovable body. "I know another way you can thank me..." She bit her lip and her brown eyes sparkled as she shot me a seductive look. "Our mating ceremony is drawing closer. I know the guys wanted to wait, but maybe I could come over tonight and cook you four dinner. We could see where things go."

I lifted my hands, placed them on her upper arms, and smoothed them down toward her elbows. "Mara," I hedged.

"Alright," Mara capitulated on a sigh, and shook her head with a little laugh. "How about just dinner?" She blushed, obviously feeling like I'd just turned her down, which I essentially had with the hesitance in my voice. I fucking hated this, but I was the one who'd convinced the guys to take a mate who didn't call to us, and I was the one who would fix it. Out of all of us, I was the one closest with Mara. And I was the alpha. Sometimes responsibility sucked.

"It's not that, Mara. Listen…" I reached for her hands and held them between my own, extracting my t-shirt from her grip. "We need to talk."

Almost as if she saw the bad news settle between us, Mara's face cleared, and I saw the hurt in her eyes before I even opened my mouth to explain.

"Come on. Let's take this outside." I took her hand and pulled her after me, glad when she acquiesced so easily. The sun was just beginning to peek through the trees on the horizon, casting long shadows along the forest floor. Leading Mara to the front steps, I motioned for her to sit, while I jogged down the last few to pace along the pine needles and moss that covered the ground.

"You're scaring me Dason." Mara's expression was confused yet guarded.

"I know. I'm sorry. I just don't know how to start."

"How about with the damn truth. What's going on?" She straightened her shoulders and peered down at me from her perch on the top step.

I stopped pacing and faced her with my hands hanging limply at my sides. "We found our true mate."

I watched as Mara's mouth popped open in disbelief. "You… what?"

"Our true mate—" I began, but Mara held up a hand to shut me up.

"I heard you the first time." She sounded angry and I didn't blame her. "How is that possible?" Her question was breathy, and she shook her head as if she was having trouble processing. Fuck, wasn't that the understatement of the day? We all were. At least, I was. The guys—really Chayton and Axel—seemed to be adjusting just fine. I knew Kota was too, in his own way. He was just struggling with his own issues of loss and commitment, but deep down I knew he was already invested in Lorn. Me? I wasn't used to change, and Lorn was a curveball I hadn't seen coming.

"She just kind of fell into our lives. It's a long story." One I wasn't sure Mara would want to hear.

"I don't understand how she just shows up out nowhere after all these years, two weeks before we're supposed to have our mating ceremony!" Mara braced her elbow on her knees and dropped her face into her hands. "Someone went searching for her, didn't they? Axel? Chayton? I always knew those two were hesitant about our arrangement."

"Chayton says it was fate. Truly, no one knew she existed. It really was a wild happenstance, but the how and the why don't matter. What matters is that it's happened, and it changes things. I needed you to know." I tried to smooth the situation. "I know how much this hurts. You've always been important to me Mara, as a friend and then more, but you have to understand, she's our mate. I have to call off our mating ceremony."

"Are you sure you can trust her? Trust this connection you think you have?" She dropped her hands, hanging them off her knees as she studied me with a sheen of tears in her eyes.

"Trust me, the connection is real." In fact, the glaring lack of connection between Mara and me now felt like a chasm, insurmountable. I'd never be able to mate with her after how connected I felt toward Lorn. The way I was drawn to Lorn—even now, from this distance away—was addicting, and it solidified my decision.

"You told me not to worry about this very thing. I knew I'd be worried our whole lives that some woman would show up and stake a claim to what was mine, and you assured me that wouldn't happen. You made me a promise. We're planning our future together..." Mara shook her head, blinked her eyes to clear them of tears, and furrowed her brow in anger as she spoke.

"I never thought it would happen for us. We spent years looking for our mate, and nothing. There haven't been any shadow touched females in twenty years. You know that better than even I do, having dealt with our histories." I pinched the bridge of my nose. "What I'm trying to say is that I never saw this coming, and I'm sorry that I have to renege on promises that were made to you."

"The invitations... the house we're building... oh gods, the bookstore." Mara jolted from her position on the steps, standing and shaking her head. "I've counted on this for so long, Dason. I've planned my entire life around you and your pack, allowed myself to hope and dream. I... I can't do this now." Mara jogged down the steps. Anger, frustration, and hurt poured off of her in nearly visible waves and her shoulder brushed into mine—hard—as she stormed past.

"Mara," I called after her and she whirled.

"No, Dason. You get to go on and live your life. You're going to go home and be happy with some other girl in your pack, in your house, in your fucking bed. And me? I get to go home to my one room cabin... alone. I've just lost my mates, my new house, and probably my fucking job." Mara stopped to suck air, tilting her head to the sky and counting silently to herself to calm down before she set her brown eyed gaze back onto my face. "I understand, logically, that you had no control over when your mate showed up, but it doesn't feel like that. It feels like you just cheated on me in the worst way and called off our wedding! So, no. I don't want to talk to you right now. I need time, and you're going to give it to me."

Feeling like dirt, I nodded and said one last thing. "I'll

respect your wishes. I care about you Mara, and I never intended to hurt you."

"I know," she whispered, "but you did." Strength, anger, and devastation warred across her features, and she pivoted on her heel and walked away with her head held high. I watched her until she disappeared through the woods, heading home.

Grabbing my hair with both hands, I tugged just to feel the pain. "Fuck." I let the word fill the tranquil morning. For the first time in recent years, the four-letter word fell short.

TWENTY

LORN

The scent of rich coffee greeted me when I cracked my eyes open on a groan. Every muscle in my body hurt in a terribly familiar way and I tensed, before pausing to assess my surroundings, just like I did every time I woke up with the type of pain that was assaulting me now. The bed was soft under my body, and when I drew in a deep breath, I scented Axel. Tentatively, I pushed myself up from where I laid on my stomach and peeked around the room. Nothing unusual jumped out at me until I glanced down out of habit. Naked, again, but this time there was a dark grey blanket in bed with me that I hadn't gone to sleep with last night.

Embarrassment flooded my cheeks as I started putting two and two together.

Shit! Not another episode! Not here!

Now that I was paying more attention, I could scent the lightest fragrance of Dason on my skin, and I closed my eyes, hanging my head on a groan. Of course the stars would align for him to be the one to find me. Out of all of the guys, why did it have to be him?

Collapsing down on the bed, I sorted through my roiling thoughts, trying to make sense of what had happened last night. As much as I wished the alpha's scent on my skin had been placed there for a sexy reason, I knew that hadn't been the case, especially because it was Dason's. That, and my entire body felt like it had been ripped apart and pieced back together with super glue.

The harder I focused, the more my dream surfaced, and the same eerie feeling that always accompanied my demon-filled nightmares made my stomach roll. I'd dreamt of another shade, this one just as large and deadly as the one we'd battled yesterday. Now that I knew more about what I was seeing, I could tell it was another class four, and I swore I could feel a phantom sting from the gashes I'd received from the last one I'd faced.

Moaning into my pillow from the exhaustion rolling over me, I eventually found enough energy to climb from between the sheets and throw on some previously worn clothing I'd neatly stacked on the computer chair. Tiptoeing my way to the bathroom, I took my time cleaning up, steaming up the bathroom in the process. Hot water soaked into my skin and I tipped my head back, enjoying the force of the spray from the shower, and letting it wash the grime and dried sweat from my skin. It was just one more clue that told me I'd been outside during this 'episode,' just like with all the others. Being outside, naked, during an 'episode' was one of the few consistencies I could cling to while the rest remained a mystery.

Finally surrendering the shower to anyone else in the house who needed it, I used the toiletries I'd been borrowing and hurried back to my room to change. I only had two previously worn outfits to choose from, and I glanced between them, unsure of which one to pick. Looking at my palms, I wondered if I should try my hand at creating clothing, but I truly had no idea where to start.

Pursing my lips, I held my hands out so my palms faced the ceiling and studied the lifelines that ran along my palms before deciding to give it a try. Mimicking what I'd seen Chayton do, I held my hands in the same position and closed my eyes, furrowing my brows together in focus, while I pictured the clothing I wanted to make.

Jean shorts. Jean shorts. Jean shorts. I pushed and pulled at my magick, asking for it to work as I kept my rhythmic chant going. When my hands began to heat, a triumphant smirk tilted my lips and I pressed forward.

My magick faded so I peeked my eyes open and gaped. In my hand was a completely formed pair of jean shorts—perfectly fit for a Barbie doll. I held up the tiny shorts in disbelief, unsure whether I should laugh in celebration that I'd actually made something, or groan from how completely off the mark they were in terms of size. The more I looked at them the more my smile grew until I was chuckling to myself and tossing the small denim bottoms on the desk. Wrapping my towel tightly around myself, I left the room and followed my nose to the kitchen.

Other than the dripping of the coffee pot, the house was nearly silent. Clutching my towel tightly, I poured myself a cup and added milk and sugar, before leaning against the counter as I eyed the clock and read the time. Just after eight in the morning.

The faint sounds of someone talking on the phone filtered into the house and I cocked my head as I listened to Dason's deep tenor.

"We need to see her as soon as possible," Dason spoke respectfully, but his tone was edged with his normal commanding tone. Only able to hear one side of his conversation, I listened to the rest. "Just let Mama Dunne know who's calling and I'm sure she will work us in." A few hums of approval and a quick goodbye, and then the front door creaked as the alpha made his way back inside.

My face heated prematurely, simply from my lack of knowledge over what had gone down last night. I could just imagine him finding me bare ass naked in his woods, and I scrambled to come up with a decent excuse as he turned into the kitchen and locked eyes with me.

His grey gaze was fathomless, and he dropped his focus from my face and down my body in a slow slide I could nearly feel. An unspoken energy slashed through the room between us, and while it was invisible, I felt the sparks shoot down my spine to my toes. The warmth from the way he looked at me settled somewhere south of my navel with a pleasant weight I wasn't ready to analyze. My body took on a mind of its own, and I preened like a peacock when his eyes darkened and heated at the same time. My breathing picked up and my cheeks infused with a heat I knew displayed as a blush, although I couldn't see it.

"You can't seem to keep your clothes on around me, can you?" His gaze narrowed just slightly with his smirk and it was enough to make my lips part in shock.

"I... what?" I stammered, yelling at my slow brain to catch up.

"This is the second time I've seen you in a towel and you've been here less than a week. Not to mention last night." He let the statement settle as he sauntered into the kitchen like he owned the place. I mean, he did... but he didn't have to act so high and mighty.

Straightening my spine, I tried to portray a more unaffected persona. "I was looking for Chayton or Axel. I need one of them to make me some clothing, seeing as how I have no belongings of my own to speak of."

Taking a jug of orange juice from the fridge, he unscrewed the cap, brought the entire container to his lips, and took a long drink. I watched the way his Adam's apple bobbed when he swallowed, completely transfixed by the simple motion that suddenly seemed so damn sexy. When he was done, he set the jug on the counter, and I didn't even balk at the fact that he'd literally just ruined the entire container of orange juice with his unsanitary manly habits. It was a trivial matter as compared to the way I suddenly needed to press my thighs together. Fuck, what was happening to me?

"If you need some help, all you have to do is ask." Dason's gaze never left mine as he spoke and the way he studied me left me feeling dizzy. Was he offering to help me... with... that? My mind skittered as it tried to keep up under the onslaught of whatever power he seemed to hold over me, and I briefly wondered if this was some kind of alpha mojo.

"I... you..."

Shut your damn mouth, woman, I scolded myself, literally shaking my head to try and jumble my thoughts back into some semblance of order. From the moment Dason walked inside, my mind seemed to have packed its bags, hopped on a plane, and was currently vacationing somewhere in the Caribbean in a sexy little two piece.

Dason stepped into my space and loomed over me, making me tip my head back to continue the stare off we had going.

"What do you want to wear?" His voice was so low that it sounded like an intimate question, although I knew that wasn't how he'd meant it.

"Shorts. Shirt," I mumbled, completely forgetting every other article of clothing I'd need.

Dason's gaze dropped to my chest, and then down and down some more in a calculating way. I shifted on my feet from the intensity radiating off of him. Then his hands were full of sparkling, stormy grey magick as he created what I'd asked for. Placing the shorts and tank top aside, he raised a condescending eyebrow, almost like he knew I needed more.

"Um... undergarments?" I hated the way it came out as a question, and it was enough to resolidify my backbone, which had apparently turned to jelly. Dason wasn't the kind of person you could let intimidate you. The second you did, he'd hold the power, and I refused to be cowed by his sexy presence and confidence. I wouldn't set that precedence in this relationship, er... friendship... mateship? Whatever it was that we had blooming between us. Begrudgingly, my brain returned to my body. "I need a bra and underwear." I shifted my stance, appearing more self-assured in front of the alpha.

His approval slid easily through the connection we had, and I smiled to myself.

"What does my mate like to wear?" Dason drawled, and my pulse skipped at the use of the possessive word. "Are you into thongs? Boy shorts? Bikini style?" Dason rattled off a list in a sultry way and I blinked at him in disbelief.

"Why do you know so much about women's underwear?" I cocked my head, studying him.

Something about my question broke some of the sexual tension building between us, and the grey color of his eyes turned stormy.

"You're not the first woman I'll have been with, Lorn," he admitted harshly. "I'm older than you. More experienced."

I narrowed my gaze on him. "You make it sound like I'm some innocent little angel. Maybe I've been with other men.

Ever think about that?" I stopped just shy of calling him on his asshole ways, even if I was bluffing.

"You've been touched by another man?" he inquired, but it wasn't nicely. Possession flashed quickly across his face. It was there and then hidden away in nearly the same second.

I jutted my chin up at him. "Maybe I have. It's not really your business."

"You're my mate." He shifted another inch into my space.

"And you're mine. Are you really saying you want to stand here and compare numbers?" I arched an eyebrow at him and propped my hands on my hips.

Bracing his arms on the counter on either side of me, he leaned over, making me arch backward and clutch my towel.

"How old are you?" The question seemed important to Dason. The set of his jaw was as hard as stone and the muscle flexed just under his skin as he gritted his teeth.

"Why does it matter so much?" I countered, but I softened —just slightly.

"How old, Lorn?" Dason sounded like he'd swallowed gravel.

"Nineteen, but I'll be twenty at the end of the summer." I felt like a child who counted their age by half years when I answered him, but it felt important that he know. I let my focus slip back and forth between both of his eyes, trying to gauge his reaction. "How old are you?"

"Old enough," he growled.

"Age is just a fucking number, Dason," I growled back. "I'm not naive. I know you're older than me. What I don't understand is why this seems to be a problem."

"I'm nine fucking years older than you Lorn." It was practically a snarl, but I didn't flinch. I didn't move at all.

"Okay," I murmured.

"Okay?" He reared back like I'd smacked him.

"Yes. Okay. It doesn't matter to me." I wasn't sure how our connection worked, but I tried to press the truth of my feelings toward him, hoping he'd be clearheaded enough to pick up on them.

"It bothers me."

My brows furrowed. "Because I'm not experienced enough?" I asked, trying to follow our previous conversation into this one. Trying to latch on to his skewed logic.

A rumbling growl flew from his mouth and he was back in my space, his chest brushing against mine. "You think I want other men to have touched you? That I want that imagery in my head? You're mine. Fucking mine. My mate." His eyes flashed yellow and I knew his primal side was right below the surface. "Only my pack will ever be allowed to touch you."

My pussy clenched around nothing and I grew wet at his fierce demand. Every heave of his chest brushed against my breasts, rubbing the course texture of the towel against my pebbled nipples. The light moan that slipped from my lips filled the room and I felt his answering growl between my thighs.

Still, I forged on. "Why then?" I whispered. "Why does it bother you?"

"Because I shouldn't want you."

Confusion broke through the lusty haze I'd been falling into, and I shook my head. "I'm not a dense person, Dason, but I don't understand what the problem is. It's not like I'm some sixteen-year-old or something. I'm completely legal."

"Barely," he spat, and I reared back as much as I could, given the limited space and the counter digging into my lower back.

"So, I'm not old enough for you." I let that reality sink in, and when Dason didn't protest, instead turning his face away from mine, offering me his profile, it was my turn to clench my jaw. "My age isn't exactly something I can change."

"I know that."

"Do you?" I challenged him, my heart aching in my chest. I wasn't sure what I could do to fix his unease. Age was just a number. It didn't matter to me at all. Why he was so hung up on it, especially when we had no choice or say about our mating, I couldn't understand.

Before Dason could respond, the front door of the cabin slammed open, admitting a panting Axel. His bare chest was on display, shining with a coating of sweat that highlighted all the dips and lines of his muscular abdomen. Even his hair was wet, curling slightly and sticking to his forehead.

"Good morning!" Axel said cheerily, until he picked up on the lingering tension between Dason and me, his attention zeroing in on my towel-clad body. "What's going on?"

I opened my mouth to explain but Dason spoke first, extracting himself from my personal bubble and letting the cool, air-conditioned air slip between us.

"I saw Lorn shift last night." He ran a hand through his short, dark hair, casting a glance my way like he hadn't just dropped a bomb on me. A bomb that clearly changed the subject from our previous conversation on purpose and gave me more to think about than the 'age' debate we'd been arguing about. As much as I didn't want to move away from our previous discussion until we'd solved it, I couldn't ignore what Dason had just said. And he knew it.

"You what?" Axel and I echoed each other, but then I continued, "Excuse me?"

Dason sent me the smallest nod of approval for following him into a new topic, clearly not comfortable airing our dirty laundry to the others yet. Instead, he gave me answers. "You were in some kind of trance. I thought you were sleepwalking, honestly." Dason pinched the bridge of his nose. "I followed you into the woods to make sure you were alright. I thought I'd be able to get you back to bed... that sleepwalking was a quirk you just hadn't mentioned to us yet, but then you shifted."

"I don't... I've never shifted." I ran my hands over my arms in a self-hug and realization dawned on me. "Oh gods. That's why it hurts so much." I closed my eyes and hung my head as every 'episode' I'd ever had replayed through my mind. The pain of waking up, the way my body felt like it'd been through a war. "I shift?" I mused to myself, but it caught Dason's attention.

"What are you talking about?" He leaned against the counter on the far side of the kitchen, watching me.

Glancing up to Axel and Dason, I told them about my 'episodes.' "I never realized. It wasn't like I had any reason to suspect I had the ability to shift."

"The question is why." Axel took a seat at the kitchen island, worry creasing his brow.

"My grandmother thinks it may have to do with her being at odds with magick and the primal spirit that resides inside," Dason informed Axel. "But I didn't know about the dreams when I spoke to her."

"You talked to your grandmother about me?" I prompted, not even realizing he had a grandmother who lived nearby. It was glaringly obvious I needed to start getting to know my mates. I wanted to learn about their lives. To know them on every mental, emotional, and physical level I could.

"She owns a bookstore and small library on pack territory. She's the most knowledgeable person when it comes to shadow touched history and lore," Axel explained for his alpha. "She's like our historian, not to mention a grandmother to all of us, blood related or not." The soft smile on his lips was full of affection.

"I'd like to meet her someday. She sounds amazing."

"That's good then, because she'd like to meet you as well." Dason grabbed the OJ and returned it to the fridge, refusing to look at me while he went about the menial task.

"Does she know..." I trailed off, staring at Dason's tense back.

"That you're my mate?" He spun around, crossing his arms over his chest.

"Yes." I didn't back down.

"She knows."

I nodded, but my mind ran away with the news. So he wasn't okay with my age, but he was willing to tell important people in his life about me? I wasn't sure if it was my limited experience with men, or simply that Dason was an uncrackable enigma, but I was more confused now than I'd been earlier. Choosing to stay on topic, I filed away all my other questions to ponder later. "So, what does this mean?" I braced my palms on the countertop and hoisted myself up onto it, making sure to adjust the towel—which had risen just above mid-thigh—to keep myself covered.

Both men in the room noticed, their eyes lingering on the line where fabric met skin. Dason cleared his throat and was the first one to avert his gaze. "It means we need to find our answers elsewhere."

"Mama Dunne?" I asked, recalling our conversation from last night, and Dason nodded.

"She's our best chance at receiving answers. Between the threats, the symbol, and now the shifting, I've impressed upon them that we need an appointment with Mama Dunne as soon as possible." Dason checked his watch. "Hopefully, we'll have

permission to seek an audience with her by the end of the day."
He lowered his arm and fixed his gaze on me. "In the meantime,
we need to add learning to shift to your training regimen. It was
already something you needed to learn, but given the new information, I'd like it to become just as much of a focus as
mastering your magick and learning the runes." He paused, as if
he was waiting for me to argue with him.

"Alright." I nodded in acquiescence. "I've been wanting to
learn to shift anyway."

"I can help teach her," Axel offered with a smirk, rubbing
his palms together in a playfully nefarious way.

Dason shook his head, already assuming the worst from his
packmate. "The basics, Axel. She needs to learn from the
bottom up."

"I can teach her from the bottom up," Axel quipped with a
wink, and I giggled at the sheer sexuality he placed behind his
agreement.

"You are trouble," I told him.

"Always, baby. Always."

"You don't even understand the half of it." Dason dug his
palms into his eyes, looking tired.

"When do we start?" I inquired, peeking at the clock on the
wall and noting the time, just as I heard rustling coming from
the top of the stairs as Chayton joined us.

A round of 'good mornings' sounded around the kitchen
while Chayton drank in my bare legs and thighs.

"I think we need to take a break today," Axel suggested.

"I'm not so sure—" Dason started but was interrupted by
Axel.

"Lorn has had nothing but stress since before she arrived. I
think it's time we did something fun for once. We all need to
relax, or the tension in this house is going to fucking break us."

Axel paused and leveled Dason with a heavy stare. "With the potential meeting tonight... we need to take our down time where we can get it." Axel looked prepared for a fight.

Dason must have noticed as well, because he relented on a sigh. "What do you have in mind?"

TWENTY-ONE

LORN

"I can't believe you downed that entire thing!" Axel smiled with wide eyes as I licked my fingers clean.

"What? I'm hungry!" I mumbled, after I popped the last bit of my po'boy into my mouth, speaking around my food. If Avalon could see me now, I knew she'd probably have a conniption over my manners and unladylike demeanor. It made me smirk knowing I was no longer under her thumb. This was the most freedom I'd ever felt in my life—even better than living at The Witching Academy—and I was already growing addicted to it. Emmaline and my father crossed my mind daily, but with everything I'd had to process, I hadn't made any progress on figuring out how to get in touch with them. My heart ached, but today was supposed to be about fun and relaxation, not falling into the pit of worry and homesickness, which I knew was waiting for me if I let my thoughts stray too far. I forced away the ominous black cloud of emotions and focused on the conversation I was having with the guys. "Besides, isn't there a law or something? I didn't think you could come to New

Orleans and not have a po'boy! I feel like it's one of those unspoken rules."

"She speaks the truth," Kota said around the last bit of his own sandwich. "It's flippin' good."

"She's eaten two!" Axel exclaimed, and Kota reached around behind me to pop him upside the head in brotherly fashion. "Hey! What the hell?"

Kota simply stared past me at Axel, who immediately held up his hands and turned his attention my way.

"You guys misunderstand," he started.

"You better clarify before you end up in the doghouse," Dason teased. He was the most relaxed I'd seen him since I'd met him.

Axel glanced around the table, finally catching on to his faux pas. "Shit, I'm not saying she's fat. The fucking opposite. I'm just damn well impressed she packed all that away," Axel replied with a hint of awe.

"I like a girl who can eat," Chayton commented, smiling at me while he scraped his bowl of jambalaya.

Smiling mischievously, I picked up my spoon, reached across the table, and swiped a small taste of Chayton's meal, humming in approval as all the flavors mixed together on my tongue with a bit of heat. Glancing up from under my lashes, I assessed Chayton's reaction.

"Good, isn't it?" He grinned at me and took another bite, completely unfazed by my meal thievery.

"And so it starts," Axel murmured, leaned back in his chair, and patted his stomach.

"What?" Kota questioned.

"The girlfriend privileges." Axel's tone was nothing but happy about the fact, and my heart pitter-pattered in my chest at the word 'girlfriend.'

Smiling to myself, I placed an elbow on the table, and leaned my chin on my palm as I stared out the window and watched the busy street. Today had been incredible and my heart was lighter than it'd been all week. After a daytime river cruise, I'd dragged the guys on a graveyard tour, instantly fascinated by the history and vaults. Then we'd gone shopping, and, thanks to the graciousness of the guys, I finally had a few items of non-magickal clothing and my own set of toiletries. It had been a good day, topped off with dinner as the lights in the French Quarter came on, creating a moody atmosphere that I loved.

I people watched from my seat while the guys chatted. A flash of black caught my eye and I peered across the street as goosebumps rose on my arms for no apparent reason. It felt like I was being watched, and the irony wasn't lost on me, since I was the one who'd been doing the watching just a moment ago. The feeling sat heavily on my shoulders and didn't relent, however, so I continued to let my gaze roam over the people outside until it landed on a man, standing at the edge of a building two doors down and across the street. He wore a black button-down shirt, complete with suspenders and a top hat tipped low over his eyes. His tailored black pants ended at a pair of red dress shoes that stood out, even on the streets of New Orleans. Dark hair curled from beneath his hat and facial hair in the form of a beard lightly covered his face. I squinted and adjusted myself closer to the window, leaning into Kota's space in my quest to get a better look.

"What's wrong?" Dason demanded, cutting through the chatter of the other guys.

"Nothing," I hedged, flicking my eyes to his, but then deceived myself by glancing back out the pane of glass and across the street.

"Lorn," Chayton added carefully. His voice reassuring even as his posture grew stiff and he went into beta mode.

"It's just… are you sure it's safe here?" I asked, prying my focus from the man outside, who did nothing but lounge against the brick wall of one of the shops, his own gaze sweeping along the street, only landing on the window I sat behind casually.

"New Orleans will never be considered a safe city when it's filled with as many magick users and other supernatural creatures as it is, but the rules if engagement have always been different here. There are rules that apply only for this area, which differ from any other place in the entire country. Each species knows what will happen if they break the treaty they've signed allowing them access to the city. Their time in New Orleans would be over if they broke it," Dason informed me and I nodded, understanding the basics.

It didn't stop me from zeroing in on the dark stranger across the street again, and this time he was appraising me as I was him. Fuck.

Dason, attuned to my tension, waved down our waitress who appeared at the table with a sultry smile she immediately turned on the guys.

"Check please," Dason asked politely, giving the beautiful woman only the briefest attention.

"Are you sure there isn't anything else I can get for any of you?" she purred, her attention skimming over each of the guys while ignoring me completely. She was one of those women who'd grown up knowing they were beautiful, and she exuded sex appeal with every graceful movement. I'd never been one of those girls, and I fidgeted with my fingers as I waited to see if any of the guys would notice the way she was practically eye-fucking them in the middle of the restaurant.

"We're good, thanks." Kota surprised me by reaching over

my head and placing his arm around my shoulders, pulling me lightly against his body while he leveled a cold glare at the waitress.

"We're here to show our girlfriend a good time." Axel winked at me and grinned mischievously. "So, unless she'd like anything else off the menu, I think we're good here."

The waitress gaped as Axel's hand landed on my thigh and rubbed lightly across the smooth skin below the line of my shorts. Her eyes narrowed in on the movement and she shot a look my way that sliced like a dagger through butter.

"Would you like anything else, sweetheart?" Chayton asked, playing into the game the guys had started.

I smiled gently at him, my heart swelling from the way they all made it clear that they were off the market. "No... I couldn't eat another bite."

"As you can see, we're all taken care of," Dason added, shocking the hell out of me by joining his packmates, his posture standoffish toward the beautiful woman—completely shut down to her attempts at flirting.

Clearing her throat, the waitress forced a smile and set the receipt we'd been waiting for down on the wooden table. "Too bad." Her tone was clipped, and she swayed her hips with a little too much enthusiasm as she sauntered away to tend to another one of her tables.

I released the breath I was holding and gazed wide-eyed at the guys, fully expecting Kota and Axel's attentions to end once the woman was out of sight. As predicted, Kota released me, moving his arm and taking a sip of his drink as he averted his attention elsewhere. My heart ached in my chest and Axel, who seemed comfortable with his intimate touch and in no hurry to end it, squeezed my thigh reassuringly, having caught my disappointment over his brother.

Pulling his wallet out, Chayton left the appropriate amount of cash on the table, including a tip, and we headed toward the exit.

As soon as I was outside, I scanned the busy street and zeroed in on the man who was still studying me intently. Waiting.

"I'll be right back." My voice was a confused mumble, and Dason gripped my elbow with enough force to stop me from taking a step forward.

"I see him too, and you're not going over there alone." His voice was a low whisper only I could hear. I saw his hand ball into a fist and felt the tingle of his magick crawl through our connection as he partially shifted.

Axel, Kota, disappear into the crowd and find a place to shift. Make it inconspicuous, and then I want you to surround the alley between those two buildings, Dason ordered, and the guys instantly faded into the sightseers. *Chayton, keep close.*

Chayton took up position on my other side, and together the three of us crossed the street. The man in the top hat turned in a fluid, elegant motion and strode into the very alleyway Dason had instructed Axel and Kota to cover.

I fidgeted with my fingers until Chayton slowly reached out and pushed at my hands.

Confidence, Lorn. Never let them see you sweat, Dason instructed, and I squared my shoulders, pushing my anxiety out of my body on an exhale. Dason was right. I'd faced a damn demon. I could face a mere man. I felt my backbone solidify as I stepped forward, only stopping when the man paused and pivoted to face us.

"Ms. Kentwell," he drawled with an accent clearly from the area, and I cocked my head to study him as I tried to place where I may know the guy from. There was something oddly familiar about him, but with the distance between us earlier, and the deep shadows of the alleyway now, I couldn't get a good read on his face.

"How do you know Ms. Kentwell?" Dason crossed his arms over his chest and stood with his feet shoulder width apart in a stance that screamed dominance. I had no doubt that he could easily kick Mr. Dapper's ass if the need arose. My magick was heavy in my limbs, growing and swirling inside of me, ready to be called should I need it. The guys flanking me, and my magick surging, helped me feel more secure, so I took a step forward.

"My boss knows Ms. Kentwell better than I do," Mr. Dapper commented, and my eyes narrowed as I put two and two together.

"You're Darbonne's apprentice." I took a step forward, heedless of the rumbling growls that sounded behind me from Dason and Chayton.

The man nodded his head deeply, and he stepped aside with a dramatic wave of his hand as a swirling portal opened and his master stepped through.

"The beautiful Ms. Lorn," Buford drawled, the heels of his shoes clicking against the pavement as he headed in my direction. His dark hair was nearly buzzed against his head and his light green eyes flashed as much as the white smile he offered. His sharp jaw and straight nose were striking, and it was hard to look away from his beautiful eyes when they locked on you the way his held me captive. Power rippled from him in subtle waves as he strutted forward before taking my hand, and placing a kiss on the back of it. His umber skin contrasted with my lighter tan coloring as he gripped my hand, refusing to let go even when he straightened. "How good it is to see you again. Especially after our last unfortunate meeting."

"You mean when the entire High Coven tried to kill me?" I sassed and arched an eyebrow, yanking my hand away from his and barely resisting the urge to wipe it against the fabric of my jean shorts.

"Surely you don't mean me." Darbonne pressed a hand to his chest. His clothing was unique and fashionable, and the black shirt he wore was more torn fabric than actual solid concealment.

"No," I capitulated, giving him that one. "You seemed to be on our side. On my side." I tucked my hands into the pockets of my shorts and cocked my head at Darbonne. "What can I do for you?"

"I think that should be my question." His brows rose. "This is my city, after all."

"You don't own it," Dason challenged, with his typical grit and gravel.

"No, not per se." Darbonne let his focus slip from me to Dason for a split second, before returning. "But I do run the coven in this area and have a right to know when one of my own is in town."

"She's not of your kind, warlock," Dason countered.

"No..." Darbonne sighed dramatically. "I don't suppose she is. However, as a close family friend, I owe it to her father to check in on her when she turns up on my doorstep." Darbonne smirked at my sharp inhale, and I realized my mistake immediately. He knew I wanted information, and that switched our positions, no longer allowing me control of our little tête-à-tête.

"How is he?" I asked, trying to keep my voice neutral but failing miserably. Both Dason and Chayton stepped forward, as if sensing the crack in my armor.

Darbonne's eyes softened a fraction of an inch. "He's doing

as well as can be expected. There has been some... fall out... due to recent events."

"Has he lost his place on the High Coven?" It was a breathy question and one my heart was fully invested in learning the answers to.

"It's complicated. He was held in captivity for questioning, but once Kingston realized he truly had no idea of your... affinities, he released him. He's on probation currently, only overseeing his own coven while the High Coven... debates," Darbonne explained in his thick, Creole accent, waving a hand in the air as if to dismiss the whole unpleasant and highly political topic.

"So, he's home? Safe?" I pressed.

"Of course." Darbonne sighed. "Your father is highly thought of. He was never truly in any danger. That's a role that's been reserved for you. I see you've found some help." Darbonne didn't hide the way his nose wrinkled when he surveyed the two men flanking me. "I hope you know what you're doing."

"I'm surviving, which is more than I can say for my welfare if the High Coven had me." I was tense and conflicted. "What are you doing here, Darbonne? Why confront me? This seems like a risk to yourself and I'm unsure why you would take it," I prompted, crossing my arms over my chest and staring down the man who thought he had all the power.

"This is my city, and as your *friend*," derision saturated the word, "has already pointed out, this isn't just my city. In an odd turn of events, I have no say over your presence here."

"Because of the random treaties?" I asked, digging for information.

"Something like that. New Orleans is her own, beautiful beast. One I tame but do not control. I'm only in control of the other witches and warlocks in the city, and again... as you've all graciously pointed out, you are neither of those things." Darbonne tucked one hand into his pocket and smirked, clearly enjoying the loopholes his city offered him.

"What about reporting Lorn's appearance in your city?" Chayton inquired.

"I'm sure I can't be held responsible to remember every citizen who graced the streets of New Orleans." Darbonne brushed away Chayton's concern. "Especially when they aren't a witch or warlock."

"What's your angle, warlock?" Dason growled.

"Can't I simply check on an old friend's daughter?" Darbonne tilted his head, crossing his arms in front of him as he studied Dason.

"No," the alpha responded. "In my experience, that's not how these things typically work."

Darbonne sighed and shook his head, an amused grin tipping his lips. "Your bodyguard here is a smart one, sweetheart."

"He's more than my bodyguard," I stated, the urge to defend not only my alpha but my mate rose inside of me, and I'd opened my mouth before I thought through the consequences. I didn't want to share too much information with Darbonne when I didn't trust him as far as I could throw him—whether he played toward my side or not—and I hadn't considered Dason's reaction to my claiming him out loud. Before I could say more, I sealed my lips shut with invisible super glue.

Darbonne's eyes seemed to gleam in the low light of the alleyway as he took in the three of us standing before him. "Interesting." He assessed us. "Your father will be interested in hear of this new development in your life, Lorn."

"What is it you want?" Chayton questioned, getting us back

on track.

"You're correct that there is something I'd like." Darbonne began pacing back and forth, tapping his chin as he debated what to tell us. Truthfully, the entire affair played into Darbonne's need for dramatics and entertainment. Stopping his stride, he turned on his heel to face me. "Your trust, Lorn."

"Yeah, that's not going to happen," Dason answered, before I could open my mouth to respond. "Asking for her trust is like asking us for ours," he growled. "We're a pack and we make our decisions together."

I held up a hand to silence him, keeping my eyes on Darbonne. "Why are you asking for my trust?"

"Because I believe we're working toward the same goal," he replied, and his response seemed genuine, but I needed more.

"And what's that?"

"To stop the evil that's been bypassing the veil." Darbonne tipped his head down, looking past his dark lashes and leveling me with his gaze.

I heard the vibration rattling in Dason's chest, but he stayed blessedly silent while I narrowed my eyes on Darbonne.

Be careful, Dason warned directly into my mind, and I sent him a wave of calm, hoping he'd realize I had this.

"You'll have to be more specific." I wanted to hook him further, lead him into divulging more information.

"We both saw the demon at the Solstice, did we not?" Darbonne drawled.

"I had nothing to do with that," I parried.

"Not directly."

I pursed my lips, thinking over my response. "I don't know who's behind the summonings."

"Neither do I."

"Then how can I help you?" I tilted my head to the side and

raised my chin, making sure to stay in control of this conversation.

Darbonne sighed, as if he was tiring of the tension that had been growing between us. He eased his stance slightly and relaxed his arms into something more casual. "When you come across pertinent information, I would be obliged if you'd share it with me. We're both on the same journey. I feel the evil pressing in on my city, and I'd like to shut it down before it affects me as it's affecting other cities. The attacks are getting worse and news of demons is beginning to spread. We need to lock the veil and I'd like to help. Don't think I don't know the information your little friends are feeding you. That it's warlocks who are summoning the beasts."

"Who else has more motive than the witches and warlocks?" Dason challenged angrily.

"I'm not saying you're incorrect. I'm simply saying I have a broader picture than perhaps you do," Darbonne replied with steely resolve. "If we combine our knowledge and work together, perhaps we can stop the impending apocalypse."

"Apocalypse?" I echoed, feeling like that was a bit of an exaggeration.

"Of course. What do you think will happen when whoever is behind breaking down the veil succeeds? A picnic?" Sarcasm coated Darbonne's words, but then he softened again. "Time is running out. The demon appearances are already increasing in frequency."

"And what do you get for your involvement in closing the veil and preventing the demons from entering our plane of existence?" Dason demanded with a stone-like expression creasing his forehead and tightening his jaw. "Leader of the High Coven?" Dason questioned, but I knew he'd already made up his mind about Darbonne, who simply shrugged.

"There are many in the witching world who are ready for a change. I'd say your Lorn is one of them after her experiences the other night. It would behoove her—all of you really—to have someone more tolerant of skinwalkers in charge of the High Coven, would it not? Besides, it can only be a helpful change for her father, who worked his entire life to earn his spot on the High Coven only to potentially lose it in one night."

I gritted my teeth, reading between the lines. He blamed me, but so did I. It was my fault in an off-handed way that my father was in the position he was in now. No, I hadn't known I was a skinwalker, but I also hadn't been honest with my dad about all the strange happenings in my life. If I had been, maybe together we could have found a way around the Solstice and avoided the entire dramatic event.

And if you had, you wouldn't be here with us, Lorn, Chayton gently reminded me, reading my thoughts from Dason and responding through the same channel.

I glanced back at him and saw the truth blanketing his face. And he was right.

There's nothing productive in your regret. None of what happened was your fault. Fate, remember? All we can do now is move forward, Chayton continued.

Turning back to Darbonne, I intended to do just that. "I'll think about your proposal and be in touch." I tried to speak as diplomatically as possible. "In exchange for your silence about my appearance in New Orleans, I can tell you that there was a recent attack in Los Angeles."

"The Fae city?" Darbonne mused. "You see, whoever is summoning the demons is growing more brash and bold."

I nodded, waiting for his agreement.

"You have my word." Darbonne bowed slightly at the waist.

"And to perhaps sway your mind to my cause, how about a goodwill gesture?"

"Such as?" I inquired.

"Meet me here in one week and I'll have a message for you from your father. If you happen to have more information for me then, that would be much appreciated." Darbonne's light green eyes gleamed when my own widened, and he knew he had me.

I... it's my father, I stuttered to Dason, who sighed through our mental link.

Go ahead. He gave me the permission I sought.

"Alright. One week. Right here." I held out my hand and shook Darbonne's extended one.

"Wonderful. You five enjoy your evening." Darbonne smirked, glancing over his shoulder at the dark cat that sat at the end of the alleyway—whom I assumed was Kota or Axel in shifted form. Either way, he'd known we'd split up. You didn't make it onto the High Coven without being smart, observant, and ready to play the game. "Until next time, sweet Lorn."

Then, Darbonne called for his wand, opened a portal, and he and his protégé walked through it, disappearing from sight.

The vibration of an incoming text on Dason's phone infiltrated the darkness we were left in, and I turned around to face the guys. Chayton stepped up and gently rubbed my back, soothing me with his closeness as I processed everything that had just happened.

"From the frying pan into the fire," Dason murmured, pinching the bridge of his nose as he stared at his phone. He glanced up as the black cat and an orange tabby converged on our group. Kota and Axel quickly shifted back to their human forms, and Dason peered around our gathering, before saying, "Mama Dunne is ready for us."

TWENTY-TWO

LORN

Sounds of jazz, street artists, and chatter from the local bars all blended together and filtered down Bourbon Street as I followed the guys toward a storefront. It had its front doors propped open and an overhead sign lit by a soft, yellow light swung gently in the breeze, the bold white lettering labeling the store as the 'House of Hex.' The closer we drew, the more I could see inside to the endless amount of shelving that seemed to hold all sorts of old trinkets, skulls, voodoo dolls, and vials. The steps up to the store squeaked and a small bell chimed as we entered the shop. An assortment of books lined the entire back wall behind the long counter, which held the cash register. The scent of sage permeated the air and I browsed the shelves full of spices and herbs in small glass jars, while Dason headed toward the front of the store, speaking to a tall, thin man working the register.

"At least this place is eyeball free," Axel commented, and cringed as he tossed a trinket in the air, caught it, and seamlessly placed it back on the shelf he'd snatched it from. "Your dad's workshop was something out of a horror movie," Axel joked, and I arched an eyebrow at him.

"About that..." I began, and Axel's jovial attitude faltered as he eyed me and winced.

"I guess we never really talked about that, did we?" he hedged, and I shook my head.

"You were in my house?" I prompted.

"Yes, but for a good reason."

"There's a good reason for breaking and entering?" I challenged. Although I truly wasn't mad, I had a feeling there was more to the story than I'd been able to piece together.

"Technically, I shifted and entered the house through the open door around back," Axel pointed out. "I didn't have to break a thing." He grinned, and I chuckled, shaking my head at him.

"So, Rook tasked you with stealing something from my father's workshop in exchange for information on a skinwalker he'd learned existed?" I concluded, dipping my head and catching his gaze.

"That about sums it up. It was important, Lorn. To me." He sobered and the serious glint in his eyes alluded to his honesty.

"I feel like there's so much more you're not telling me. I want to know you, Axel."

"I know, and I will share my past with you. Soon, I promise. Just not here." He motioned to the store around us and our lack of privacy. Even though we were cocooned between the rows of shelves, I knew anyone could be listening to our conversation. "It's not a light topic and it doesn't just concern me." The tenor of his voice dropped as he spoke quietly, and when he glanced around, I knew he was talking about Kota.

I nodded and bit my lip, looking forward to the day when

we'd have more uninterrupted time together to delve into deeper subjects.

Addressing our previous discussion, Axel continued, "Besides, as it turns out, you were the one I was searching for all along, and if I hadn't been at your house that day—" He shuddered out a breath.

"Things could have turned out very differently," I finished for him.

Axel moved closer, leaving only a few inches between us. "I'm so glad I found you that day, Lorn. I don't regret a thing, even if you're upset at me for my actions that day." He reached out and his thumb swept over my cheek in a tender caress. His forest fresh scent surrounded me when he pressed closer, and then his lips were on mine in a sweet, gentle brush that left me wanting more. He pulled back a few centimeters, rubbing his bottom lip against mine, as our breath intermingled before I wrapped my arms around his neck and popped up on my tiptoes to seal my lips to his once more. His happiness surged through our bond and I kissed him harder, enjoying the hard planes of his chest as I leaned into him. Strong arms wrapped around my waist and he hauled me into his body with a groan. His tongue slid across my lips and I opened, meeting every stroke and lick with one of my own.

I was completely lost in Axel, uncaring of the world around us or who may be watching. His body and the way his lips played with mine were like a lifeline, offering me air when I'd been drowning for days. For those few moments I was in his arms, I forgot everything and let myself fall into the haven he offered.

Someone cleared a throat—twice—before it infiltrated my heady haze, and when I pulled back I saw Kota appraising us with an unreadable expression on his face.

"Mama Dunne is ready to see us," he informed us, then turned and disappeared through a doorway covered in a beaded curtain.

"Shit," I mumbled, and pressed my hands to my cheeks to cool my heated face.

Grabbing my chin lightly, Axel turned my face toward his. "Don't let my brother bother you. Honestly, he's probably just jealous that he didn't do that first."

"I don't know about that. I'm not sure he's too keen on me." I sounded more disappointed about that than I meant to, but the truth was, our encounter from the kitchen the other day still played through my mind. None of us had gotten to choose this connection we now shared, and it bothered me to think that the guys may not want me. I was already growing more and more attached, and my feelings were becoming... involved. How much of that was the magick of the connection versus the time I'd been able to spend with the guys, I couldn't fully judge, but either way, I was invested now, and I wanted to see where our relationships could go. How much they could develop and grow.

"Trust me, he's keener than you know, but Kota doesn't let people in easily anymore. Just... don't give up on him, alright? He just needs time," Axel pleaded his brother's case and I smiled gently.

"I won't. I never intended to."

Happy with my answer, Axel took my hand and pulled me after him through the beads, which clanked and jingled a melody as we entered the back of the store, following the sounds of the other guys' voices.

"Ah, 'dere's the chil'." The Cajun woman who spoke was old, aged by time, but beautiful nonetheless. Her hair was dark, and I could only guess she kept it dyed to stave off the grey. The wrap-style dress she wore accentuated a body she still strove to show off, and around her neck hung various necklaces of all shapes and sizes. Heavy perfume surrounded her, and I tried not to cough from the scent of it as she marched forward and surprised me by taking my face between her soft palms. "Hello *cher*. I've been waitin' a long time to meet ya." Pulling me down a few inches to match her height, she placed a kiss on each of my cheeks. When I straightened, I peered wide-eyed at the guys who all wore varying expressions ranging from shock to laughter.

"It's... uh... nice to meet you as well?" I didn't mean for it to sound like a question, but after the overly familiar greeting, I was feeling out of my element.

"You don't know who I am, and it's understandable that you will be hesitant, but you and I'll be great friends, you'll see." She patted my cheek in a grandmotherly way and abruptly turned, heading back behind her table. It was obviously a meeting space. Warm lamps lit the room and a burgundy brocade rug covered the old, scratched hardwood floor. A table sat in the middle of the room covered in a deep red tablecloth, with a throne-like chair sitting on one side and a multitude of eclectic, mismatched chairs on the other, which I assumed were for us. When Mama Dunne took her seat, the guys shifted until Chayton pulled out a chair and motioned for me to take it.

I sat down and the guys all filed in around me, taking the remaining available spaces, and the room fell into an awkward silence as Mama Dunne stared at each of us in turn.

"It has been many, many years since I've seen someone of your talents, *cher*." Mama Dunne leaned back in her seat when her attention returned to me. "Dat you would appear now, when we need you da most, can only be fate."

"What talents do you think I have?" I asked with confusion.

"More dan you even know you possess chil'. Your Dason filled me in on da strange happenings in your life, and none of dem are a coincidence, my dear, but rather destiny."

"Destiny?" Dason pressed, looking for more answers.

Mama Dunne held out her hand, her palm facing the ceiling. Her attention lingered on Dason before landing on me. Jutting her hand toward me one more time, she waited with raised eyebrows. I scooted forward in my chair, perching myself on the edge, and offered her my hand. With movements far faster than I would have assumed she was capable of, she gripped my hand in hers, flipped it palm up, and withdrew a small dagger that she placed against the fleshy part of my hand near my thumb. The irony of the last time I'd had a dagger threatening the flesh of my hand was not lost one me. What was it with hands, blood, and magickal rituals?

"Hey!" Kota was nearly out of his chair in protest by the time she sliced a thin line into my flesh and let blood slowly pool.

The thick, red liquid ran across my lifelines as Mama Dunne started to chant. I felt simmering power radiating from her, but I couldn't place her supernatural race to save my life. Her scent didn't come across distinctly—especially through her heavy fragrance—but she was without a doubt otherworldly.

Her dark, nearly black eyes lost all their color, bleeding to white while she chanted, and I gasped from the sight of it as she leaned over my hand, tracing her finger along the outside part of it. I almost missed the way the blood moved preternaturally along my palm as she read my bloodied lifelines.

"I am not mistaken. You are who I think you are, Lorn Kentwell. You, the adopted chil' of a skinwalker. You are shadow touched, and your destiny as the gatekeeper awaits you." The trance she was under ended abruptly and she collapsed back into the chair, letting go of my hand. I began pulling it toward myself, but Kota grabbed it and started dabbing at the blood that now dripped off my fingers with a handkerchief that appeared out of thin air before healing the wound.

"I am adopted, and I am shadow touched. What do you mean 'gatekeeper?'" I asked, my heart racing inside my chest. I wanted to look at the guys, to gauge their reactions to all of this, but I couldn't seem to pry my gaze from the woman whose eyes were slowly returning to their normal color, working through every shade of grey as they reverted to their previous dark depths.

"You have more responsibility dan any one chil' should have, *cher*. You, and only you, control the gates of the veil. You are the veil keeper, and we have been waiting a very long time for you to rise," Mama Dunne answered, and my mouth open and closed while I struggled to respond.

"I... that..." I turned to Dason with pleading eyes.

"Are you sure?" he inquired, with enough force to cut through my scattered thoughts. I was pretty sure I was suffering from shock.

"When am I not, Dason?" Mama Dunne shot him a hard look that would break a lesser man, but Dason just nodded his head.

"Mama Dunne has never been wrong. Not in all the years I have known her, or the many lifetimes before that," Dason spoke lowly, angling his words and attention my way.

"I don't understand how I became the veil keeper, or even what that means," I implored Mama Dunne.

"No one knows how keepers are chosen, chil'. Fate rarely reveals her mysterious ways to us mere mortals." She paused and let that sink in. "What I do know is dat only a shadow touched woman can fill the role. Since dey already have access to the veil, it makes sense. Your mother, bless her soul, was a veil keeper, Lorn, and da veil has been left unguarded since her death." My heart stuttered to a stop in my chest, the air in my lungs wheezing out as I absorbed that information. I'd always suspected that my parents could be dead, but having it confirmed was like having Mama Dunne's dagger plunged into my heart. The pain was sharp, the blade deep.

"You..." the words barely made it past the tightness in my throat, "you knew my mother?"

Mama Dunne's eyes softened a fraction, and she shook her head, "Not well, chil'. I knew of her, but she never did seek my council." My bleeding heart dropped to my toes. "I know dat is not da answer you were looking for." She said nothing else, giving me a moment to digest my disappointment. Kota's hand landed on my knee lending warmth, and he squeezed with silent support. That small touch grounded me and gave me the strength I needed. It took all my mental effort to shove the agonizing truth and the millions of questions I had into a box and bury it in the deep recesses of my mind, saving it to open another day. When I was alone and could let myself feel it. Nothing I could do or say now would change my mother's fate, and I needed to hear the rest of what Mama Dunne said, because I had a feeling she wasn't the type of woman to repeat herself.

Mama Dunne waited until I nodded. It was the slightest movement. I wasn't even positive it was visible, but she dove right back in where she left off and I tried my damndest to pay attention, battling away the numb fog that threatened to slip into my mind. Later. Later I could fall apart, but not now.

Kota's hand surprisingly stayed anchored on my upper leg, each minute he touched me healing the internal injuries my heart had sustained, and I wondered if he had the ability to heal emotional and mental health the way he could heal physical ailments.

"You have been called at da perfect time to take your mother's place and right the wrongs dat have been done. Thankfully, we've had shadow touched men to protect our world while we waited for you to rise. Without da shadow touched, dere is no way da gates would still be standing. Dier demon fighting ways are da only thing that has kept any sort of balance between the dark world and ours."

"Are you saying that the demons are escaping on their own?" Even as I asked the question, it didn't sit right.

"Heaven's no," Mama Dunne spat. "There is evil in our world, just as well as da next, and dey are da ones who are summoning the demons past the gate, allowing them to wreak havoc on our lives, in our cities, and against our own peoples. It started slowly but has been building and growing worse dese past twenty years the veil has been unguarded."

"Do you have any idea who could be behind the summonings?" Chayton piped in for the first time, and I was grateful I wasn't the only one responsible for the conversation. I shifted in my seat while I waited anxiously for her answer, and Kota's hand slipped away. The absence of his touch was as impactful as ice water over flames, and I had to resist the urge to re-establish contact.

A dark cloud passed over Mama's face, recapturing my full attention. "I wish I did, chil'. I wish I did. Dat is a mystery that you will have to solve on your own. They've cloaked their identity from even me for all dese years." Her eyes flashed with potent anger and I let them return to normal before I spoke again.

"What do I do now?" It was a question that was burning inside me, and I let it hang in the quiet room.

"Now, you learn, sweetie. You need your mother's grimoire. The Book of the Keepers. It's been passed down from keeper to keeper for longer dan I've been alive, and I've been around for longer dan you know. Everything you need to know resides in dat book." Mama Dunne tipped forward in her chair and narrowed her eyes. "Find da book, find da answers you seek."

"Find the grimoire." I nodded absently, clearly overloaded.

"Where can we find the book?" Axel interjected, asking the pertinent questions while I slumped back in my seat and rubbed my temples.

"Dat is a journey for Lorn to embark upon on her own, but what I can tell you is dat she will need you. Each and every one of her mates." Mama Dunne gazed at each man in turn. "She needs you now more dan ever. You are her anchors in dis world. It's why the veil keeper is always female. The center of her circle, protected by her males. Da veil is a treacherous place, and da creatures dat are trying to break into the living world are more dangerous dan you know. If the gates fall…" Mama Dunne trailed off, but her sentence didn't need finishing. The doom written across her face was all I needed to see. "Da bond you share will be strengthened when you confirm your mating. I suggest you do dat sooner rather than later. She will need dat connection to you if she wants to survive. Da more anchors, da more stable she and her powers will become." Mama Dunne turned in her chair, and a strange hissing sound pierced the air. "Shush, Clarice," she scolded the noise, as she reached for something beside her chair.

Peeking over the table, I glanced toward the floor to see what she was talking to, and my eyes bugged out of my head at the sight of an alligator lounging near the woman's feet.

"Holy fucking shit!" I squealed and pulled my feet up onto

the chair I was sitting in, squishing myself into the small space. The guys all chuckled, and I glared daggers in their direction.

"Clarice won't harm you. I've never seen her do anything to any of Mama's guests," Chayton soothed, reaching out a hand and running it over my back.

"That you've seen," I pointed out the obvious.

"You fight demons and dat is what you are afraid of?" Mama Dunne cast an amused glance over her shoulder and chuckled to herself, before she pulled a black bag out and faced us once more. "You have nothing to fear from Clarice. She's my companion. Here, chil'." Mama handed the black bag to me and I began to peek inside when she stopped me. "It might be best if you wait until you get home to open dat, love," she said with a wink.

I cinched the bag back up and side-eyed the guys, who looked just as confused as I did. "Well, thank you." I motioned to the bag awkwardly, and then Axel reached for it, magicking it away before my eyes—a handy trick I'd seen them do with my shopping bags earlier. It was like having giant, invisible pockets and I couldn't wait to learn that skill. I'd never need to carry a purse again.

"Just a few small dings dat you will need, is all." Mama's smile was teasing and there was a glint in her eyes that made me want to snatch the bag back from its invisible hiding place, and dump its contents onto the table for inspection. Instead, I offered her a tight smile and shifted in my chair, placing my feet back down on the ground tentatively.

"As for payment..." Mama Dunne peered at Dason, who nodded and offered his hand toward her.

"We know the cost and are prepared to pay." Dason waited patiently.

"And I appreciate dat, but yours is not da promise I have my heart set on, handsome." Turning her gaze to mine, Mama Dunne held up the dagger once more. "A drop of blood to seal a promise."

I scooted forward once more to the protest of the guys, but since I'd been the one to benefit from the information Mama had provided, I felt it was only fair to take the promise she required as payment upon myself. I held my hand out, but Dason quickly covered it with his own.

"No, I made the appointment, I'll be the one to swear a promise," he stated vehemently.

"You defy me?" Mama Dunne asked in a hard tone accentuated by the hissing of her alligator friend.

I swallowed hard. "I've got this Dason, really. I'm the one who benefited from the information tonight. It's okay." I had a feeling that Mama would accept nothing else. As helpful as she'd been, there was a dangerous air just below the surface, and we all knew we didn't really have a choice.

With a tic in his jaw, Dason extracted his hand and I held out my finger, allowing Mama Dunne to prick it with the point of the dagger and press my bloody fingerprint to a document she procured from thin air. I felt the sting of magick bonding me to the promise, before she released me and allowed me to pull my hand back. Sucking on my finger to rid it of blood, I watched as Kota rolled his eyes, his lips pulling up slightly on one side, and reached for me again, healing the small cut with a flash of blue magick.

"A peace offering, Dason." Mama Dunne handed the alpha a small satchel that smelled strongly of an herbal concoction. "Dis is for your grandmother. Please send her my warmest regards and tell her I will try to visit her soon. In my old age, I don't get out and around like I used to." Mama shook her head sadly, but then huffed out a breath and let her gaze slide across my men, landing on Dason again last. "And as for da girl," Mama's Dunne's voice dropped an octave, and at first, I thought she was talking about me. "She will be fine without all of you. She has her own future ahead of her. Her own story to live. You need to rid yourself of guilt and embrace your future." Mama peered pointedly at me and I blinked, studying her and then Dason as I tried to catch up.

"Girl?" I whispered, glancing to Chayton and the others. When they shifted awkwardly and no one answered me, my heart sunk straight into my stomach. "There's another girl?" I repeated myself, my voice growing harder, each word pronounced with fervor.

"No," Axel started, then stopped and cleared his throat. "There's not. Not anymore. Isn't that right Dason?" He shot a look over my head to the alpha.

"Lorn, I can explain," Dason began, but a gasp from Mama had us all tensing and facing her again.

Her eyes had bled white once more, this time without the chanting, and her face went as pale as her tan complexion allowed. "It is time for you to leave!" The strangled way she spoke had me out of my chair in an instant as concern for her shot through me, just before a loud, quaking roar pierced the air. "They know she is here," she warned breathily. "They will stop at nothing to end her life. You must protect her. Always."

A quick glance down at Axel's ring told me all I needed to know as a deep, garnet color replaced that of the normal blue stone, indicating a demon was nearby.

"Lorn, let's go." Dason gripped my arm and hauled me toward him in a protective way as the other guys surrounded me.

"Heed what I have said," Mama Dunne pleaded. "Go out the back way. Hurry now." Pushing up from her chair with more speed and grace than I assumed was possible for someone her age, she ushered us toward the back of the store, throwing open a door that led behind the row of shops. When I went to step past her, following Dason, she stopped me and I halted. "Don't be too hard on da boys. Dey mean well and dey all care for you. Da bond will continue to grow stronger, and you need dem as much as dey need you, sweet chil'. I will see you again."

Taking a deep breath, I leaned forward and hugged Mama Dunne. "Thank you for helping me get some of the answers I've been looking for."

"Aw, sweetie. Your journey for answers has only begun, and you will find what it is you seek most. You've already started."

"What's that?" I asked, to Dason's chagrin.

"A family and a place to belong." She squeezed my arm and then gave me a push toward Dason, saying a quick goodbye to the other men before she hollered to the man at the front of the store. "Louis, let us defend our city and show dem how ignorant dey are for targeting our New Orleans!" Mama's voice faded as she rushed back into her store while Dason pulled me after him, rounding the building and pressing me against it, shielding me with his body.

"What do we know?" he ordered.

"Only that based on the roar, the beast has to be a class four, at least." Kota was already drawing runes into his skin, preparing for battle just like Axel and Chayton were.

"Lorn, do you think you're up for this?" Dason gazed down at me, leaving the decision in my hands for the first time since I'd met him. My magick flared in my fingers, growing in a steady buzz I let it fill me.

The fact that he didn't argue or try to waylay me from joining them spoke volumes, and with a sharp nod, I answered his question. Holding out my arm, I began to draw my runes.

TWENTY-THREE

LORN

"I s this really necessary?" I asked, as the hooded cape fluttered behind me while I ran with the guys, keeping up with the pace of their much longer legs.

"We need to keep you as unrecognizable as possible, babe," Axel said, barely huffing or puffing the way I was. Fuck, I was out of shape for this kind of activity, and I made a disgruntled mental note to add running to my training regimen. "Besides," Axel eyed me for the millionth time, "you look like a sexy little red riding hood, except in black." He smirked and sent me a sinful smile.

"Badass," I corrected him, but my gasp for air diminished the point I was trying to make. "A badass little red riding hood."

"Sexy and badass," Axel relented with a laugh. "Best two words to describe my mate."

The other guys blessedly slowed and peered around the corner, right as a floater rounded on us, swirling past the guys and shooting through me on its way to cause mayhem. The chill the class one shade left behind was heart-stopping and I rubbed at my chest as I caught my breath.

"There needs to be a rune for speed," I complained briefly, sucking air into my lungs.

"There is." Kota smirked at me and I sighed.

"Why wasn't that the first one I learned?" I grumbled.

"Probably because we didn't want you to run away," Chayton teased, grinning at my dismay, and even though we were in danger, I couldn't get over how handsome he was. A long braid fell down his back and he cracked his fingers, preparing for the impending fight.

"Now, Chayton," Dason ordered, and Chayton let his magick build into the familiar red blast that shot out over the city.

"This one just blocks the mundanes," Chayton explained, his voice strained as he molded the magick to blanket the part of the city we needed to contain. "They won't see anything or hear anything. It will be business as usual for them, and they'll be compelled to stay indoors until the fight is over."

"Good call," Dason praised. "We'll need all the help we can get. You guys ready?"

"As we'll ever be," I replied, swinging my arms and bending my neck from one side to the other.

"Lorn, you only engage if needed. Do you understand?" Dason loomed over me, going alpha with his penchant for protecting.

"Yes, sir," I said, squaring my shoulders and facing off against him. The flare in his eyes when I called him 'sir' stirred something deep inside of me and my ovaries woke up.

Not now, girls, I chided my body. *Fuck, maybe not even when we get home.* And that was *if* I could even get Dason to move from alpha status to mate. First, however, was the need to address what I'd heard Mama Dunne say. The ache of hearing there was another girl in their lives—or had been—was still heavy on my heart and I needed answers. From all of them.

Our main objective is to keep Lorn safe. Do you understand? She's the one they're targeting, which puts her at more risk than all of us combined, Dason directed the guys as they headed toward the action, the roar of the demon growing more deafening as we ran into the danger instead of away from it.

Agreement rang through the mental connection our alpha had created with his shift.

If things go south, one of you portal Lorn home. Axel, I'm assigning her to your care. Cover her with your life, Dason growled, and Axel gave full-hearted assent.

I can handle this, I tried to reassure the guys, but nothing I said or did was going to change the possessive protection mode they'd all activated. Truthfully, it made me feel cared about, and I wouldn't deny I loved that feeling.

The scene that greeted us when we reached the demon was gruesome. Witches and warlocks were strewn about the streets in various conditions, and the crimson blood flowing across the asphalt, along with the groans from the injured, were a testament to the power of the demon they were battling. Kota paused for a mere second in indecision before resolve covered his face in a hard mask, and he rushed forward to tend to the injured, no matter their supernatural class.

A mixture of Fae and warlocks were shooting magick at the creature who shrieked into the night, before swiping its deadly claws down and knocking another mass of defenders to the ground in a mixture of blood and bone.

My stomach wanted to retch, but I swallowed, hard, and watched as Dason and Chayton exchanged a look, and then rushed into the action, shifted in mid-stride, and picked up their routine of shifting and attacking the demon.

"Holy fuck!" Axel exclaimed, pulling me toward the side of the street and blocking me in against a storefront window.

"What if... will they attack them?" My gaze followed every movement Chayton and Dason made, tracking them and their progress as they attacked, defended, and lunged.

Axel's silence was enough of an answer. Not only was the demon a threat, but so were the other magick users who would know by now what my men were. Shadow touched.

"They'll probably wait until we take care of the threat first, but..." he trailed off and I ground my teeth together, eyes flying over the street and all the supernaturals in it.

"Tag Chayton out," I ordered Axel, hoping he'd catch on to what I was saying. His gaze was confused, however, when he peered down at me. "Trust me. I have a plan." My magick thrummed, pulsing in time with my heartbeat, which was growing faster from watching every deadly swipe of the demon's claws. The class four shade was just as lethal as the last one we'd faced, and worry clawed at my heart.

Except this time, when we banished it, we'd be taking on a host of other supernaturals—the ones who wanted us dead.

Axel searched my eyes and must have seen my resolve and determination, because he cupped my face, stroking his thumb over my cheek once, and then disappeared.

Do you ever follow orders? Dason growled through our mental link.

Not when they put my mates in more danger than they need to be in, I snarked right back.

Chayton, you need to use your persuasion to move the rest of the magick users off of this street—like you did back in Los Angeles. Can you do that? I waited with bated breath for his answer.

Sure can. I could feel Chayton's shortness of breath even in his thoughts, and when the timing was right, he slipped out of the fight, allowing Axel, who shifted into his small feline form before darting under the demon, to take his place. Transforming back to his human half, Axel slashed into the demon with a stream of orange magick.

Lava-like blood spilled out onto the road as the magick users started to retreat, disappearing one by one. Soon, the only ones left were either already dead or too severely injured to move. I could see the outline of Kota moving in the shadows from fallen form to fallen form, trying his best to save the ones he could, his blue magick flaring to life and sinking into the injured.

When the next roar rent the air, it stopped me cold. Because it wasn't the demon's.

I turned just in time to see the demon pulling its claws from Dason's chest, and excruciating pain shot through the bond I shared with the alpha, stealing the air from my lungs and leaving me in agony.

Dason! I cried through the mental link, while a sob escaped my lips. Heedless of all the warnings, I rushed forward, flying past fallen magick users and skirting around the demon, who Chayton and Axel kept occupied and away from our fallen packmate. Leaving the shadows, I hurried to Dason and fell to my knees beside him. Blood pooled around his body and bubbled from the puncture wounds in his chest, and I pressed my hands against the worst looking one, trying to stanch the bleeding.

Strong arms wrapped around me and pulled me back, and I clung to Kota, the world moving in slow motion as I gazed up at him with tears streaming down my face.

"I've got him. It's okay Lorn. I've got him." Kota's litany finally broke through, and with bloody hands, he smoothed my hair away from my face and gazed into my eyes. "Are you okay?" he asked, and I nodded.

"Go," I rasped. "Save him!" The cry tore from my throat.

"Take cover!" Kota's eyes meant business as he released me and turned to Dason, setting his hands on his body and calling his magick. The blue glow pulsed into Dason again and again while Kota worked, and I stood, backing up small step by small step, unable to pull myself away enough to find a place to hide out.

I didn't want to hide. I wanted to fucking fight. Rage replaced my heartbreak at seeing Dason so injured, and before I knew what was happening, a wave of purple magick exploded from my body, bypassing Dason and Kota, and crashing full force into the Demon that Axel had been doing his best to occupy.

The corresponding roar pierced my ears and nearly knocked me over from the sheer strength of it. The next thing I knew, Chayton was swooping down and helping Kota drag Dason off the road and out of the way of the demon, while Axel came to stand at my side.

"What the fuck was that?" he panted.

"Magick and a pissed off female." I flung the reply in his direction, not taking my eyes off the Demon who was gushing lava blood from the penetrating wound I'd managed to put in its chest. A little tit for tat. I wanted to do worse than that. I wanted to see this thing decimated.

I'd never known anger so strong nor so heady, but I latched on to the feel of it and let it build, using my emotions to fuel my power.

Like I knew it would, the demon turned and locked on to me, following me without hesitation.

"Run with me," I ordered, grabbing Axel's arm and pulling him as I turned and fled, while the storming footsteps of the monster trailed behind us as it roared again.

"You've got a plan, right?" he asked.

"I seem to recall asking you something similar that first night," I quipped, grinning at the memory as Axel and I were chased by yet another demon.

"I don't think we should make this our thing!" His laugh was edged with a maniacal note, and I smirked at him before turning down a side street, leading the demon far enough away from Kota and Dason to keep them safe.

A sardonic smile curved my lips as I turned and let a fresh bolt of magick fly when the demon rounded the corner. I didn't let myself bask in the roar that sounded as I ducked, quickly moving to avoid the swipe it aimed at me in retaliation. The magick gathered in my fingertips once more and I released it, throwing as much power behind the blast as I could. Shifting back and forth, Axel bounced around the creature and peppered it with slashes that helped decrease its health and vitality. The demon finally started to wear.

Sweat covered my forehead and made my black t-shirt cling to my body while my cape fluttered around me making me feel like a dark superhero. Careening toward the beast, I loosed another bolt that shot straight through its shadowy body without doing any damage, and my eyes widened as the demon gave me the creepiest version of a smile I'd ever seen.

Did you think you could defeat me? You, a tiny child? the beast hissed into my mind, and waves of nausea rolled over me as its evil presence drew closer, despite Axel's attempts to waylay it. Breathing rapidly through my nose, my gaze flew over its form, looking for a spot of weakness to aim for next.

I backed up and the creature stalked toward me, making me the prey instead of the predator.

Hands raised, I let the magick within me build again, calling on my power hard and fast.

It cackled a laugh as if it found me amusing, and my eyes hardened.

You don't even know how to use your magick. How do you plan to kill me, little keeper? Something in its words registered in the back of my mind, reminding me of the attack I'd suffered during training, and for one split second, I paused. That one second of self-doubt was enough of an opening for the beast to rear back and swipe at me with its powerful, deadly looking hooked claws.

The pain when its talons met my skin was sharp and searing, but I wouldn't allow myself to feel the brunt of my injuries. Not yet. Not while the demon was still standing. Not when I didn't know if Dason would make it.

Pulling myself from my pain, I danced around the creature, releasing blast after blast of magick into the whips of smoke that made up its body. The closer I aimed toward its center, the more the hits seemed to rack up damage. Axel danced with me, soon joined by Chayton, and together we worked to take down the shade.

Lorn can do better than that, the beast taunted, and I ground my teeth, refusing to reply or let the demon know it was creeping me out. How the hell did this thing know my name? And how was it even speaking into my mind?

Slithering forward, the beast bent down and got into my face, and I stumbled backward from the closeness, not having expected it to cross so readily into my personal space.

Lorn is dead girl walking. A strange cackling sound slipped past its dripping maw, but I ignored the rotten stench coming from its mouth while I let the magick in my fingers build to an inferno that needed to be released. With the demon this close, I had a clear shot, and I took the advantage. Magick poured from my hands, and I aimed it directly at the demon's head just as it sunk its claws into my side. Crimson blood stained the dark fabric I wore, pooling quickly and dripping down my body, but I didn't stop. The anguish was hard to ignore as it wrenched itself free from my flesh, but I kept my thoughts focused on Dason and the way he'd looked on the ground, letting the images keep me standing while Axel and Chayton joined their magick with mine.

I staggered back, looking for something to keep myself upright, when a hard chest appeared behind me, and arms banded around my body, holding me up while being mindful of my wounds.

When a fourth stream of magick joined the rest, my eyes widened. The silver sheen of it reminded me of Dason's, but he was definitely not the one wielding the magick to my right.

I kept my hands trained on the beast as I felt my life force draining, but I didn't give up or ease off. I wouldn't until the beast was dead.

With a primal call, the demon screeched, and I smirked as I watched the life begin to leave its red, glowing eyes, but my smirk vanished just as fast when floaters from all around New Orleans answered the beast's cry, swarming down the side street and making me release a gurgling gasp.

Moving one hand, I pressed it to my wound, staunching the bleeding to the best of my ability. I grit my teeth and decided to try my hand at healing, and I begged my magick to work as I siphoned some of it from the stream I still had trained on the demon, deviating it into my injury. I couldn't contain my cry of pain as the magick did a rough and brutal job of singeing vein, muscle, and skin back together in a patch up job that I would need Kota to fix later.

Finding a reserve of strength I didn't know I had, I stood straighter and pushed off whoever was holding me, standing on my own. My breath sawed in and out of my lungs as I watched the floaters sacrifice themselves to the class four shade, giving it their power as it consumed them into the large mass of its smoky body.

When it threw its head back, arms out, claws extended, and roared, I knew the tides of the fight had shifted. We were already battle weary, injured, and exhausted, and now the demon had a seemingly endless supply of lives. We didn't stand a chance.

My pulse was a pounding whoosh in my ears when I heard a small voice whisper to me, and me alone. *Trust yourself.*

My magick warmed inside of me in a way I'd never felt before. It came from a peaceful place rather than one of anger or heightened emotion, and I followed it on instinct. Without another thought, I gave it control and felt the exact moment my magick left my body, this time wavering in front of me like a shield rather than a stream of destruction. I watched it spread, listening to every breath I took as it engulfed the class four demon and all the floaters buzzing around its head like bees to a hive.

And then on instinct I disconnected from my body and dropped. The rush of falling had a scream leaving my lungs before the world shifted and changed, and the sky turned a blood-red. When I finally stopped, the ground beneath my feet was an ashen grey and a million hissing voices called out to me, causing all the hair on my body to stand on end. When I finally gazed upward, I saw the demon and the floaters consumed by my magick.

Unsure of what to do next, I took a minute to look around, finally noting the tall, iron gate behind me. Pointed spires were spaced evenly along the gate, jutting into the sky like the black, twisted trees that dotted the dead landscape. Walking to the gate, I reached out a hand and touched it, pulling back when it sizzled and burned my skin.

Shaking my hand out, I added the injury to the tally of what I needed Kota to help me heal if I could figure out how the hell to get out of here.

And by here, I was pretty sure I meant the veil.

Without any means to open the gate, I worried my lip and studied the demon when an idea came to me. Reaching for the coiled magick in the center of my being, I let it lash out and wrap around the demon. Sizzling ropes confined it.

"That's going to have to hold you for now. Until I can open that gate." Working off instinct, I bent down, placed my hand on the dark ground, and released my magick into the ashen dirt, tethering the rope of magick to the veil that would act as a prison. I had no idea how I knew to do that, but it felt right in the moment, so I ran with it—adding more questions to my never-ending list.

When I was done, my magick snapped back into my body, and I focused on my connection to each of the guys. While they were faint, they were there, and I reached for them. After a few frustrating tries, I finally had a good enough grasp on the connection to pull myself out of the veil and anchor myself back in the mortal plane.

My ears were ringing when I gasped for breath when a

distinctly male voice cut through the fog of pain, swiftly yanking me back into the present.

"Holy hell! Are you alright?" A warm, large hand landed on my shoulder, and my eyes flew open to meet a pair of concerned blue orbs that were staring back at me from a very handsome face of a stranger. Wavy, black hair tipped with silver, which was clearly dyed that way, framed a golden face with dark eyebrows, a straight nose, and a pair of full lips that were turned down in a frown as the man, who knelt in front of me, checked me over.

For a moment, all I did was stare until I pulled my scattered thoughts together enough to realize I was being cradled in the arms of another guy I didn't know. I noted his long, dark hair and square jaw as I looked up into the second man's face. His dark, expressive eyes seemed to communicate with me, and they were full of concern and something far more tender than I expected to see from someone I didn't know.

Taking a deep breath, I let the men's combined scents fill my lungs. The mixture of citrus, honey, and leather went straight to my head in an alluring way, and I swayed before the man holding me tightened his group.

"Who are you?" I rasped, trying to get the words past a throat that was determined to undermine my efforts. Finally, my brain began to function on a basic level and panic built rapidly in my chest. Struggling to sit up, I glanced around in alarm, looking for my guys.

Every motion made my head spin and black dots swam in my eyes as I fought for consciousness. I just need to see them. To know they were okay, and then I could let go.

"Oh, fuck." The male with the silver-tipped hair leaned closer, inhaling deeply, those same blue eyes now drinking me in. I watched his eyes dilate as a shudder raced through his body.

Somewhere in my brain alarm bells were sounding, trying to tell me something, but I couldn't make my thoughts align long enough to reason out anything other than trying to stay awake so I could check on my men.

"Chayton, Axel," I murmured, finally catching sight of them hurrying toward me. Knowing they were alive and well was all I needed, and I lost the battle I'd been trying so hard to win, slipping into the darkness that was waiting to carry me away.

Familiar scents of the cabin greeted me as I woke up on the couch with a hint of déjà vu. For a girl who'd never passed out in her life, it was becoming a rather annoying habit I wanted to break. Shoving the blanket off my body, I tried to sit up.

"Easy, you've had quite a night," Chayton cautioned me and reached his hand forward to pull me into an upright position. Settling on the couch beside me, he checked me over to make sure I was all in one piece. He was tender in the way he handled me and it sparked a warmth in my chest that helped chase out the cold icy tendrils from the veil that had taken root.

"I told you I healed her." Kota shook his head at the way Chayton double-checked his work.

"It doesn't hurt to make sure she's back to one-hundred-percent." Chayton's eyes were like chocolate and his voice was smooth honey. I reached for him, running my fingers along the line of his jaw, letting the light scruff of his face abrade my fingertips.

It was like my touch brought life back into his eyes, and

they regained their light, flecks of glimmering cooper warming the deep brown. "I'm okay," I whispered, reassuring him.

"This time," Dason mumbled, but the sound of his timbre had me turning, wide-eyed, and nearly jumping off the couch.

"You're alive!" The sheer emotion in my voice was enough to be embarrassing, but I didn't hide my relief or the tears that filled my eyes. I blinked rapidly, trying to hold them at bay, sure that Dason would see them as weakness rather than gratitude that he was still with us.

"So are you," he replied, surprising me by smiling gently. It only lasted for a minute. "You were foolish to rush into the fight, Lorn."

"It's not foolishness to try and keep my mate from potentially dying in the street, Dason." I put a little extra sass behind my words. "You wouldn't leave me bleeding out like that any more than I would you."

"You are going to be a handful." Dason shook his head, but I didn't miss the way his lips tipped up just slightly at the corners.

"You know it." I grinned and swung my body so my feet were planted firmly on the floor. "Maybe I'm just as alpha as you are," I mused.

"That's what I'm afraid of." Dason let a full-out grin cover his lips and for a moment, my heart stopped.

A knock on the door caught everyone's attention, sharply cutting through the celebratory mood we'd been in as we basked in the simple fact that we were still breathing, and thanks to Kota's healing abilities, relatively unscathed. Chayton sighed like he'd been expecting the intrusion.

I peered over the back of Dason's couch as I watched Chayton swing the door open, admitting two men I didn't know.

"Jolon." Dason stood from the couch, shirtless, and turned

toward the door, addressing the man who stepped into the living room first. His hair was wavy and black, tipped with silver, and while I couldn't place him as someone I knew, he seemed oddly familiar.

"Dason," the man replied, reaching out and clasping wrists with my alpha in semblance of a handshake. A god walked in behind him, tall and broad with long hair that hung loosely around his shoulders. His white t-shirt was stained in blood that smelled like mine, and memories of other men at the battle filtered back to me slowly.

"You helped us," I stated, and the long-haired man nodded. "Thank you." I stood on shaky legs and Kota reached for me, making sure I was steady on my feet before letting me go. Remaining by my side, he stared down our guests.

"What are you doing here, Jolon?" Dason's usual alpha command infiltrated his tone and Jolon widened his stance, facing off with Dason with just as much alpha power permeating the room.

He cast a heated look at me, his voice was full of surety when he replied, "I just found out that our mate lives here."

"Your what?" I asked, swaying on my feet from the news, and Kota reached for me again. Wrapping his arm around me to keep my upright, he braced me against the hard line of his body in an uncharacteristic display of possession.

"Mate, Lorn." Chayton gazed at me with his open, truthful brown eyes. "We all knew it was a possibility that you'd have more mates than just the four of us."

Shock rang through me and curse words flew through my mind at the news. I gaped like an unattractive fish as I stared around the room. The guys gave me a few moments to digest that information, and my anger surged. There was so much they weren't telling me that I wanted, no needed, answers to. Would it kill these men to actually communicate?

"And I'm just learning about this why?" My tone had a hard edge to it that made all the men in the room shift on their feet. My feelings were all over the place and exhaustion was making it hard to think straight.

Mates. I had more mates. As in *six* mates. I wasn't sure if my life was lucky or simply sinking into pure insanity at this point.

"I knew it was a possibility. There hasn't been a shadow touched female in so long that it made sense you would probably take a number of mates," Chayton mused. "Our ratio of males to females is wildly unbalanced. Taking on more mates helps tip that scale a little."

"You're sure about this?" Dason leveled Jolon with a hard glance, and then did the same for the giant man who stood silently behind him.

"We are. Her blood called to Syler and me the second we scented it. The bond, on our side, has already formed. I can feel her confusion, anger, and curiosity as I stand here now." Jolon's blue gaze settled heavily onto me, and everything that happened after I'd returned from the veil came rushing back. While I hadn't smelled their blood yet, their scent had drawn me in. In fact, I couldn't deny the mixing fragrance of all the men in the room set me at ease rather than on edge, and it helped to lessen my anger. There was a rightness to it that I had no control over. It just existed. "We can prove it, make ourselves bleed so you can scent us now," Jolon offered, and I held up my hands to ward off the idea.

"No!" I said, a little too hastily as I remembered my last reaction to mating. My cheeks flushed. "Maybe not right this minute. I believe what you say, and we'll know soon enough," I mumbled quickly. "What I don't understand is why I have so many mates?"

"When Mama Dunne explained that you were the veil keeper and needed anchors, I had a feeling you'd end up with more than just us, especially with the incredible amount of magick you already possess. My best guess? The number of mates you'll need will correspond to how much power it's going to take to anchor you in the mortal realm when you're in the veil," Chayton explained.

Truthfully, it made sense. I just wasn't ready to throw my arms out in welcome. I was still getting to know Dason, Chayton, Kota, and Axel, and now I needed to add Jolon and Syler to my list of suitors. None of us had a choice in the mating, and I wasn't sure if I should simply fall back on fate and faith, or continue to question the magick behind the bonds forming. Never in my wildest dreams had I ever considered I'd have more than one mate, and now I had half a dozen. Call me a romantic, but I wanted these guys to like me for me, and not just because of what my supernatural ID card would list as my species. Relationships took time to grow, and we needed to give ourselves that time. Being the only option—the only shadow touched female—made the whole situation both a blessing and a curse.

Deciding I couldn't handle the weight of the mate discussion right now, I chose to table it. "I know this is an important topic, trust me when I say I realize that more than any of you, but I'm not in a place where I can discuss our mating right now. I need time to adjust."

"That's understandable, Lorn," Chayton relented, and the other guys added their agreement.

Satisfied with their acceptance, I changed the topic. "You know about veil keepers?" I questioned Chayton, unwilling to dismiss the way he talked about it so casually. If he had information on what I was, I wanted to learn everything he knew.

"I've heard the stories. They've been passed down from generation to generation in my family. You're going to be strong, Lorn. Powerful."

"I want to know everything and there's already so much to process," I murmured, looking from one man to the next until I'd surveyed them all.

I was the veil keeper and I had six mates. Six men looking to protect me and anchor me to the mortal worlds, so I could man the gates that essentially led to hell, and I only knew four of them. Threats surrounded us on all sides, and everyone seemed to have their own agenda, their own motives for wanting power in a world full of powerful creatures. Demons plagued our cities, the destruction I'd witnessed tonight was only a small piece of the havoc they rained down on the supernatural and mundane realm, and whoever was summoning them wanted me dead. Talk about your average week.

"I'm not ready for all of this." I sent a pleading expression to Axel and I shook my head as I swallowed the bittersweet pill life had dealt me.

"You're not right now, but you will be. We'll find the grimoire, we'll train you. This is only the beginning, Lorn," Axel soothed, stepping up to my other side and wrapping his arm around me, mirroring his brother. "For all of us." Pressed between two of my mates, I drew in a calming breath, letting their similar combined scents wash over me. "What do we do now?" Axel looked to Dason as he drove his free hand through the long strands of his shaggy, dark hair. "You heard Mama Dunne. Whoever is summoning these demons is after Lorn. They want her dead."

"That will never happen." The vehemence in Kota's voice

warmed my heart, even as dread descended on me at the thought of the threat.

Dason looked around at each man in the room—including the newcomers—and I knew they were having some kind of silent conversation I wasn't privy to. Finally, he turned to me, his grey gaze set and determined as he made a decision and spoke. "Now, we protect what's ours."

AUTHOR'S NOTE

Thank you for reading Shadow Touched!
I hope you enjoyed it!

Are you ready for the next Veil Keeper book?
Find it on Amazon in early 2020!

To stay current on our release dates, read extra content, get
sneak previews into the next book, and follow upcoming series
by Harper Wylde, come join her on Facebook!

The Wylde Side Facebook Group

www.harperwylde.com

ALSO BY HARPER WYLDE

The Veil Keeper Series

Shadow Touched

The Phoenix Rising Series

Born of Embers

Hidden in Smoke

Spark of Intent

Forged in Flames

Blaze of Wrath

The Huntress Series

An Assassin's Death

An Assassin's Deception

An Assassin's Destiny

The God Trials

The Selected (Coming Soon)

ABOUT HARPER WYLDE

Harper Wylde is a paranormal romance author who lives in the countryside of Pennsylvania. As a wife and a mother of two young children, she spends her days chasing after little people and making crazy notes about story ideas all over her home. As a serial entrepreneur, Harper also dabbles in photography and graphic design...but has found that her favorite occupation is the one she's doing now—writing fantasy and paranormal romance. She loves coffee, cooking, chocolate covered pretzels, and characters with hidden strength and endearing flaws! To connect with Harper, follow her on Facebook where you can join her author group called The Wylde Side and stay up to date on sneak previews, teasers, and new releases!